BROKEN COUNTRY

A NOVEL

CLARE LESLIE HALL

SIMON & SCHUSTER

New York   Amsterdam/Antwerp   London
Toronto   Sydney   New Delhi

Simon & Schuster
1230 Avenue of the Americas
New York, NY 10020

Originally published in Great Britain in 2025 by John Murray (Publishers)

First Simon & Schuster hardcover edition March 2025

SIMON & SCHUSTER and colophon are registered trademarks of Simon & Schuster, LLC.

For information about special discounts for bulk purchases, please contact Simon & Schuster Special Sales at 1-866-506-1949 or business@simonandschuster.com.

The Simon & Schuster Speakers Bureau can bring authors to your live event. For more information or to book an event, contact the Simon & Schuster Speakers Bureau at 1-866-248-3049 or visit our website at www.simonspeakers.com.

Manufactured in the United States of America

5   7   9   10   8   6

Library of Congress Cataloging-in-Publication Data is available.

ISBN 978-1-6680-7818-1
ISBN 978-1-6680-7820-4 (ebook)

For Jake, Maya, and Felix, my tristar

BROKEN COUNTRY

Part One

Gabriel

The farmer is dead, he is dead and all anyone wants to know is who killed him. Was it an accident or was it murder? It looks like murder, they say, with that gunshot wound to the heart, so precise it must have been intended.

They are waiting for me to speak. Two pairs of eyes relentless in their stares. But how can I tell them what he wants me to say, the words we have practiced over and over in the minutes before the police arrive?

I shake my head, I need more time.

It's true what they say: You can live a whole lifetime in a final moment. We are that boy and girl again with all of it ahead, a glory-stretch of light and wondrous beauty, of nights beneath the stars.

He is waiting for me to look at him and, when I do, he smiles to show me he is fine, the briefest nod of his head.

Say it, Beth. Say it now.

I look at his face again, beautiful to me then and now and always, one final glance between us before everything changes.

1968

Hemston, North Dorset

"Gabriel Wolfe is back living in Meadowlands," Frank says, the name exploding at me over breakfast. "Divorced now. Just him and his boy rattling around in that huge place."

"Oh."

It seems to be the only word I have.

"That's what I thought," Frank says. He gets up from his side of the table and walks around to mine, takes my face in his hands, kisses me. "We won't let that pillock cause us any grief. We'll have nothing to do with him."

"Who told you?"

"It was the talk of the pub last night. Took two huge great lorries to bring all their stuff from London, apparently."

"Gabriel hated it here. Why would he come back?"

His name feels strange on my tongue, the first time I've spoken it aloud in years.

"There's no one else to look after the place. His father long gone, his mother on the other side of the world. Up to her neck in dingo shit, with any luck."

Frank always manages to make me laugh.

"What's here for him, anyway?" Frank says, casually, but I see it, the unsaid thought that flits across his mind. *Aside from you.* "He's bound to sell up and move to Las Vegas or Monte Carlo or wherever it is these . . . "—he grapples for the word, looks pleased with himself when he finds it— "*celebrities* hang out."

Frank spends all the daylight hours and a fair few at nighttime out on the farm, caring for our animals and tending the land. He works harder than anyone I know but

5

always takes time to notice the beauty of a spring sunset or the sudden, dizzying soar of a skylark, his attunement to weather and wildlife set deep in his bones. One of many things I love about him. Frank doesn't have time to read novels or go to the theater. He wouldn't know a dry martini if someone chucked one in his face. He's the very antithesis of Gabriel Wolfe, or at least, the one we read about in the papers.

I watch my husband leaning against the door to pull on his boots. In twenty minutes' time his skin will be permeated three layers deep with the stench of cow dung.

The door, rapped hard from the other side, makes Frank start. "Bloody hell," he says, yanking it open so quickly his brother falls into the room.

Our mornings invariably start this way.

Jimmy, still ruddy from last night's beer, eyes screwed half shut, one strand of hair sticking straight up as if it's gelled, says: "Aspirin, Beth? Got a banger."

I take down the medicine box from the dresser where it lives primarily in use for Jimmy's hangovers. Once upon a time it was full of infant paracetamol and emergency plasters.

There are five years between them but Frank and Jimmy look so similar that, from a distance, even I struggle to tell them apart. They are well over six foot with dark, almost black hair and eyes so blue people often do a double take. Their mother's eyes, I'm told, though I never had the chance to meet her. They are both wearing shabby corduroys and thick shirts, soon to be covered in the navy overalls that are their daily uniform. In the village they are sometimes called "the twins," but only in jest; Frank is very much the older brother.

"What happened to 'just going to finish this pint and call it a night'?" Frank says, grinning at Jimmy.

"Beer is God's reward for an honest day's toil."

"That from the Bible?"

"If it isn't, it should be."

"We'll be with the lambs at midday. See you then?" Frank calls to me as the brothers go out of the door, still laughing as they cross the yard.

With the men out milking and the kitchen cleared there are plenty of jobs to get on with. Washing—so much of it—both brothers' overalls rinsed and waiting for me on the scrubbing board. The breakfast washing-up. A floor that always needs sweeping, no matter how often I take the broom to it.

Instead, I make a fresh pot of coffee and put on an old waxed jacket of Frank's and sit at the little wrought iron table looking out across our fields until my gaze meets its target: three red chimneys of differing heights peering above the fuzz of green oak on the horizon.

Meadowlands.

Before
1955

I don't know I am trespassing, I am lost in a dreamworld, my head full of romantic scenarios in which I triumph. I picture myself beside a fountain with an orchestra in full flow, receiving an impassioned declaration of love. I read a lot of Austen and Brontë at this time, I have a tendency to embellish.

I must have been staring up at the sky, head in the clouds quite literally: The collision comes out of nowhere.

"What the hell?"

This boy I bump into, his shoulder bashing into mine, is no hero. Tall, slender, arrogant, like a teenage Mr. Darcy.

"Don't you look?" he says. "This is private land."

I find the whole "private land" thing slightly absurd, particularly when it's accompanied by a curt, cut glass accent like this one. This meadow we are in, green and curving, oaks with their cloud-bloom flowering, is England in its full glory. It's Keats, it's Wordsworth. It should be for everyone to enjoy.

"Are you smiling?" He looks so annoyed, I almost laugh.

"We're in the middle of nowhere. There is no one else here. How could it possibly matter?"

The boy stares back at me for a moment before he takes in what I have said. "You're right. God. What is wrong with me?" He holds out his hand, a peace offering. "Gabriel Wolfe."

"I know who you are."

He looks at me expectantly, waiting for my name. But I don't feel like telling him yet. I've heard talk of Gabriel

Wolfe, the famously handsome boy from the big house, but this is the first time I've seen him in the flesh. He has a good face: dark eyes framed by eyelashes my girlfriends would kill for, wavy brown hair that flops across his forehead, sharp cheekbones, elegant nose. A patrician kind of beauty, I suppose you might call it. But he is wearing tweed trousers tucked into woolly socks. Draped across his shoulders like a cape is a jacket of matching tweed, belt dangling. Old man's clothes. He's not my type at all.

"What were you doing here?"

"Looking for a place to sit and read." I draw my book out of my coat pocket—a slim volume of Emily Dickinson.

"Oh. Poetry."

"You sound a little disappointed. P. G. Wodehouse more your thing?"

He sighs. "I know what you're thinking. But you're wrong."

I'm smiling again, I can't help it. "What are you, a mind reader?"

"You think I'm a brainless, upper-class twit. A Bertie Wooster."

I tilt my head and consider him. "He'd love your getup, you have to admit. He'd say it was spiffing."

When Gabriel laughs, it changes him completely.

"These are my father's old fishing trousers. I nicked them out of a box of stuff going to the jumble sale. I wouldn't have worn them if I'd known you'd take such offense."

"Is that what you're doing, fishing?"

"Yes, just down there. I'll show you, if you like."

"I thought it was out-of-bounds for plebs like me?"

"You see, that's why you have to come. I've been rude and I'd like to make it up to you."

I stand before him, unsure. I don't want to get caught up in something that is hard to get out of. All I wanted was a pretty spot to sit and read.

He smiles again, that face-changing smile. Handsome even in his old man's garb. "I've got biscuits. Please come."

"What kind of biscuits?"

Gabriel hesitates. "Custard creams."

Fountain, orchestra. Lake, biscuits. It's not so much of a stretch.

"Well, in that case . . . " I say, and this is how it begins.

1968

Of all the seasons, early spring, when the air is sly with cold and the birds are starting up and the fields are filled with lambs, has always been my favorite. Bobby was mad for our lambs. He fed the waifs year after year with a bottle, that was his job, he wouldn't let anyone else touch it, even stayed off school to do it one time. A spirited boy, he wore shorts right the way through winter and no coat, even when the headmistress sent him home for one. A golden boy, he sang so much when he was little we called him Elvis. He was tall and skinny with brown hair that stuck up just like his uncle's.

Jimmy has the transistor radio playing, I can hear it well before I reach the tin barn. It's the Beatles: "Hello, Goodbye" at full volume. Not very pastoral, but it's clearly working for Jimmy's hangover. I watch him as I come in through the gate at the top of the field, he has one hand resting on a ewe's backside, hips swaying from side to side, left foot jiggling.

"Where's Frank?" I say, and Jimmy points to the bottom of the field.

Together we stand and watch as my husband vaults the fence. One strong arm placed on the top rail, his body swung out at a right angle before he clears it like an Olympian hurdler. I see him doing it most days but it still gives me a small rush of pleasure, the simple joy of it in a man whose life is dominated by hard work.

He walks up the field toward us, swinging his arms energetically; even from here I know he is probably whistling. This is Frank where he most loves to be.

Most of our ewes have delivered, we have forty-six lambs out to pasture with a handful still in the stalls. Only one bottle feeder and one stillborn. Frank and Jimmy look over the pregnant sheep, palms against their bellies to check for a breach, examining their rears for signs of birth. It's more instinct than anything; they could do it in their sleep. Jimmy is the soft touch, he chats to the ewes while he works, gives them Rich Tea biscuits when he's done. Frank is always in a rush, in his head an unending checklist of tasks, a brain that holds too much.

"Think we could wrap up the mothers' meeting and crack on?" Frank says, and Jimmy rolls his eyes.

"Bossy so-and-so, isn't he?" he tells the ewes.

The sheep have a long, sloping field to themselves but they don't spread out much, always clustered up here, next to the barn. In a week or so the lambs will become more independent, and that's when they start frisking off in one direction or another, spindly legs buckling. The stage Bobby loved the most. He was a farm boy, he understood how it worked, but every single year it broke his heart when it was time to ship his babies off to market.

I don't know which of us hears the barking first. We spin around to a golden-haired lurcher tearing toward us.

A stray dog, no owners with him, charging our lambs.

"Get out of it!" Frank tries to block the lurcher. He is six foot two, broad and fierce, but the dog just darts around him, straight into the thick of our ewes.

The sheep are moaning, tiny offspring bleating in fear; only a few days old, but they sense the danger. A flick-switch change in the dog. Eyes black, teeth bared, body rigid with adrenaline.

"Gun, Jimmy! Now!" Frank yells, and Jimmy turns and runs to the shed.

He's fast, Frank, racing at the dog with his primeval roar, but the dog is quicker. It picks off a lamb, nips it up by its neck, throat ripped open. The appalling red of its blood, a jet of crimson pools on the grass. One lamb, two lambs, then three; guts spilling out like sacrificial entrails. The ewes are scattering everywhere now, stumbling out, terror-blind, their newborns exposed.

I'm running at the dog, shrieking, trying to gather up the lambs but I hear Jimmy yelling, "Out of the way, Beth! Move."

And then Frank has grabbed me into his arms so tightly I'm pressed right into his chest, and I can feel the thundering of his heart. I hear the gunshot and then another, and the dog's quick, indignant howl of pain. It's over.

"Bloody hell," Frank says, pulling back, checking my face, a palm pressed against my cheek.

We walk over to the dog, the three of us cooing and calling out to the sheep, "Come on, girls," but they are shivering and bleating and giving the three infant corpses a wide berth.

Out of nowhere, like a mirage, a boy comes running up the field. Small and skinny in shorts. Maybe ten years old. "My dog," he screams.

His voice so sweet and high.

"Fuck," Jimmy says, just as the child sees the bloody heap of fur and yelps, "You killed my dog!"

His father is here now, panting and flushed, but scarcely different from the boy I knew. "Oh, Jesus Christ, you shot him."

"Had to." Frank gestures at the butchered lambs.

I don't think Gabriel has any idea who Frank is, or at

least, who he is married to, but then he turns and catches sight of me. Momentarily, panic flits across his face before he recovers himself.

"Beth," he says.

But I ignore him. No one is looking after the child. He is standing by his dog, hands covering his eyes as if to black out the horror.

"Here." I'm beside him in seconds, my hands on his shoulders. And then I kneel in front of him and wrap my arms around him. He begins to weep.

"Keep crying," I say. "Crying will help."

He collapses against me, wailing now, a boy in shorts in my arms.

And this is how it begins again.

The Trial
Old Bailey, London, 1969

Nothing could prepare me for the agony of watching the man I love sitting high up in the dock, flanked by two prison officers, as he awaits his verdict.

A man accused of an unthinkable crime.

He never glances up at the gallery to search for my face and he doesn't look at the jury either. Doesn't observe them, as I do, examining each one, panic pounding through me, as I ask myself: Will this tired-looking, gray-haired woman believe in his innocence? Will this middle-aged man in his banker's garb of pinstripe suit, blue shirt with a white collar and cuffs, be the one to vote against him? The young man with shoulder-length hair, who looks kinder than the rest, might he be our ally? Mostly they are inscrutable, the seven men and five women who hold his fate in their hands. My sister says it's good there are plenty of women. They are more compassionate, she says, as a rule. It feels like clutching at straws, but a part of me hopes the female jurors might understand the derailing passion that made us risk everything.

After months of our talking about it, the trial has begun. Everything about this courtroom seems to emphasize the severity of our situation: the high ceiling and wood-paneled walls; the judge, resplendent in red on his high-back chair, like a king on his throne as he surveys his court; beneath him the barristers in wigs and black gowns, looking through papers as they wait for proceedings to begin; and the court clerk quietly pompous as he stands before the dock and makes his chilling proclamation: "You are charged with the murder . . . "

The press bench is filled with journalists in tweed jackets and ties, not a single woman among them. And then there is the gallery, where I sit with Eleanor, along with all the rubberneckers. Not so long ago I shared their thirst for human drama. How avidly I followed the Profumo scandal and the subsequent trial of Stephen Ward. I remember, as if it were yesterday, the photos of Christine Keeler and Mandy Rice-Davies leaving court, how stylish they looked, how the press still managed to denigrate and cheapen them.

It's very different when the prisoner in the dock is the person you love. *Look up. Please, my love.* I try to engage him telepathically, the way we always used to, but he stares ahead with his strange, blank eyes. The only giveaway of the distress I know he is feeling—felt in every waking moment since—is the angry clench of his jaw. To an outsider, perhaps, he looks hostile, but I know better. It's the only way he can stop himself from crying.

Before

If I were to paint a picture of a classic English lake it would look just like the one at Meadowlands.

The surface is covered with clusters of water lilies, the flowers a fist of white and pink with bold yellow hearts. At the far end a pair of willow trees stretch out across the water, and three white swans are gliding toward us in a uniform line, as if the gaps between them have been measured with a ruler.

Gabriel has set himself up with a rug, a picnic hamper, and a folding canvas chair, a pair of fishing rods propped up against it. He gestures to the chair—"Be my guest"—but I choose to sit next to him on the rug instead. From the hamper he produces a tartan thermos of tea and a packet of Garibaldi biscuits.

I raise my eyebrows and he grins.

"I thought you might not come if I told you it was squashed-fly biscuits."

I watch him pour tea into a white tin mug with a navy rim. He has beautiful hands, with long elegant fingers. He adds milk and sugar without asking and hands it to me.

On the far side of the lake, near to the willows, there's an ancient-looking khaki tent, the kind you see in safari films. I can imagine Grace Kelly sitting outside it, sipping a gin and tonic, a neat shirt tucked into her fawn-colored breeches.

"What's the tent for?"

"I camp here in summer. Wake up and swim every morning. Fry bacon and eggs on a little stove."

It seems odd to me, a boy who lives in a house the size of Meadowlands, choosing to rough it instead under canvas.

Like everyone else in the village I've been to Meadowlands for the annual summer fete. I've eaten wedges of Victoria sandwich in the tea tent, hooked myself up to my sister for the three-legged race, come last but one in the egg and spoon. I've seen Gabriel's mother, Tessa, dressed like a fashion model in head-to-toe black: her neatly tailored suit more fitting for Paris than Hemston; a wide-brimmed hat, huge sunglasses; scarlet lips her only hint of color. Compared to all the other mothers in their plain print dresses and sandals, she always seemed exotic and untouchable. I can picture his father, Edward, besuited, bespectacled, and much older, gamely lobbing balls at the coconut shy.

What I can't remember is Gabriel.

"Why have I never seen you at the village fete?"

"I've always been away at school. Not anymore, though. I sat my last exam two weeks ago. Three months at home before I go to university, not sure how I'll stand it."

I gesture to our view. The glittering water and overhanging trees, their fronds reflected in a mirror image of feathery gold. The irregular stipple of white and pink. "How hard can it be?"

He glances at me, then shrugs. "It's not a sob story, if that's what you mean. I know how lucky I am. But I've been at boarding school most of my life. I don't know anyone my age here. I suppose what I'm saying is, I don't much like being at home."

"What about your parents? Don't you get on with them?"

He swivels his hand in a so-so gesture. "My father is quiet, scholarly, spends most of his time shut up in his study, reading; I don't quite know how he ended up with my mother—a moment of madness, I think. They could not be more different. He doesn't ask me anything, she never leaves me alone. She wants to know every detail of my life, who my friends are, which parties I've been invited to, whether or not I have a girlfriend. Especially that. She has a weird fascination with my love life. And she can be difficult. Especially when she drinks, which is most of the time."

I met Gabriel fifteen minutes ago, perhaps less, but already I can tune into the words he doesn't say. I can picture him aged ten or twelve, sitting beside a tall, exquisitely dressed Christmas tree, surrounded by presents but craving something else: teasing and chaos and banter.

When I begin to talk about my own family, I catch the wistfulness on Gabriel's face. I tell him about my sister, who is about to finish her first year as a secretary for a solicitors' firm in London. Her days may be spent taking minutes for short-tempered men, but at night she explores London in all its postwar glory. She writes to me of jazz clubs in Soho and after-hours drinking dens, wandering at dawn through the flower market at Covent Garden, waking hours later to a bedroom strewn with red roses.

To a country girl, the life my sister is leading seems one of unparalleled color and richness; I cannot wait to join her.

I tell Gabriel we have spent most of our adolescence leaning out of Eleanor's bedroom window, sharing cigarettes filched from our father's packet of Benson & Hedges, spinning daydreams for one another.

"What do teenage girls dream about? James Dean? Marlon Brando?"

"Bit more highbrow than that," I say, immediately defensive.

But Gabriel is right, we spoke of boys and love mostly.

"And"—he looks up as if he's examining the thin trail of cloud above us—"were there any ordinary mortals in these dreams of yours? I suppose I'm asking if there's someone in particular you care about?"

Actually, there is, though I'm not about to tell Gabriel that. There's very little to tell. A boy who takes the same bus to school and always smiles at me. A boy who is tall and broad and handsome, who looks too big for his uniform, as if one day he might burst out of it. His skin is always sunburned from weekends working on the family farm. He has let it be known in time-honored fashion, from his friends to mine, he would like to take me out one day. I have filtered back that if he asked me, I would be likely to say yes.

It seems simplest to evade the question. "Mostly we'd make up futures for each other. The dreams I spun for Eleanor were always more elaborate than the ones she made up for me. Eleanor gets bored easily. And I could get so lost in the detail, hours of conversations, wrong turns leading to right ones, I'd always make her wait for her happy ending."

"You're a storyteller, then. You'll become a writer, I bet."

"I write poetry."

I never tell anyone about the poems I write, probably because I suspect they are bad. I can't stop writing them, though, filling notebooks with lines of verse, half phrases, and pleasing word pairings when I should be crafting an essay on the Russian Revolution.

He taps the Emily Dickinson on the rug between us. "A poet," he says. "I had a feeling you might be."

"A bad poet. Maybe even a terrible one."

"Don't say that. You have to fool yourself into thinking you already are the thing you want to become. That's what my father says. You write, therefore you're a writer."

There's a moment's silence, and then he says, "I write too," and I recognize the sheepishness with which he says it.

We smile, perhaps both thinking the same thing: two would-be writers, two dreamers, two lonely teenagers waiting for their lives to begin. Who would have thought we'd have so much in common?

"What kind of things?"

"A novel I've started over and over. It always collapses at the same point, about seventy pages in."

"What's it about?"

"I'm embarrassed to tell you."

"Does it, by any chance, feature a boy from a big house with questionable taste in clothes?"

Gabriel looks crestfallen and I am filled with sudden self-loathing. Why am I behaving like this? I don't know him well enough, and my humor is clearly misjudged. "I'm sorry. I'm teasing you but I shouldn't. I know better than anyone how painful this whole thing is."

"You're right about the autobiography aspect. The main character is a drunk. A beautiful woman, unhappily married to a much older man. The only thing I want in life is to write novels. I used to want to be Graham Greene. But then I read *Lucky Jim* by Kingsley Amis and it changed everything for me. It's such a funny book, but daring too. And that's the kind of novelist I'd like to be. Taking risks. Surprising people. A bestseller before I am thirty, if I'm lucky. There. I've told you my innermost secret. You can laugh at me now."

"I don't want to laugh at you," I burst out. "I want to take back every mean thing I've said. Can we start again?"

This time it's me who holds out a hand for him to shake.

"You're a strange girl, Beth Kennedy," he says, taking my hand.

"Good strange or bad strange?"

"Good strange, definitely. My kind of strange. I have a sixth sense for these things."

The light is beginning to drift from the sky by the time I get up to leave. We have been talking for several hours.

"I'll walk you to the road," Gabriel says.

"Escorting me off your land?"

"More eking out the last minutes with you."

I feel a rush of pleasure at this, not that I show it.

"When will you come again?"

I like that for him it's a foregone conclusion we will see each other again.

"At the weekend?"

"Come on Friday evening. The lake is magical at night."

There's a frisson of awkwardness when we say goodbye, as if we should shake hands or kiss or something, but we do neither.

"Goodbye, then," I say.

"The tweed is going straight in the dustbin," he calls after me.

"Good," I shout back.

At the bend in the road, I turn around to wave and I can sense his eyes following me until I disappear from view.

1968

In all the fantasies over the years of meeting Gabriel Wolfe again, driving his child and his dead dog home was never one of them. Leo is sitting in the back of the Land Rover, the dog wrapped in an old coat of Frank's. His weeping cuts me to the bone.

Gabriel occasionally tries to bridge the impossible task of placating us both, and excusing the dog. "It was instinct," he tells his son. "Lurchers were bred to hunt and kill. The farmer did the only thing he could. He had to stop him."

"He murdered Rocket," Leo says.

"Oh, honey," Gabriel says, with a slight twang that makes me think of his American wife. "He had to protect his lambs."

Gabriel says this without much conviction, and I understand. How can a lay person appreciate the true cost to a farmer in losing his sheep? It's not the money, although we rely on the sale of each lamb to keep us going through the winter months. It's the heartbreak of seeing your animals destroyed. The absolute terror of the flock as they watch their own being slaughtered. Five months of nurturing the pregnant ewe, the joy of its lamb being born, which doesn't diminish no matter how many times you see it, only for the lamb to be lost to a savage, bloody death.

Even so, the boy's pain is hard to bear.

"I'm sorry," I say.

"Beth?"

I glance at Gabriel. He has not lost any of his handsomeness with age.

"This is not your fault."

It's surreal seeing him like this, a normal person, a father dealing with a bereft son, instead of the alter ego I have become used to seeing in newspapers and magazines. Gabriel Wolfe, enfant terrible of the literary world. In the years since I knew him, Gabriel has become the thing he desired more than anything else, a respected author. His first novel, published when he was just twenty-four, was a bestseller; his dream had come true in the space of six years. A combination of his edgy writing and indisputable good looks kept the press attention rolling in. If publishing had rock stars, then Gabriel was Mick Jagger and his pretty, blond wife was Marianne Faithfull. And our lives, his and mine, became polar opposites. I was now a farmer's wife, my days filled with bitterly cold mornings, the magic of a lamb being born at sunrise.

I wouldn't have changed a second of it.

We turn into the gates of Meadowlands. Gabriel's childhood home is still one of the most beautiful houses I have ever seen. It has the feeling of a chateau on a small scale with that lovely yellowy stone; steps ascending to a huge oak door; arched windows, their frames painted pale blue. I always loved the blue windows. I'm glad they haven't changed them.

Gabriel gets out of the Land Rover and carries his bundle of dog toward the house, his boy following.

"I'll leave you to it, then," I call after them.

Gabriel turns, looking perplexed. "I don't know what to do with the dog."

"You should bury him."

I am thinking of Bobby, my sensitive boy, how we buried every bird, every rabbit, a hundred little funerals.

"Where?"

"Not exactly a shortage of space, is there?" I say, and he gives me that sideways glance of old.

How quickly we have slipped into our personas from the past, he the landowner's son, me the acerbic dissident.

But we are not who we once were. He is a father, and I was a mother, our identities as merged as they once were separated. You can never change back once you've had a child, even if that child no longer exists.

Leo says: "I have an idea where. Would you come with us, Beth?"

He asks so politely—considering we have just murdered his dog—and looks straight at me with his wide brown eyes. Bobby's eyes were brown too; I used to say they were the color of freshly churned mud. He always laughed at that.

"Come on, then. Let's find a nice spot."

We cross the perfect green lawn, past a tree house that is new since my day—Gabriel must have installed it for Leo. I think how much my son would have loved it, a boy who was happy enough sliding down a stack of hay bales or riding on a tractor with his dad, who was never spoiled with toys but understood every single day, the way Frank does, the glory of our farm.

"Where are we going?" I ask and Leo replies.

"The lake."

Gabriel looks over at me and smiles but it's a regretful sort of smile, as if the ache of memories are the same for him. I cannot allow myself to think of it. When my relationship ended with Gabriel all those years ago, I was devastated for a while, and then I did what every self-respecting woman would do: I shut the door on it, on him. I taught myself to think of Gabriel as someone who belonged to my teenage years, a first crush, little more to me than my brief fixation with the singer Johnnie Ray. Seeing Gabriel again, like this, in the place where we once meant so much to each other, could shake me to my core if I let it.

Father and son choose a spot beneath one of the willow trees.

"If you fetch some spades, I'll help you dig," I say.

While Gabriel is gone Leo and I stand together, looking out at the lake.

Leo is no longer crying, but he stares out at the water morosely. I wonder if he feels awkward being left alone with me, a stranger.

"Do you think you're going to like living here?"

"I doubt it. I miss my friends. And I don't like the kids in my class. They're mean."

"Who is your teacher? Mrs. Adams? She's nice, isn't she?"

"I guess," he says, sounding American. His accent is in and out, certain words sound American but mostly he's more English. "How do you know her?"

"My son used to go to your school."

I've had two years to practice but it never gets any easier, waiting for the next question.

"How old is he?"

"He died two years ago. He was nine."

"Almost the same age as me."

Leo takes my words at face value, the way only a child can. But then, in a gesture so kind and unexpected it takes my breath away, he reaches for my hand. "You miss him, don't you?" he says.

"I do," I say, and Leo must hear the fervency in my voice for he gives my hand a quick squeeze.

When Gabriel comes back with three spades, one for each of us, Leo and I are still standing in the same spot. We don't talk, but there's a peculiar sense of peace between us. Perhaps it is the proximity to this boy, not my boy, but there's an energy and sweetness that brings Bobby back to me.

It's laborious and physical, the digging. The ground is too hard for us to make much progress and Leo soon gives up and sits a yard or so away, watching.

Gabriel and I dig in silence for a while. Then, I say: "I hear your mother is living in Australia now."

He glances up at me. "A mere ten thousand miles between us. Turns out there is a god, after all."

"Of course there's a god, Dad," Leo says. "Why would you think there wasn't?"

"Just a figure of speech. I'm joking."

"Dad doesn't like my granny much," Leo says, in a confiding tone.

"I can't think why."

I had forgotten Gabriel's laugh, how he gives himself over to it until it becomes infectious, and I can't help laughing too, in spite of myself; or rather, in spite of the way I feel about his mother.

"Beth had a son, Dad," Leo says. "But he died. She's still so sad."

The laughter dies on both of us, instantly.

"Oh, I know," Gabriel says, looking everywhere but at me. "I wanted to write and then I wasn't sure—I didn't know if you—"

"It's fine," I say. "Really."

I find myself in this situation often: managing other people's awkwardness around my grief, my loss. But talking to Gabriel about Bobby, a child he never knew, will hurt me in a very specific way.

"It isn't fine. I should have written, I thought about you so much but—"

"Gabriel?"

"Yes?"

"Stop. Please."

"All right. But can I say something?"

"So long as it's not an apology. I hate that."

My voice is harsher than I'd intended. But the endless sorrys get you down. The soft, sad eyes, the reverent tones: It makes me want to scream.

"Is there any way you and I could be friends?" He sticks his hand out in a gesture that reminds me of our beginning.

I think, looking at Gabriel's anxious face, how much I like him. I always did. In spite of everything.

I reach across the grave for his hand. "Friends," I say.

Before

Gabriel is waiting at the end of his drive but looking the wrong way, as if he has forgotten the direction I am coming from. It gives me a second to regard him. He is dressed in dark clothes tonight—a navy sweater, gray trousers—and from twenty yards away his silhouette is long and lean. I cannot see his face but I absorb everything else, his tallness, his slightness; the way he keeps running one hand through his hair, the other stuffed into his trouser pocket.

"I'm missing the tweed already," I call, and he spins around.

Instantly we are grinning at each other. Wide, foolish grins. Does this mean he feels the same? The past week has been almost unbearable, my head filled only with Gabriel, replaying every conversation I could remember, wondering if I'd imagined the feeling of connection.

"You look quite different in your own clothes." By which I mean he is beautiful. Almost shockingly so.

We are standing a few inches apart and I have an irrepressible urge to kiss him. Just for a second. To see how it would feel, see what he would do. Instead, I turn away. I have the sense Gabriel can read every thought that flits through my mind.

"I wasn't sure you'd come," he says.

"There was no danger of that."

I'm rewarded with his slow smile as he takes in what I've said.

Gabriel has made a pathway down to the lake with a dozen candles burning in jam jars. In front of the lake is a little card table draped in white linen and laid with wine-glasses, silver knives and forks, a jug of pale pink roses at its center. There are two folding wooden chairs with cushions on them and blankets draped across their backs in case it gets cold, which is unlikely because, a few yards away, a fire has been lit in a low cast-iron bowl. The moon has begun its slow rise, turning everything around us silver white: the willow trees, the surface of the lake, even the grass glimmers as if it's made of crystal. It is the most romantic thing I've ever seen: a stage set made for two.

"This is wonderful. You've taken so much trouble."

"Told you, way too much time on my hands. Unfortunately, my mother caught me at it, so now she's all agog wanting information. Don't worry, I made her promise she wouldn't come down here."

"I wouldn't mind meeting your mother," I say, and Gabriel laughs.

"I'll remind you of that when you've actually met her."

He pours us each a glass of wine. There is a cooked chicken and potato salad, tomatoes and lettuce from the greenhouse. A little jam jar with ready-mix vinaigrette. And there is Gabriel, untying the paisley scarf looped around his neck before he smiles at me and raises his glass.

"To trespassers," he says, and we clink.

It's strange, the patchwork stories we tell someone when we want them to catch up, a shortcut to knowing us, as if such a thing were possible.

I tell Gabriel my family are Irish, or at least my father is, even though he was born in London and his family moved to Shaftesbury when he was eight. He has never lived in Ireland, and has no trace of an accent, but he pines for it all the same.

"He once told me he felt all wrong in England. As if he'd been displaced from his natural habitat. I asked him how that could be when he's scarcely set foot on Irish soil. He said it was just a feeling he had. That it must be his genetic inheritance and it was driven into his bones, whether he liked it or not. All he knew was that in Ireland the pieces would suddenly fall into place."

My mother is a Dorset girl, born and bred, just like me. She met my father at sixteen and has been with him ever since. They went to the same teacher-training college and married straight after graduation, both their daughters born before they were twenty-five. They adore each other with simple, unfaltering devotion and I sometimes think it has left Eleanor and me with unattainable romantic expectations. How can we ever hope to follow that?

We touch on religion. Catholicism for me, another inheritance from my father, schooling via nuns from the age of five.

"What are they like, your nuns?"

"A few of them are all right. Some of them can be pretty unpleasant, particularly the headmistress. She has her favorites and, unfortunately, I'm not one of them. Thank God I have only one more year to endure before freedom."

Gabriel is going up to Oxford to study at Balliol College, where his father and grandfather went before him. He thinks he will have the same rooms his father had, overlooking the quad.

"Would they have taken you even if you were thick?"

"Probably. The Master is a contemporary of my father's, they are still good friends."

Gabriel laughs, perhaps expecting I will.

I look down at my plate, willing myself to say nothing, while my indignation burns. It's so easy for someone like Gabriel, with his future mapped out from birth.

"I know you're thinking it's unfair. But you could go to Oxford if you wanted to, Beth. There are quite a few colleges that admit women these days. You could apply to St Anne's. It only became a college recently and it's pretty radical, by Oxford standards."

No one at my school has ever gone to Oxford or Cambridge. Very few make it to university at all. The ones who do stay on for sixth form often seem to view it as a waste of time, just waiting for the starting pistol to release them into a life of child-rearing and domesticity, as if these things are the holy grail.

"You love literature," Gabriel persists, when I say nothing. "At Oxford you'll get the best teaching in the world. You can't imagine what the libraries are like. Beautiful buildings filled with first editions. They have handwritten manuscripts of Gerard Manley Hopkins and Shelley. Think of all the writers that went there before you. You'd be walking the same streets as Oscar Wilde and T. S. Eliot."

"Any women?"

"If it matters to you, I will find some."

We move our chairs beside the fire as the evening begins to cool. Gabriel feeds it with more logs, stirring up the embers with a poker and blowing on the flames until they shoot into the air. The stars seem to blaze more brightly here than they do in our back garden; same stars, set like jewels into a navy sky.

"It's getting late," I say. "I'll have to go home soon."

"Stay five more minutes. Ten. This evening has gone too fast."

Something changes in the atmosphere. The look on Gabriel's face makes my heart begin to race. He leans forward in his chair and presses his mouth to mine. A kiss that is tentative and gentle.

"I've wanted to kiss you all evening."

"What took you so long?"

Gabriel laughs and I love the way it animates him. Most

of the time I get the feeling he's observing, but when he laughs his guard comes down.

"I was nervous, I suppose. Wasn't sure if you felt the same." Gabriel takes hold of my hand and pulls me onto his lap.

We kiss again and this time it is everything, his tongue searching mine, hesitantly, then more confidently. We clamp ourselves together, kiss deeply, our fingers entwining.

I didn't know a kiss could be like this, that you could lose yourself in it, no thoughts in your head, your whole body alight to the touch and taste of another.

Gabriel walks me home from Meadowlands on the outskirts of the village to our cottage right in its heart. Outside our gate we kiss again, a chaste goodbye on the cheek in case my parents are watching from the upstairs window.

"Is it too soon to say I already like you more than anyone I've ever met?" Gabriel says.

I can't stop smiling as I walk up the path.

At the sound of my key in the front door, my father comes bustling out of the kitchen. He's clearly been waiting up for me.

"Look at that face," he says, when he sees me. "Goodness me, I think my baby might be in love."

"Dad," I protest, laughing. "Stop."

But I float up the stairs to bed, holding the thrill of his words to me. Perhaps that's what it is, this feeling never experienced before, elation, excitement, a furious kind of happiness. Perhaps this is love.

1968

Frank has left me a note telling me to come to the pub.

I put the kettle on to boil and make myself a cup of tea, but I don't drink it. I'm listless and pacing, churned up with feelings I won't allow to become thoughts. It's the boy mostly. The grip of his hand. I'd forgotten how young children, much like animals, can sense your pain without being afraid of it. Frank and I dance around each other's sadness. Any couple who has lost a child will tell you the same. You see it in the other, of course you do, but it's like you're on a seesaw of grief, and all you want is to avoid tipping the other one down.

Sometimes when I'm like this, I'll give in to it. Sit still and think of Bobby, everything I miss about him, the boy he was. Other times, I get up—as I do now—find my coat, and head out. I need the distraction of others, the softening that only alcohol and conversation can bring.

The Compasses Inn, thatched, dark, and rickety, with uneven slate floors and shadowy corners, is where the village convenes of a Friday. There's a knackered piano which is always in use at closing time, most often by the people who can neither sing nor play. The pub decor, if such a word can be applied, veers toward grim, with fearsome-looking farming equipment displayed on its walls: a rusting scythe from the eighteenth century, an antique plow, even a gamekeeper's mantrap. The beer is regularly off, the crisps always run out, the floor is sticky with cider. There is no better place on earth.

Frank and Jimmy are sitting at the bar, half-drunk pints

in front of them. I tap Frank from behind and he grins broadly as he turns to me, as if seeing me is the best thing ever. One time, after my sister, Eleanor, had overheard me talking to Frank on the phone, she said: "You don't sound married when you talk to Frank. You sound like you've just met."

I am lucky, I do know that.

Jimmy's girlfriend, Nina, is behind the bar. They have been together since they were nineteen. She is a glorious-looking girl with her reddish-blond hair, back-combed to-night into an immaculate beehive. She loves to dress up. Nina and I often laugh about the so-called Swinging Sixties, how there's no sign of it around here. Looking at the pub's regulars—pipe-smoking men wearing corduroys, women in plain sweaters and slacks—you could be forgiven for think-ing you'd stepped into a time warp. Not so Nina, who shops in London whenever she can, blowing her wages on the lat-est craze.

I love watching Nina at work. She coasts a perfect line between flirtation and censure. No one messes with her, not even the drunks. Although, to be fair, the drunk she manhandles from the pub most often is Jimmy.

"How was the boy?" Frank says, as soon as I am sitting beside him.

"He was very upset. Probably a bit shocked too, at his dog killing our lambs like that. He's grown up in the city, hasn't he?"

"And Wolfe? What was he like?"

I feel him watching me carefully. Frank picked up the pieces when Gabriel and I broke up. He knows, better than anyone, how long it took me to recover, how great the cost.

"He was nice," I say, smiling at the blandness of the word. "Grown up, different. A dad, you know?"

"Once a posh nob, always a posh nob," Jimmy says.

As far as I know, Jimmy has never met Gabriel before today, but he dislikes him regardless, out of loyalty to Frank. The bond between the brothers is fierce. When I read *Of Mice and Men*, I felt almost dizzy with recognition, as if Steinbeck had peered into my life. It's insulting of me to compare them to George and Lennie. I'd never say it out loud. There's nothing simple about Jimmy, yet he has an unerring, childlike devotion to Frank which sometimes feels too much. But mostly there's a real sweetness to him. He can charm anyone from the church ladies to the local bobby; he's a cap doffer and a door opener and usually the first to buy a round, even when he can't afford it.

Helen is in the pub tonight; she has been my closest friend since school. When Bobby died, the whole village mourned for a week or two. Then they seemed to forget. Or perhaps, they didn't want to remind Frank and me of our loss, aiming instead for breezy conversational chat that contained what was left unsaid like a layer of silt beneath. You could see the anxiety ticking across their faces. *What can we talk about? I know, the weather!* Helen was different. She came to our house every week, without fail, for the first year. She let herself in and washed up anything that needed to be washed up, cleaned the kitchen, changed the beds. She didn't speak much; she just let us be while she worked in the background, cooking, tidying, making tea, quietly helping our lives to work better. I have never forgotten it.

Helen waits until Frank and Jimmy are talking. Then she says, in a low whisper: "Gabriel's back? What the hell?"

"And we managed to kill his dog on his first afternoon."

We burst out into the kind of laughter reserved only for the most inappropriate of moments, just as we did at school.

"Share the joke?" Frank says, turning around.

"Nothing interesting," Helen says, smoothly. "Did I tell

you our spaniel got herself knocked up? One-night stand with a Lab by the looks of things, the minx. Six puppies in all. We've one left to find a home for. A boy, very handsome."

"I'll take him," I say, and Frank laughs in surprise, kisses the side of my face.

"Consultation is not something my wife chooses to engage in," he says. "Why not? Be nice to have a pup on the farm."

But already an idea is forming. I know full well the healing charms of a puppy. And there is someone who needs that even more than me.

Before

It follows that an order of nuns who named their school the Immaculate Conception Convent should be violently opposed to sex outside marriage, and quite possibly within it. Sister Ignatius, our current headmistress, has demonized it enough over the years that we are predestined either to develop lifelong sexual hang-ups or—as in the case of my sister—set upon a trail of wild promiscuity the moment we are set free. Rumor has it a sixth former did fall pregnant not so long ago—she was hustled out of the school before the pregnancy had even begun to show.

The head takes us for religious studies every Monday, last lesson of the day.

"Elizabeth." Sister Ignatius snaps out my name but, at first, I am too lost in thought to react.

My body has been aflame since the last time Gabriel and I were together, there is no other word for it. I have kissed a few boys but never one who connected me to this sharp and insistent desire. I long now for things never imagined before, I think of him undressing me, of his fingers trailing across my skin, of our bodies pressed together, of more. There is an ache I have that was not there before, as if I have been catapulted into a foreign universe; where previously lust did not exist, now it's all there is.

"Elizabeth Kennedy!"

"Yes, Sister?"

"Would you stay behind after class, please? I'd like a word."

When the rest of class has filed out, I stand beside Sister Ignatius's desk, waiting.

"I hear you're thinking of applying to Oxford?"

When I told my English teacher I was hoping to read English literature at Oxford, she cautioned me against it. Oxford was not meant for "girls like me," she said. She didn't elaborate, but I caught her drift.

"That's right."

"The school would be very proud, I'm sure, to have one of our girls there. You're bright enough, so long as you apply yourself."

This is unexpected, I can't help beaming back at her.

"The school will help you however we can." The nun nods to signal the end of our chat. "Hurry now, Elizabeth, or you'll miss your bus."

My head is full of Gabriel on the bus journey home. On Saturday I am spending the whole night with him and it's hard to think of anything else. I have told my parents I am staying at Helen's. I don't like lying to them but I know my mother would worry if she knew the truth. She'd tell me it was too soon.

When we arranged it, Gabriel said: "Please don't think I'm planning on taking advantage of you."

I thought, but did not say, *Oh, I hope you do.*

I am so lost in thought I don't notice someone sitting down next to me until a voice says: "Hi, Beth."

It's Frank Johnson. For once, not sitting in his usual place at the back of the bus with his friends. I do like Frank. He always seems more grown-up than the other boys my age. We see each other at the parties of school friends or the annual village hop, and he always asks me to dance or offers to fetch me a drink. For a while, I'd hoped our easy friendship might develop into something else.

When Frank was thirteen his mother died from a bleed on the brain.

She'd been helping with the afternoon milking when a cow kicked out and caught her full thwack in the temple. Accidents happen frequently on farms, everyone knows that. What shocked me was how Frank was back on the school bus the following day.

We'd had art that afternoon, two hours of sticking pressed flowers onto porous blue paper. Most of the girls had brought in daffodils from their gardens but I'd taken the trouble to plunder bluebells from the woods. When I got up for my stop, I passed by Frank, white-faced and silent in his seat. I took my picture out of my satchel and handed it to him, no words needed. I remember his look of surprise, then the merest hint of a smile. We have been friends ever since.

"I wanted to ask you something," Frank says, and my heart dips with dread.

This thing I wanted, daydreamed about, in fact, for weeks and months, has come too late.

"I think you know what it is."

I do, oh, I do, and I want, more than anything, to stop it from happening.

"Beth." My name again, the beginning of a speech I fear Frank has rehearsed.

"I have waited far too long to tell you this. I think about you all the time. Seeing you on the bus is the highlight of my day. It would make me so happy if you would let me take you out this weekend."

Frank has delivered his speech without looking at me, his eyes held just out of reach of my own. But now he does look, and he sees instantly my expression of regret.

"Oh," he says. "It isn't what you want? I don't know why I thought it was."

I put my hand onto Frank's arm, my fingers splayed on the cheap black material of his school blazer. His hand is clenched into a fist, a scattering of black hairs between his wrist and his knuckles.

"It's just—I'm sorry—I've met someone."

Frank looks heartbroken. "I left it too late."

"I'm sorry," I say again.

I want to make it better between us, to find a way of bringing back some light into his handsome, healthy face.

But Frank gets up and heads to the front of the bus. And when the driver stops, he gets out, miles from home, as if he cannot bear to be near me for a moment longer.

For the rest of the journey, it's Frank who is the headline in my thoughts, my heart churning at the thought of his long walk home and the burning humiliation he must have felt to get off the bus. And beneath this, a gnawing sense of regret or remorse or confusion that I might have thrown away the chance of something great.

1968

Leo is in his tree house, peering out at whoever it is coming up the drive, and when he sees it's me, he waves and clambers down his rope ladder. It's electrifying looking at him, the shape of him, the size of him, a reminder of the boy we lost; part of me wishes Frank were here to see it too. Since Bobby died, we've spent very little time in the company of children, and never one the same age. That was our choice and I know why we made it, but I hadn't realized how lonely it would feel living a life that had no children in it.

Leo shrieks when I bring the puppy out from the car. "Is he yours?"

"He doesn't really belong to anyone yet. He's in between homes, let's say. Would you like to hold him?"

Leo makes a cradle of his arms and the dog settles instantly.

"Look how relaxed he is with you."

"Let's show Dad. He's in his study."

I'm curious to catch Gabriel at work. There have been countless features over the years, Gabriel looking thoughtful in a black polo-neck. "Pretending he's Hemingway again," Helen said once, flashing a copy of *Vogue* she'd stolen from the hairdresser's in which Gabriel appeared at his typewriter, tumbler of whisky beside him. I read his books in secret, looking for traces of familiarity, for the boy I once knew. I always found them. Sharp-tongued women with a fondness for drink, and lurid, provocative sex scenes which forged his reputation as a brave writer, and sometimes made me weep.

Into the house with its head rush of memories. The hall

smells the same, wax polish and old wood, so much of it, everywhere. Oak panels on the walls, parquet on the floor, the worn circular staircase I always loved, slippery to a socked foot.

And here is the writer in a room off the kitchen where once we came to hunt for his father's cigarettes. Gabriel has his back to us, typing at great speed with two fingers, the famed glass of whisky in situ at a chaotic desk covered with books and papers. I spy the spines of W. H. Auden, Graham Greene, and Henry James.

"Dad, look," Leo says.

Gabriel spins around, taking in me and the puppy at the same time. His hair is a little wild, as if he's been running his fingers through it, and there's a streak of blue ink on his cheek.

"Beth," he says. "And who is this? My God, he's cute."

He comes over to stroke the pup.

It's disturbing, our proximity. Seeing him again feels new and exciting in a way it definitely shouldn't. In my head, I've mastered the readjustment, telling myself our past doesn't matter, we are adults now, we can try, or at least pretend, to be friends. It's my body that betrays me.

"What's he called?"

"I haven't named him yet."

"But you're keeping him?" Leo asks.

"If no one else wants him, then yes. I'm helping out my friend Helen."

Leo looks at Gabriel. They smile in exactly the same way. A grin that spreads slowly until, in the last seconds, it can no longer contain itself and becomes a suppressed laugh.

"What type of dog is he?" Gabriel asks.

"Half spaniel and we're not one hundred percent on the rest. There's some Labrador in there. Fully weaned and house-trained, apparently."

"So, we could have him, if we wanted to?"

"Yes."

"Can we, Dad? Please?"

"Why not? So long as you promise to look after him."

Leo puts the puppy down. Instantly he starts to pee on the floor.

"Charming," Gabriel says, looking at me and Leo. "Good thing he's house-trained."

It feels good, our sudden, shared laughter.

"If you're going to keep him, just make sure you teach him to behave around livestock. This is farming country, cattle everywhere."

"Could it happen again?" asks Leo, anxious.

"Not if he's properly trained. If you like, I'll help you." I've said it without thinking through the consequences.

Before I can change my mind, Leo throws both arms around my waist, presses his face to my chest. For a second or two, it throws me. I close my eyes, willing myself not to think of Bobby, and when I open them, I see Gabriel watching, a gentle, sad sort of smile on his face.

"Hey," Frank says, when he comes in from the farm at suppertime. "Where's our pup? Weren't you picking him up this afternoon?"

"I gave him to Gabriel's boy. Thought it would help."

Frank says nothing.

"I'm going to help Leo train him. Don't want the same thing happening again."

"I see."

Conversations between Frank and me are always easy. We talk about the farm mostly, our shared labor and passion. Since his father, David, died last year from a heart attack— out in the fields, exactly the way he always said he wanted to go—Frank, Jimmy, and I have run the farm together. But this is new territory.

His face is stern, a seriousness I don't often see. What he wants to say is, *Don't get involved with this child, Beth. He's not our boy. We'll never get him back.*

Instead he says: "Should I be worried about you spending time with Wolfe and his son?"

And I want to tell him, *You risked his life. You did this, not me.*

But I say: "I don't think so. Are you worried?"

"Not if you tell me there's no need."

I reach for his hand and smile at him until it triggers his own reluctant grin.

"There is no need, I promise."

Back then, at the beginning, I believe this to be true.

The Trial

Heads turned to look at me when I took my place in the public gallery. I have a new identity now. The woman who loved two men, one of them worthy of pages of newsprint, the other an ordinary farmer.

When the story first broke, photographers snuck out to the farm for shots of our beloved, ramshackle house with its peeling windows and chaotic yard until I spied them from the kitchen and ran out, screaming like a wild woman. Next day, that was the photo they chose. I learned the hard way to conceal my face and never answer the questions they hurl at me. *Why did he do it?* The question I'm asked most often. From reporters, villagers, friends, even my own family at the beginning.

I tell them the story we have come up with, honed, practiced, perfected, day after day after day, hoping it will be enough.

How much easier it would be if we could tell the truth.

Before

The inside of Gabriel's tent is like nothing I've ever seen, it feels like entering an alternate universe. There's a double mattress made up with sheets and blankets and a very regal-looking bedspread in red velvet; I can imagine it topping Louis XIV's four-poster. Sheepskin rugs cover the floor, there's a little bedside cabinet with a water decanter and two glasses; he even has a small bookcase filled with paperbacks. He has pinned swathes of bright-colored silk to the ceiling and there are candles burning in glass lanterns in every corner of the tent.

"What do you think?" he says.

"It's like *Arabian Nights*. If it were me, I'd never sleep anywhere else."

Gabriel sits down on the bed and holds out a hand to me. "Come here."

I've done nothing but imagine this moment and now that it is here, I freeze.

"I can't," I say, in a tight voice. "I'm too nervous."

"Don't be. We're just talking. We might progress to holding hands at some point. But only if you want to."

I sit down next to him and, as promised, Gabriel begins to talk. He tells me about his dog, Molly, a Labrador who lived until she was sixteen.

"She was the soppiest dog you could imagine, loved everyone, including a couple of burglars who climbed in through the kitchen window. Just wagged her tail while they lifted the family silver."

He picks up a novel which is open, face down, beside the

bed and holds it up for me to inspect. *Swann's Way*, the first volume of Proust's novel *In Search of Lost Time*.

"I only chose it so I could show off in my tutorials next term, but it's better than I thought. Quite funny at times."

Now he smiles as he looks at me. "Sometimes," Gabriel says, "it's almost light before I fall asleep, I'm so busy thinking about you. And all the things I'd like to do with you."

"What things?"

In answer Gabriel takes my face in his hands and kisses me. A long, slow, intense kiss. "Better?" he says, drawing back.

"Yes."

We lie back on the bed and turn toward each other, faces inches apart.

Gabriel reaches out to trace a line from my forehead to my nose, resting his finger above my top lip. "I think about this little dip here," he says. "How it would be exactly the right shape and size for the tip of my finger."

Gabriel takes hold of my hand.

"Just because you're staying the night, don't think that means we have to do anything more than this."

"What if I want to?" I say.

"Then we would discuss it."

"I want to."

He looks at me, half laughing, but then his face changes and the desire I see in him ignites something in me. A sort of daring, a need.

"I really want to."

I would freeze this moment, if I could, the two of us watching each other hungrily, knowing and also not quite knowing what is going to come next.

Gabriel and I continue kissing, and it's me who takes things further, unbuttoning my shirt, reaching out to take his hand and putting it on my breast.

Everything is done slowly. The removing of my clothes, one by one. Then his. The two of us naked in each other's arms, the electricity of that. Taking our time to look and appreciate the secrets of each other unclothed. The hardness of his muscles beneath his smooth, suntanned skin, the line of black hair that runs from his navel to his groin, the surprise of him aroused, his gasp when I run my finger lightly across his penis.

His touch is hesitant and questioning as he traces patterns across my skin but our bodies begin to drive us, the path starkly clear. I pull him down on top of me and we kiss more passionately. It's instinct that makes me lift my hips to meet his and I feel the hardness of his erection pressing against me before he draws back.

"No, Beth, we shouldn't," Gabriel whispers.

"Why?" I whisper back.

"You know why."

"Just for a second?"

He presses the tip of himself inside me.

We begin to move against each other slowly and soon we're giving in. It wasn't planned; it was inevitable. And it feels good until Gabriel thrusts more deeply inside me and I yelp in pain.

"Oh, God, I'm sorry." He tries to pull away, but I clamp my thighs around him.

"Stay," I whisper.

And so, he does.

What can I say about these long moments where we just look at each other, allowing ourselves to feel the sensation of him inside me, the two of us connected in the most intimate way? I'd imagined it so many times but it's nothing like I thought. My heart is so full of feeling, emotions I cannot name, neither joy nor sorrow but something in between. *This is us*, I think. *This is us.*

After a while I move against him again, just a little.

"Is it OK?" he says. "Am I hurting you? Should we stop?"

"Gabriel? Please stop talking."

"I'll try."

We smile at each other. Part of me still can't believe it is happening, as if I am outside looking in.

The pain begins to shift into something more pleasurable, a kind of ache. We seem to fit perfectly together and we find a slow, gentle rhythm, rocking back and forth in our makeshift bed. Not once do his eyes ever leave my face.

"I'd stay here forever if I could," he says.

Afterward we marvel at the fact it was the first time for both of us and yet we seemed to know exactly how to be. We lie together, heartbeats fading, wrapped up so tightly in each other's arms I cannot see his face when Gabriel says: "By the way, I love you. I think I did from the first moment I saw you."

"Yes," I say, because I believe it is true.

This is a love story and it is better, by far, than any of the ones I have dreamed up in the past. If I'm allowed a wish, just one, then it is this: I wish for our story to have a happy ending.

1968

Frank, Jimmy, and I are out in the sheep field the first time I leave to meet Leo. We have fed and watered the ewes and checked over the lambs, revising the list of which ones will be sold first at next week's auction.

Even with a fresh trough of water and the buckets of feed, some of the sheep stay clustered around Jimmy, braying and butting his thighs for attention. It's always this way—Jimmy is their rock star.

"Away with you now, Mrs. Tiggywinkle, we've work to do," Jimmy says, with a slap to his favorite ewe's rump.

It was Bobby who began the tradition of naming our ewes, Jimmy who insists on upholding it.

"Bloody hell," Frank says, glancing at his watch. "You're right, how did it get to half three already? The cows will be bellyaching. Give us a hand, Beth?"

"Sorry, I've got to go," I say. "Puppy training."

Frank spins around. He'd forgotten I was going to Meadowlands today. And I see—the way his face changes from resentment to a forced placidity—that he is never going to feel all right about me and Gabriel.

I watch him registering my clothes, not the old Viyella shirt of Frank's, the cords and wellies I normally wear, but a black polo-neck and a pair of dark jeans, a castoff from Nina that is still more fashionable, with the slight flaring at the ankle, than anything else I own.

I flush beneath his scrutiny, feeling self-conscious and overdressed.

"Why are you bothering with that clown?" Jimmy says.

He's seen Frank's face too.

"Because, Jimmy," I say, and my tone is too defensive, too spiky, "sometimes it's nice to put yourself out for other people."

"Even when that person is a complete asshole?"

"He's joking, Beth," Frank says, before I've time to rise.

"Half joking," Jimmy corrects him, and we eyeball one another for a second, but that's all before we're both smiling. I can never stay cross at my brother-in-law for long.

I decide to walk to Meadowlands rather than drive, I need the time to think. I've told Frank he has no reason to feel concerned about these afternoon visits, my spending time with Leo but, inevitably, seeing Gabriel too. Told myself the same. But my body, my mind, refuse to listen on the ten-minute journey from my house to theirs. There's a knot of tension in my stomach, I can sense the blood pulsing, pulsing in my veins, an anxious rhythmic tattoo. There were things that happened back then that no one knew of; I live in dread of those secrets worming their way out. And something even more unnerving—a gathering feeling of excitement at the prospect of seeing Gabriel again.

I knock on the door, pushing from my mind the memory of the time I once stood here, heart pounding, for very different reasons.

Gabriel answers, smiling when he sees me. He is wearing jeans and an untucked white shirt, a tattered black jumper on top, full of holes. He looks as if he hasn't shaved in days. Dark circles beneath his eyes. I wonder how he's managing, a single parent who still has to fulfil his writing obligations. Not very well, by the look of things.

"Beth. Come in. Someone's very excited to see you."

Leo runs into the hall on cue, the little dog in his arms.

"Have you named him yet?" I ask.

"Hero," Leo says.

"I like it. Suits him."

"Cup of tea before we get started?" Gabriel says. "I was just about to make one."

"No, thanks. And don't worry about coming with us. We'll go out into the garden, you carry on."

Something passes across Gabriel's face here and I wonder if he's been looking forward to some adult company for a change. So be it. I'm determined to spend as little time with him as possible. I owe that to Frank, to myself.

"All right," he says, evenly. "I'll leave you to it."

The swoop of disappointment as I watch him walk away is almost as pronounced as my relief.

Out in the garden, Leo and I begin with the command "sit," rewarding Hero each time he manages it with a little cube of cheddar or a piece of ham, treats I have brought with me from home. He catches on quickly, so we progress to "stay." I demonstrate first getting Hero to sit, then showing him the palm of my hand, and repeating "stay." Then Leo tries it and, each time, the puppy stays put, even when we start to walk away from him, one step at a time.

"This is going to be a cinch," I say.

"Is he a genius?"

"I think he might be. But we should leave it there for today. Geniuses need their rest."

"You're not going already?" Leo says. "Do you have to?"

I can tell he's spoken without thinking. And, in a flash, I see his loneliness. "How about you show me your tree house first?"

He looks so delighted.

Inside, the tree house is a revelation. It's a fairly big space, tall enough to stand up in, around eight feet wide, with a big open window looking out over the grounds. The walls have been painted sky blue and the floor is covered with giant velvet cushions in gorgeous jewel colors: emerald green, ruby, sapphire blue. There's a pile of comics and Tintin books, candles, an old-fashioned kerosene lamp, a box of dominoes, packs of cards, a Ludo board.

"I wish I had a tree house like this. It's a proper den. Have you slept up here?"

"In the summer we will, my dad says. He loves camping. He used to camp by the lake when he was a boy."

My heart lurches, but I ignore it.

"We painted it one weekend. We had our supper up here and played cards by candlelight. It was the best."

I catch the wistfulness in Leo's voice. "You need to invite some friends over. They'd love it up here."

"Maybe," he says.

"How are you liking school?"

"It's fine, I guess."

"Doesn't sound it."

I see him weighing up whether or not to tell me the truth. "It's no better? I thought you might be settling in now."

"I hate it so much." He looks angry suddenly.

"Did something happen?"

"I'm always in trouble. Every day I get sent to the head-mistress. Or I'm made to stand outside the classroom."

"Why?"

"I get cross. Sometimes I shout at the other kids. I hit a boy yesterday. He was saying mean stuff and I punched him. It just happened. I didn't mean to do it."

"Does your dad know?"

"Not everything. Only what the teacher tells him."

"That sounds hard. No wonder you hate it. It'll feel better when you're more used to it."

"Doubt it." He looks so glum, this young boy, it doesn't feel right for him to be so unhappy.

"Fancy a game of Ludo before I go?"

"Yes," he says, his face brightening as he reaches for the box.

I'm glad to keep him company and yet there's a slight feeling of sorrow nagging at the edges of my mind. I'm not sure it's even about Bobby, the usual thing. I can feel myself starting to care about this boy already, even though I've promised Frank, promised myself, I wouldn't get involved. And it feels a little dangerous, opening my heart like this, just a chink. Knowing I should stop. Knowing I'm not going to.

Before

For one glorious week in August, Gabriel's parents go on holiday to the Highlands.

"Grouse shooting," Gabriel says. "And yes, it's cruel. But look what we get. The run of the place for seven whole days."

Gabriel often decries his inheritance, but I sense his pride as he shows me around. The entrance hall alone feels as grand as a ballroom with its dark wooden paneling and an enormous crystal chandelier, which hangs from the ceiling like a statement of decadence. It smells of wax polish and fresh flowers and something less distinct: a rich, dry scent as if even the air has been filtered for refinement.

Hard not to be intimidated by the beauty of this house, not just its size and grandeur, but also the way it is furnished—the gilt-framed pictures, the tapestries and dark polished wood, silver everywhere, all of it with a fierce, mirrorlike shine. I count four flower displays as I wander through the rooms, not daffodils plonked in a jug, but artful arrangements in porcelain. Gabriel's mother is a woman with a passion for flower arranging; mine sits by the fire late into the night marking essays and planning lessons for the next day.

In the drawing room I examine the family photographs on top of the piano. Tessa Wolfe, as a bride in the 1930s, is more beautiful than any Hollywood star, and it's easy to see where Gabriel gets his good looks from. Her dress is a column of ivory silk, worn with a feather headdress and long white gloves. There is something cold and intimidating about her, even on her wedding day. Her half smile seems scornful, as if she despises the photographer, the guests, perhaps even her husband.

The photo I love best is Gabriel, aged around nine, in shorts and a white shirt, sitting cross-legged with his arms around the neck of a fat black Labrador. I can't stop looking at this picture, his smile, his frank, dark-eyed stare. Something about it unravels me.

In a week of unbroken sunshine, we spend our days playing tennis and swimming in the lake. We become more daring, knowing we have the place to ourselves. Aside from their "daily," Mrs. W, who comes in to clean first thing, we are entirely alone. In the afternoons we sunbathe naked, we make love in the open air and almost every room of the house, imprinting our passion on the antique furniture—a dimpled leather sofa, a gilt-tooled desk.

As I was leaving, my mother surprised me with a diaphragm she had requested from the doctor. We hadn't discussed my sleeping with Gabriel, but I'd spent so many nights with him at the lake, she must have guessed.

"You don't mind?" I asked her.

"You seem serious enough about each other. Men have lovers before they marry, why shouldn't women?"

"You're not like other mothers," I said, and she laughed and kissed me.

"Thank God for that."

Something changes in this week of liberation, which feels twice as long as its actual hours. Time no longer matters, it stretches before us like elastic. We scarcely sleep, for one thing. There is the novelty of being naked together in a proper bed, one we can return to at any time of day. I tell Gabriel we have become like one of those old-fashioned weather clocks where the man and woman pop out at different times; when one of us is asleep, the other is invariably awake, pulsing with longing.

We live in this week like one person. We take baths together, head to toe and up to our necks in delicious-smelling bubble bath he steals from his mother's bathroom. This, for me, is the epitome of luxury. At home we restrict ourselves to a twice weekly "bath night," heating up water to fill the tin bath, Eleanor and I taking strict turns as to who goes in first.

Gabriel and I cook increasingly bizarre meals as the fresh ingredients run out and we are forced to rely on the larder. Consommé soup studded with tinned ham, rice we overboil to the consistency of glue, roast potatoes with marrowfat peas. We abandon our own books so we can read the same one, matching our pace as we scan each page, sometimes stopping to talk about what we have read, so in tune we often say the same thing at the same time.

"It's starting to feel like we share a brain," Gabriel says. "How will we integrate ourselves back into the real world?"

My favorite times are the evenings, when we help ourselves to wine from his father's cellar and play records on the gramophone. We listen to Dickie Valentine and Chuck Berry and Bill Haley & His Comets. Over and over we play "Rock Around the Clock," the hit of the summer, while Gabriel attempts to teach me the jitterbug, snapping out instructions like a ballroom dance teacher: "Under the arm now, two steps back and swing!" It invariably ends with us collapsing onto the sofa, laughing.

It is on these nights, tongues loosened by wine, we begin to talk in a way we have never spoken before. I confess to Gabriel that there was someone who loved me before he did and I fear I might have broken his heart.

Rumor has it Frank Johnson has dropped out of school, choosing to work full-time on the farm instead of finishing his A levels.

"You can't help who you fall in love with," Gabriel says,

kissing me. "But poor fellow, whoever he is. I wouldn't want a life without you in it."

"You don't think I'm a heartless monster?"

"I think you're utterly and completely wonderful."

One night, Gabriel trades a secret of his own.

A few years ago, his mother told him she was having an affair. The man was young, around her age, and handsome, but virtually penniless. She didn't care. Over the course of a few weeks they had fallen in love and she decided to leave Gabriel's father. But only if Gabriel would come with her.

"She looked so happy when she told me about him. Like a lovestruck young girl. She was euphoric. A side of her I'd never seen. Just like us." He pauses, as if the next words are too hard. "I told her if she left, she wouldn't see me again. A stupid, idle threat, I didn't mean it. I was just worried about my father. She stayed because of me and I think the heartbreak destroyed something in her. She changed almost overnight. The daytime drinking started. The bitterness. The pointless cruelty to my father and, occasionally, me. Sometimes I think I ruined her life."

For a moment I pause, trying to find the right words. I am shocked by what he has told me, not just his mother's affair, but also the way she resented Gabriel and his father once it had ended. She sounds selfish and unkind.

"You mustn't think like that. You weren't responsible for your mother's happiness."

Gabriel pulls me against his chest. "It wasn't enough for her to be unhappy herself, she had to make my father and me miserable too. I hated being here, until you came along."

"You won't leave me?" Gabriel says, on our last night together.

It's late or very early, a ghostly light beginning to edge around the velvet curtains in his bedroom.

I am half-asleep, lost in that pleasurable haze where dreams and reality bleed into one another.

"Beth?"

"Mmm?"

"Promise you won't leave me."

"As if."

"Then promise."

"Are you actually serious?" I open my eyes.

He nods. "Very."

"You first," I say, and he laughs.

"So competitive. Even when you're asleep."

He promises, then I do, and it doesn't mean anything, not really, it's just silly talk, the kind of thing lovers say, but it feels, for a moment, before I drift back to sleep, as if our future is written.

1968

The men are out on the farm and I am spending the morning at home trying to finish some of the endless chores I set for myself.

Busyness is the only thing that helps. People spoke to me of meditation after Bobby died, I was lent library books on Buddhism and the ancient art of yoga. And I thought, *Really, you think a few minutes of intense breathing will modify my pain?* In the agonizing first months when I still saw Bobby everywhere and nowhere, I could not even read. I'd taken solace in books for my entire life. As a child I'd become so absorbed in my favorite stories, the characters sometimes felt more vivid to me than my friends. Even as an adult, I could still lose myself in fictional worlds, feeling the wrench when I was forced to return to real life. And, quite suddenly, I didn't have the heart or the mental capacity for any of it. I could not listen to the radio. I could not manage a conversation with anyone other than my own family and, even then, only at the most cursory level. But what I could do was work, really hard. It was my father-in-law, David, who put me back to work on the farm, understanding hard physical labor, twelve-hour stretches of it, was a necessary outlet for my grief. I can do everything the men do, milk cows, herd sheep, mend fences, heft hay bales. Me and Frank and Jimmy, the hardest workers you'll ever come across.

When the doorbell rings, I am kneeling on a sill furiously shining a window with newspaper and white vinegar. It is annoying to get down and answer the door but I do it—

country people usually do. We live a more courteous life than town folk, or so I have always imagined: We greet each other, we lend things, we share useful information.

What I am not expecting when I throw open the door is to find Gabriel on the other side of it.

"Hi," I say, attempting to sound nonchalant though my heartbeat tells a different story.

"Am I interrupting?"

"Not at all. Would you like to come in?"

Country manners, ingrained and inescapable.

Gabriel looks around him with open curiosity when he comes into the room, and I wonder what he sees. It is a classic farmhouse kitchen, I suppose. A huge oak table that belonged to Frank's grandparents and has endured three generations of eating and laughter and arguments. An assortment of dining chairs, some I have painted, others in dark old wood. The huge fireplace at one end of the room which always draws admiration—it feels medieval as if it should have huge black cauldrons dangling in front of it. The dresser with the pretty blue-and-gold china we inherited from Frank's parents and rarely use. A framed picture of pressed wildflowers, the same ones I gave Frank on the bus all those years ago, now fading beneath its glass. And, blown up to poster size, a picture of Bobby on his third birthday, chin smeared with chocolate, eyes crinkled in his trademark grin.

I watch Gabriel taking him in.

"Your son? Beth, he's you exactly."

"People say that." If my voice is too crisp, I can't help it. "Was there something you wanted?"

He hesitates, thrown, perhaps, by my directness.

"I'm horribly behind on my deadline and I've realized I need someone to look after Leo for a couple of hours each day. A paid job, I mean. Picking him up after school and keeping him busy while I write. Would you consider it?"

"I have a job. I run the farm with Frank and Jimmy."

"The thing is, he adores you. It would only be a couple of hours. You quite often spend that with him now. The only difference is that I'd pay you."

Gabriel is right: In the past few weeks I've spent more and more time at Meadowlands. Leo's easy friendship—his quick laughter, his chatter, his curiosity—has consoled me more than anything else. It began with dog training. Before long I was pointing out wildflowers and teaching him to tell different birds apart, their colors, their sounds. All the things an urban child grows up without knowing.

"I wouldn't like taking money from you."

"You'd be taking it from the publisher, not me. I got a decent advance on this book, I'd want to be generous."

Gabriel Wolfe as my employer, how would that feel? And how can I possibly expect Frank to agree to it?

He steps closer to me, so close I can smell the woody, cedary aftershave he's wearing. I can see the muscles working in his jaw. "Can I say something?"

I nod, not trusting myself to speak.

"It's made such a difference to Leo—and me—having you around. I only wish you didn't feel you had to avoid me. I know it's awkward with everything that happened. What I'm trying to say is, I'd really love it if you and I could be friends."

"We are."

"We're not. You hardly ever come into the house. You always rush off as soon as I appear. You never stay for a cup of tea."

"I have things to do here."

"Beth. Look at me. Please."

63

I do look and it becomes a kind of staring contest, the two of us gazing at one another long enough for it to become comical. Both of us smiling. In this moment, I feel like Beth Johnson, the farmer's wife. There is nothing of Beth Kennedy, the teenager who once fell crazily in love with the man standing before me. I think, *Perhaps we can do this. Perhaps we will be all right after all.*

"I'll have to talk to Frank. We decide everything together."

"Of course," he says. "And thank you."

Over dinner Frank and I talk about the farm, its growing debt, a looming meeting with the bank that is worrying him. Smallholder farming doesn't pay, it's not something you do for the money. We struggle a little but never enough to sell up; the farm is our mutual passion, Frank's and Jimmy's and mine.

"Guess what I saw earlier?" Frank says. He's watching me carefully, a look on his face I can't quite read. "The kestrels are back."

"They are not."

"Yup. Didn't have the binoculars so I couldn't tell if the chicks have hatched yet, but I don't think so. They've just arrived, I'm sure."

We had nesting kestrels in one of our ash trees three years in a row, and Bobby was obsessed with them. Frank built him a hide opposite the tree out of a wooden stepladder with a beer barrel for its seat and he'd spend hours up there, binoculars trained on the nest, counting the chicks as they hatched. Every day after school we'd go to the hide, waiting for the male kestrel to fly off in search of food, which he always did, sooner or later. Our favorite thing was when the chicks were a little older, big enough that we could see them waiting for the male to return, pink mouths open. We were always sad when they left the nest at around six weeks old, thrilled when they came back the following spring. The year Bobby died the kestrels stopped coming.

"Tomorrow I'll come with you and take a look," I tell him.

We carry on eating, but the conversation we need to have is nagging away at me, until I can no longer hold it in. "I've got something to tell you and you're not going to like it. But it's money."

Frank laughs. "If it's money, I'll like it."

"Gabriel has asked me to watch Leo after school. A couple of hours each day. Sometimes I'd be at Meadowlands but I'd like to bring him here. He'd love the farm. He's mad about animals."

"No, Beth."

The change in his face, I hate it. You spend years looking at someone night after night across a table, you know every inch of him. I know from the set of his mouth, the hurt in his eyes, what Frank is thinking. It's a precipice we are on, I don't need him to tell me.

"We don't need his charity. I'm surprised you'd even consider it after everything that happened."

"It's hardly charity, it's a job. If I don't do it someone else will. But I'm going to do it. For the money, yes. But mostly it's the boy. It helps me, Frank."

"It's dangerous what you're doing," he says, quietly.

And there is nothing I can do but nod.

"I don't want it to come between us," I say, but he shrugs.

It already has.

Before

Tessa Wolfe is astonishing to look at close-up. Her hair and eyes are dark, like Gabriel's, but her features are finer: a delicate nose, a mouth that might be thin but is painted defiant scarlet, a slender neck glistening with a band of diamonds that are almost certainly the real thing. I've never been up close to beauty like this or, for that matter, such extravagant jewelry, and it is all I can do not to stare.

She is also, according to Gabriel, well on her way to being drunk.

"Just agree with her on everything and you'll be fine," he told me when I arrived for a dinner I have been dreading since it was first suggested.

"I've been dying to meet you," Tessa says, gesturing to the chair next to hers. "And Gabe has selfishly kept you to himself all summer long."

"Very wise, if you ask me," Edward Wolfe says, winking as he shakes my hand. He is instantly likable, and I wish I were sitting beside him rather than next to Tessa on the other side of the table.

I have never seen such an ornately laid table, with its terrifying number of glasses, knives, and forks. It feels excessive for a dinner for four people and when the food is brought in by a girl from the village, there are things I have never even heard of before. Smoked salmon and beef Wellington, which turns out to be a whole fillet of beef cooked in pastry and served almost raw in its middle. Rationing only stopped last year and, aside from the introduction of sugar and a little more meat, at home our diet has scarcely changed.

The serving girl, Sarah, is a couple of years older than me; we both went to Hemston primary school. When she waits for me to help myself to a slice of beef, I feel like a fraud.

"Hi, Sarah," I say, softly. "How are you?"

But she simply nods an acknowledgment and looks away.

"I hear you're applying to Oxford," Edward says. "Good for you. Which college?"

"St Anne's, to read English."

"Oh, one of the *new* colleges," Tessa says.

"Actually St Anne's has a wonderful reputation," Edward says. "Of course, in my day, there were no women at Oxford at all. I'm really quite envious of Gabriel."

"The other girls will probably have been to boarding school," Tessa continues. "I hope you won't feel left out?"

"For goodness' sake, Mother, don't be such a snob," Gabriel says, and I see the vivid color in his cheeks.

"Oh, I'm an incorrigible snob, according to my son."

Tessa says it with pride. And I catch something that explains her to me, better than Gabriel has ever been able to. I don't think she's from this world originally, much as she pretends otherwise. One she almost walked out on but didn't, that's why it matters to her. It's a consolation prize, and she guards it closely.

I was expecting this evening to be tough, but I imagined Gabriel would be on hand to rescue me. Instead, he strikes up a long conversation with his father, leaving me to fend off Tessa's intrusive questions by myself. I sense Tessa Wolfe circling, hungry for something, but I cannot tell what.

"Your parents both work, isn't that right? I expect your mother feels she rather missed out on your childhoods?"

"Not really. They teach, so we've always had the school holidays together."

"Where do you like to holiday as a family?"

It feels like some kind of test, this, and I don't have the right answer for it. She is looking for me to say the south of France or wherever it is the fashionable people go. We spend our summers at home and my parents fill them with day trips to the coast, visits to museums, twice-weekly trips to the library, where we take out our full quota of books. On rainy days we light a fire in the sitting room and all four of us read and, when I think of it now, I can feel the quiet contentment of those days.

Tessa doesn't seem to notice my silence. She refills her glass and fires off another question. "Tell me about you and Gabe. Do you love him very much? No need to answer that, it's all there in your eyes. And he's terribly fond of you, I do know that."

In a low, confiding voice she says Gabriel is the kind of boy who makes friends easily. "Trouble is, he can spread himself a bit thin sometimes. Once he's at Oxford I imagine he'll be very taken up with his social life."

"I'll be very taken up myself, studying for A levels."

Tessa leans closer so our faces are only inches apart, I can smell her intensely floral perfume and the wine on her breath.

She lowers her voice until it's just above a whisper. "I think what I'm trying to say—I hope it's helpful—is that Gabriel tends to put himself first. It's why he makes such a success of things—he's very blinkered on what he wants. And then, quite suddenly, he can move on to the next thing. I've seen it happen with friends of his. Probably my fault for making him the center of my universe. I treated him like he was God's gift when he was a little boy. I still do."

I console myself with the things Gabriel has told me about his mother. That she's a mean drunk, that she obsesses over his life because she doesn't like her own.

I see also Tessa doesn't really know Gabriel, not the way

I do. She doesn't know, for example, about his desire to write, the fear he will never be good enough, of being railroaded into something he would hate, like banking or law, the professions his mother has in mind for him. Tessa has no idea Gabriel doesn't want to inherit Meadowlands, that the pressure of being an only child depresses him and he dreads being left with the responsibility of looking after his mother when his father dies.

"All right if we head off to the lake now?" Gabriel asks, breaking off his conversation, not a moment too soon.

"Of course," Edward says, half rising in his chair. "Wonderful to meet you at last, Beth."

"Let me help wash up first," I say, thinking of Sarah in the kitchen, guilty and embarrassed I've been eating the extravagant food while she's been waiting on me. I stand and begin to pile the plates, one on top of the other, knives and forks moved to one side, but Tessa reaches out to still my hand.

"We don't stack here, we leave that to the school dinner ladies."

I leave the room, with my eyes smarting, clutching a single plate between my hands. Perhaps Gabriel didn't hear, perhaps he finds it easier to allow his mother's put-downs to drift over his head. In my chest, anger is rising.

In the far corner of the kitchen, Sarah is standing in front of the butler's sink, a pile of plates beside her. She doesn't turn as I come in.

I hesitate, wondering if I'll make things worse by going over to talk to her, but before I can decide Tessa comes in.

"You can leave the washing-up, thank you, Beth. Our girl is perfectly capable, there's really no need." She lowers her voice to just above a whisper. "Before you go, a quick word, if I may. You are being sensible and using precautions, aren't you?"

I stare back at her, too horrified to speak. There's no way Sarah could hear across the other side of the room, but even so, I feel mortified.

"No need to look like that, I'm quite unshockable. And most grateful to you for keeping Gabe occupied all summer. He can get terribly bored at home. I do hope you haven't compromised yourself?"

I'm saved answering by Gabriel, who arrives in the kitchen and wishes his mother good night.

Outside a fine rain is falling and the sky has turned electric blue, with ribbons of light at its edges. One time, by the lake, we were caught in a rainstorm. We kissed until our clothes were soaked through and then we tore them off and danced and whirled and bathed ourselves in the rain like weather gods. It is the freest I have ever felt.

"You're very quiet. Was it awful?" Gabriel says, reaching for my hand.

For a moment I don't trust myself to speak. There are so many emotions swirling in the pit of my stomach, it's hard to know what I'm feeling. Angry, humiliated, insecure. Wretched, ashamed. I don't regret a moment of the time I've spent with Gabriel or the things we have done, but his mother was clever in the way she managed to plant a seed of doubt in my head. What if she's right? What if Tessa does know her son far better than I do?

"Your mother made me feel so cheap, like some tart you'd picked up for the summer." The words burst out of me like poison. "Foolish for considering Oxford. Arrogant for thinking you and I could be anything more than a convenient fling." There's a weight of pressure in my chest, tears I need to shed in the privacy of my own bedroom. I feel sudden, aching loneliness. I don't belong in this place with these people. "And you abandoned me."

Gabriel's face is incredulous, then he seems amused. "It was only dinner. Don't you think you're overreacting?"

There's no way to control the rage as it spills out of me. "You don't understand. And why would you? Look at you."

"What's that supposed to mean?"

He sounds hurt, but it's not enough to stop the outpouring of thoughts I have hidden from everyone, especially myself. "Everything is given to you on a plate, with a silver bloody spoon attached! No one tells you you're not good enough. Not rich enough. Not posh enough. You get welcomed with open arms wherever you go. You can do whatever you want. Sleep with whoever you want. And get applauded for it. You will never be made to feel small or unworthy, never have to endure the sneering I had from your mother this evening."

"Can I say something?" Gabriel asks.

"Yes."

"I'm sorry," he says, and I burst into tears.

He puts his arms around me, presses my face to his chest. He smells of laundry powder and soap and the aftershave he always wears. "You're right," he says, pulling back a little so he can look into my face.

His eyes are shining too brightly; I see he is close to tears himself.

"The truth is, I'm scared of her sometimes. She can be so cruel when she wants to be. But I should have protected you. Forgive me?"

We kiss, his mouth warm on mine, his hands cupping the back of my skull as he holds me to him. *This is us*, I think. Not the people we were inside the house, but the boy and girl who have spent a whole summer together, pledging their love beneath a hundred starry nights.

1968

I have known Jimmy since he was an angry thirteen-year-old whom Frank acted as father and mother to, when he could find the time. Frank's father, David, when I first met him, was still reeling from the loss of his wife years earlier and he'd allowed his younger boy to go feral.

Sonia died when Jimmy was just nine years old. One minute she was there, the next she was gone, a loss he was too young to comprehend. Frank says it was when he became a teenager the trouble started. Jimmy was sent home from school for bringing alcohol onto the premises and, after a particularly nasty fight one lunchtime, he was asked to leave. It was Frank who talked the school into taking him back. Jimmy was a motherless boy, he said, whose response to bereavement was occasional violence. Back then, you got the feeling Jimmy's wildness concealed the fact he didn't care about himself at all.

Jimmy and Nina are having supper at the farmhouse tonight and I sense it's a relief to us both: Since I began looking after Leo, the nightly conversations between Frank and me have become strained, the two of us doing our best not to mention Gabriel, whose name will always trigger an uneasiness in Frank, or Leo, who causes him pain, the same way he causes me pain, by the simple fact of not being the boy we want. I'm getting used to it, though: Every day Leo becomes more himself in my eyes and *my* boy, *our* boy, fades into the background that little bit more.

I have made a chicken and ham pie, which is Jimmy's and Nina's favorite, and Frank has brought home two bottles of red wine, a gift from an old farming friend, which is an event in itself. We never normally have wine at home.

Frank pulls out the cork with a ceremonial pop and pours wine into two glasses.

We are listening to *Aftermath* by the Rolling Stones when Jimmy and Nina arrive. Nina cries: "I LOVE this song"—it's the opening track, "Mother's Little Helper"—and dances into the room, her bright hair flying behind her as she executes a perfect spin. She is wearing a pink, yellow, and green minidress in a bright graphic pattern, legs clad in clashing turquoise tights, a pair of patent leather Mary Janes on her feet. I love the effort Nina puts into her appearance; she is like a rare and ornate flower in the shabby surrounds of our kitchen.

Nina hugs Frank, then moves toward me, pausing to sniff the air like a bloodhound. "Don't tell me you made the pie?"

"'Course I did, you idiot."

"I love you, Beth Johnson. Did I ever tell you that?"

"Many times. And ditto."

We embrace by the stove, her long hair whipping into my face. She smells of Pears shampoo and Nivea face cream.

"Looks like we're going to be gooseberries tonight," Jimmy says to his brother.

"What else is new?" says Frank.

"Tell us about the new job, Beth," Nina says, the minute we're sitting at the table.

She's always been one for confronting the elephant. I catch the glance between the brothers, the quick flash of scorn on Jimmy's face. He will hate Gabriel unless Frank tells him not to; that's how it works with them.

"I really like it," I begin. "It's different, you know? I thought going to the school would be too hard but, actually, it's helping. I'm facing things I've avoided for two years— the playground, the teachers, the mothers—and it's easier than I thought. Already, I'm used to it. And Leo is not like

Bobby at all. I know you were worried me spending time with Leo would bring it all back. And it does, sometimes, but I feel I'm doing something worthwhile, something that's making a difference to him and to me. I feel sorry for Leo. His father works too hard, and his mother has begun a new life in America without him. He's lonely."

While I've been talking my eyes have never left Frank's face, I am saying all this for him. And what I see reflected back is his comprehension. He gets it. I smile in relief, and he reaches to take my hand. We have always been good at communicating without words.

I notice, as the next bottle slips down, the tension has drifted from Frank's face. His skin is slightly flushed and his eyes have a glitter to them. He looks happy, younger. Like his old self.

"Wine drunk suits you," I say, and he kisses me, quite hard, on the mouth. A kiss that is really a full stop, and says, *OK, enough now.*

"Look at you, bloody lovebirds," Nina says, but she's happy to see it. Our relationship means so much to them both. "How did you know you were meant to be together? You were so young."

"I knew from the age of thirteen," Frank says.

No need to tell the wildflower story—my drawing is pinned up on the kitchen wall, so familiar I hardly see it.

"Beth took a little longer."

"But once I was sold, I was sold," I say, and I lean into him, my head against his shoulder. It's not just the booze, in Frank I find reassurance when I most need it. He is mine and I am his and we've been together forever. This is the story I tell myself.

"You two know, don't you?" Frank says. "Come on, you've never had eyes for anyone else. How many years is it now, five, six? What are you waiting for?"

The strangest, most unexpected thing happens.

Nina gets up from the table and kneels in front of Jimmy.

We all realize, at the same moment, she is down on one knee. Jimmy looks over at Frank—*Is this really happening?*—then his face slides from sheepishness to wonder.

"Jimmy Johnson, love of my life, will you marry me? I'll be an old maid if I wait for you to ask me."

Jimmy pulls Nina onto his lap and the two of them start to kiss as if there's no one else in the room. Frank and I just look at each other, eyes wide while we wait.

"Is that a yes?" Nina asks, when they part. "You didn't say."

"Of course it's a bloody yes! All I've ever wanted is you. Ask them." He gestures at me and Frank; we are still watching them in amazement. "I've been in love with you since the very first time I saw you. I was too scared to ask you in case you said no."

Nina rolls her eyes.

"Thing about you, Jimmy Johnson, is you have no idea what a catch you are. You're the best man I know. And not so bad to look at either."

And then we are all embracing and the sight of the brothers, these two giant men clinched in a bear hug, moves me, almost to tears. I wish David were here to see it. He longed to see his younger son settled, worried about him constantly—not that he'd ever say.

Nina climbs back onto Jimmy's lap, both arms wound around his neck. I can't take my eyes off them. When did I last look at Nina properly? Nina, who has a radar-like sensor for Jimmy's changing moods and weathers the worst of them effortlessly. Nina, whose beauty is matched by her vivaciousness, her willingness to laugh, to dance, to find the best outcome. Nina, who might have had anyone, but has been firmly stuck on Jimmy since she was nineteen.

"A wedding, then?" I say. "Let's have it here."

"Oh," Nina laughs. "Forgot about that bit."

"We'll invite everyone," Jimmy says. "The whole damned village. It's about time we had a party."

The concept of a wedding at Blakely Farm envelops us in a cloud of excitement. Glancing up, I see Frank looking at me. He smiles fractionally and nods his head. I know we are thinking the same thing. This wedding is what we need. This wedding is going to be good for us all.

Before

I am in my mother's bedroom getting dressed for a dinner party at Meadowlands. My sister is here too, lolling on my mother's bed, dishing out fashion advice and snippy remarks about the Wolfe family.

"Is it too much?" I say, staring at myself in the long, gilt-framed mirror.

I am wearing an off-the-shoulder top of Eleanor's, with a circular skirt my mother and I have sewed painstakingly over the past four days. My mother has lent me a wide patent leather belt and Eleanor has put waves into my hair with my mother's rollers. Makeup too, borrowed from my sister: red lipstick, rouged cheeks.

"Oh, Beth," my mother says, when I turn around. "You are lovely."

"You look great," Eleanor says. "Although that dreadful woman will no doubt tell you your clothes are completely out-of-date."

It was probably a mistake to tell my family about Tessa's behavior the first time I met her.

Gabriel came here for supper a few nights ago. He was his most charming self, talking to my mother about the Brontë sisters, her favorite; to my father about Dublin, where Gabriel had holidayed as a child; and asking Eleanor all about London's nightlife.

It did no good. When Gabriel left, Eleanor said: "He's all right, I suppose. Very good-looking. But how do you put up with that voice? Frightfully posh, isn't he?"

*

The dinner party is in full flow by the time I arrive.

"There you are, dear Beth," Tessa says, when I walk into the dining room where Gabriel, his parents, and some visiting American friends are gathered. "The silly girl brought our soup out before we were ready for it. So I'm afraid we've had to start without you."

"And here's your place next to me," Edward says, rising in his chair. "Let me introduce you."

The guests are Richard and Moira Scott and their daughter, Louisa, who has just finished her first year at St Hilda's, Oxford. Gabriel gave me no other information about this evening other than there was some dreary American girl coming for the weekend whom he was being forced to look after, and please would I help.

He's giving a good show of being willing rather than coerced is my first thought, as I watch him listening to Louisa, his head tilted toward her. Perhaps no one had told him how pretty she was, although "pretty" does not do justice to her pink-and-white skin and glittering eyes, a mouth that curves upward as if in permanent readiness for a smile. She has a doll-like perfection, dainty ears, elegant little nose, curvy rosebud mouth, like a prototype for classic beauty.

I thought I had dressed up for this evening, but it is nothing compared with Louisa. She is in strapless black satin, a choker of pearls around her lovely neck, a daring suggestion of cleavage on show for this family party.

It's interesting seeing mothers and daughters together, particularly when they are the mirror image of each other, like Louisa and Moira Scott. It bodes well for Louisa, her mother's smooth, unlined skin, her slim body encased in a narrow black dress. Good genes, great bone structure. Strong white American teeth. They laugh a lot, perhaps to reveal these excellent smiles.

Louisa waves at me from the other side of the table. "It's lovely to meet you," she says. "Gabriel has been telling me all about you."

"And Louisa has been filling me in on Oxford."

"Some of my best friends at Oxford are poets and play-wrights. They are always on the lookout for other writers."

With sudden clarity I understand two things: Louisa and Gabriel are going to become close, and I will feel excluded.

Whether out of politeness or design, I am soon distracted by Richard Scott, who is sitting on the other side of me. I've never known someone so curious—he asks a stream of questions about my family, my school, my favorite authors, what sort of music I like, whether I'm a confirmed country person or could picture myself living in town?

He treats me like an adult, asking how I feel about Anthony Eden, our new prime minister. Was I sad to see Churchill go?

I repeat what I have heard my parents say, that Churchill was once a brilliant politician but it was time for him to retire, and Eden had waited a long time. My parents are not fans of the Conservative Party but I decide to keep that to myself.

We talk about the recent hanging of Ruth Ellis. Like everyone else my age, I was appalled by the death sentence. "She was a mother," I say, and Richard must hear how my voice falters for he reaches out to pat my hand. "And her boyfriend was abusive. It was so wrong."

From time to time, I manage to steal the occasional glance at Gabriel and Louisa, still talking intently. I see the way she looks at him, not quite with adoration, but with full, rapt attention.

With some pressing, I manage to piece together informa-tion about the Scott family. They live in California, in the

Hollywood Hills. I picture a white mansion with a shimmering pool, a row of sports cars parked outside, Marilyn Monroe dropping in for sundowners. Richard is a film producer, recent credits include *Sabrina* and *Rear Window*, both of which I have seen.

"You know Alfred Hitchcock?" If my voice is starstruck, I can't help it.

"Yes. Well, as much as anyone knows him. He keeps himself to himself."

"What was he like to work with?"

Richard takes a sip of his wine. "'Challenging' is probably the best way I can put it. He is not an easy man."

"And do you know Marilyn Monroe? I've been trying not to ask but I can't help it."

Richard laughs. "Oh, ask away. I have met her. Hollywood is a very small world, everyone goes to the same parties. But I wouldn't say I know her. We haven't worked on anything together and she usually has an entourage around her."

"Daddy?" Louisa calls out across the table. "Gabriel is writing a novel. I was telling him you'd probably have someone read it for him?"

"I can do that," Richard says. "What's it about?"

This is the thing about Gabriel. If it were me presenting an idea to a Hollywood producer in front of a room of people I knew, including my parents and my girlfriend, I would fall to pieces. Gabriel does the opposite. He takes his time to think about what he's going to say, composing his thoughts while we wait.

"I'd describe it as an upside-down love story. Instead of the girl being desperate to marry the boy, it's the other way round. The girl wants to explore her sexuality and live freely like a man. She's batting off his proposals while she sleeps with whomever she chooses and he's left at home waiting for her, hoping she's going to come back."

"I like that," Richard says. "Subverting the trope. How does it end?"

Before he can say any more, Tessa interrupts. "No prizes for guessing who the racy heroine is modeled on." She allows her gaze to rest on me, her meaning clear. "Beth, answer me honestly," she continues. "If the offer of a great marriage came along, would you turn it down?"

There is a sudden hush in the room. Across the table I see Gabriel watching, and I know what he is thinking. *Don't rile her. Please, let it go.* It's a tightrope Edward and Gabriel walk when Tessa is drinking.

"What constitutes a great marriage?" I say, avoiding the question. "I think we'd probably have different ideas on that."

Yours, Tessa, for example, is more flawed and destructive than any I've ever seen.

Across the table, Gabriel shakes his head at me. And I realize, once again, he is leaving me to flounder. Or defend myself alone. When it comes to Tessa, Gabriel doesn't have it in him to stand up to her. He doesn't want me to spoil his chances with Richard Scott either. This is how inner circles work: You meet the right people, doors open, you are ushered through. Join the club. You'll fit right in. So long as your drunk of a mother doesn't ruin things for you.

"Marriage is the last thing on my mind, to be honest. This beef is delicious, Tessa. So tender."

I notice, when the meal is finished and Louisa starts to pile the plates nearest to her, one on top of the other, Tessa simply thanks her.

"Stay where you are, Louisa," she says. "We have a girl in the kitchen washing up. Beth and I will fetch the pudding."

Another girl from the village has been serving the dinner, so there's no need for me to help, unless it's an excuse for Tessa to talk to me alone. My stomach clenches with dread.

"Louisa seems lovely," I say, as soon as we are in the kitchen.

"Isn't she? She and Gabe hit it off immediately. I knew she'd be his type."

"It was a good idea of yours to invite them. So nice for him to start university with a friend."

I'm saying everything Tessa wants to hear. But it's no good. She fixes me with dark, contemplative eyes, and a small, pitying smile.

"Dear Beth, I do worry about you."

"Oh? I don't know why."

"I hope you're going to cope with him leaving you."

"It's only one term and then he'll be back."

She laughs. "You think it's going to last that long?"

I'm so shocked by her unkindness I cannot find anything to say.

"I'm fond of you, Beth, and I hope you haven't thrown everything away on a summer fling. You've let my son take advantage of you rather, haven't you?"

I feel my face flush with anger. Day in, day out, men are admired for their sexual prowess, for the "conquests" notched upon their bedposts. Whereas women, who dare to do the same, are derided, and, most often, it is other women dishing out the derision.

Didn't Tessa hear what Gabriel's novel was about? His attempt to expose double standards so ingrained nobody ever questions them? Her son gets it, even if she doesn't.

"Boys like Gabriel don't tend to end up with girls like you. I don't mean to be unkind. Quite the opposite. I'm just trying to warn you, so you don't get hurt."

For the rest of the evening, I cannot shake myself free of

Tessa's insinuations. I look at Gabriel and Louisa and see them as a perfect inverse of each other, one dark and tall, the other blond and slight. Handsome, clever, and well-bred, they are ideally matched, like a pair of Henry James protagonists destined to fall in love.

1968

Every day at Meadowlands the phone rings dead-on six o'clock. It's my signal to go home, and let Leo speak to his mother, who is calling from California to say good night. She's coming over for a visit soon and Leo talks of little else.

Leo races to pick up the phone. "Hello, Mama!"

He sounds so happy to hear her. I can't imagine how it must tug at his mother's heart, being on the other side of the Atlantic, hearing her child's voice but not being able to see him. I wonder how she bears it.

Gabriel told me the only reason he has temporary custody of Leo is because his wife was feeling so guilty about falling in love with someone else, she gave Leo the choice: America with her, or England with his father? For now, he's chosen England.

I am only half listening to Leo as he tells his mother about his day, a story he wrote during English, the boy in his class who was sent out for saying a rude word.

"Bollocks," Leo says, just as Gabriel comes into the room.

"Charming," says his father.

We both turn in alarm when Leo shouts: "Are you kidding me? You're not coming?"

He's silent for a few seconds, listening, and although his body is turned away from us, I read his despair in every curve.

"That's not a reason, that's an excuse, you just don't want to come," he yells, dropping the phone and running from the kitchen.

Gabriel starts berating his ex—"For God's sake, do you think you might have told me first so I could have broken it to him gently? Can you really not come?"—when the front door slams.

I am torn, wondering if I should leave Leo alone with his anger or go after him. Sometimes I get the feeling Leo is hanging on by a thread and the only thing that has kept him going is the thought of his mother's visit.

I find him sitting in front of the lake. He doesn't look up as I approach.

"I'll go away again if that's what you want."

Leo says nothing.

"I know how much you were looking forward to seeing her."

"She only cares about the baby."

"Why can't she come?"

"Because of him, of course. He's teething. Too miserable to fly. It's just an excuse."

"I suppose that might be hard. Babies aren't very good at traveling."

"She could leave him behind."

"Easier said than done with a baby. They take a lot of looking after."

"I thought you were meant to be on my side."

He doesn't sound like him; there are brittle, hard edges to his voice, and something else, a thickness that makes me think Leo is holding back tears.

"I am on your side. One hundred percent. And so is she. That's all I'm trying to say."

"You'd never have left your son behind in a different country. I've seen your face when you look at the photo of him in your bag."

His words knock the breath out of me. I keep a photo of Bobby with me and I look at it so many times during the day

I'm almost unaware I'm doing it. But to think of Leo, a boy who always tries to hide the missing of his mother, watching me, a woman who always tries to hide the missing of her son, shocks me. It is all the more obvious to me why Leo and I clicked straightaway, but it also feels increasingly dangerous. It's not the real thing. I need to keep a grip on that.

"Look, here's your dad," I say, and we watch Gabriel hurrying across the grass toward us.

He sits down on the other side of Leo, puts an arm around his shoulder. "I'm really sorry," he says.

"I don't want to talk about it."

"Fair enough."

Gabriel doesn't say anything else and I think how sensible that is, his not trying to make things better, just accepting the disappointment and sadness which cannot be fixed for now.

After a moment, Leo drops his head onto Gabriel's shoulder.

A hawk swoops from the sky in a dramatic curve, skimming the surface of the lake before settling on the grass.

"Look, a buzzard," Gabriel says. "Beautiful creatures, aren't they?"

"It's a sparrow hawk, Dad. Buzzards are bigger, and their feathers are brown not gray."

"Get you." Gabriel punches him on the shoulder. "What else have you been learning behind my back, country boy?"

The lake is surrounded by woodland; it's a haven for birds, particularly in early summer. Leo and I have been identifying them using a pair of binoculars that used to belong to Bobby.

"Bobby knew the names of hundreds of birds," Leo says. "I only know a few so far."

"Bobby?" Gabriel asks, then catches himself. "Beth's son. Of course."

Is it strange I talk to Leo about Bobby sometimes? He's curious about him, probably because he is ten, just a year older than Bobby when he died. I like telling him about the things we used to do together. I like the fact Leo is getting to know Bobby, even a little bit, and talking about him helps me to keep his memory alive.

I listen as Leo tells Gabriel about the things Bobby could do. Milk cows, trill like a blackbird. He sounds almost proud of Bobby, a boy he will never meet. I feel touched by how much he has taken in.

But then Gabriel turns his gaze upon me and I see the question in his eyes. *Why are you doing this? Why are you telling Leo about your dead child?*

Before

Summer fades and Hemston is transformed by the changing season—trees showing off in coppery gold and beetroot red and banana yellow, and Gabriel is not here.

To begin with he writes constantly, letters that burn with longing and read like poetry. As the term progresses and he becomes more immersed in university life his letters change, the heat goes out of them, they feel rushed, or worse, written out of duty. One thing nags at me—how often he mentions Louisa Scott, for they are the best of friends, apparently. Gabriel has been absorbed into her circle, an arty, literary crowd whom I picture smoking and drinking Campari while they dissect the works of Jean-Paul Sartre.

I spend my time studying for my interview at St Anne's in November, forgoing invitations to parties and reading day and night until my eyes hurt and at last I am forced to close my books.

"It's too much," my father says, cajoling me to come for a walk with him for fresh air, a change of scene.

"Let her be," my mother says. "Only a few more weeks to go."

She is almost as ambitious for me as I am myself. When my mother left school in the 1930s hardly any women went to Oxford, it simply wasn't an option for her. I know, because my father teases her about it: She intends to vicariously live the life she wasn't able to have through me.

"We'll visit so often you'll be sick of the sight of us," she says, laughing.

"Never," I say. "We'll punt on the river and eat cream teas

and spend a whole day in the Ashmolean looking at broken bits of pottery."

It is almost two months before Gabriel and I finally meet. He is waiting for me to finish my interview, sitting on a low wall outside the college, reading. When he sees me, he leaps to his feet, flings his arms wide, his book clattering to the ground. "It's you," he says, enveloping me in his huge woolen overcoat. "And you are not wearing enough clothes."

"I'm planning on wearing even less," I say, and then we are laughing and running through the streets, faster and faster until we reach his college rooms.

As soon as the door closes behind us, we start tearing off our clothes. We are naked, on his bed, the feeling of his skin against mine, after all this time, my fingers tracing a pathway across his chest, his stomach, hip bones, the places I love and miss the most. Gabriel's lips press to my neck over and over, him telling me he has missed me, how much he wants me, and everything is the same. There's the desperate craving I remember so well, not wanting to wait even though Gabriel always says it will be better if we do, then the feeling of him inside me again, the intensity of it, pleasure that is almost unbearable, the way he cries my name, Beth, Beth, and then lying together afterward so tightly wrapped around each other we can barely breathe.

"How many times do you think we can make love in twenty-four hours?" Gabriel says. "Shall we see?"

I feel so happy knowing what we had, what we still have, was real, wondering why I doubted it, why I pored over his letters looking for proof he had stopped loving me.

"I need to show you Oxford," he says, when we are still in bed, hours later.

The light has gone. Outside his window, Oxford looks spectral against the blue-black sky.

"There's a birthday party we could go to," he says. "But I'd rather keep you to myself."

"Whose party?"

"Thomas Nicholls, Tom. He's in the second year."

I pick up on something, a slight hesitation, which makes me question his reluctance to go to the party. Does he feel awkward introducing me, still a schoolgirl, to his writerly crowd? Or is there something—or someone—he wishes to keep from me? In my head, I'm sifting the spare details for specks of hidden truth.

"Where does Tom live?"

"He has rooms on Magdalen Street. He lives with Louisa."

Louisa. Just her name invokes a chill, as if my body has stored the weeks of suspicion and jealousy and is ready, in a moment, to be reactivated. As if the hours of lovemaking, the endless passionate declarations—I love you, I missed you—now vanish into air.

"I'd rather stay in bed. But what will I tell my parents? They'll be wanting a blow-by-blow account of my twenty-four hours in Oxford."

"You're right," Gabriel says, throwing back the blankets and leaping from bed. "We can go for half an hour and then we'll sneak off and find somewhere for dinner."

At first, the party thrills me. Tom and Louisa share a house that feels surprisingly large for a pair of students and there are people everywhere, crowded into the drawing room with its shiny black piano, smoking on the staircase, shouting to be heard in the kitchen, where we go to find our hosts. *This is what it's going to be like*, I think, drinking it all in: a boy in a purple velvet suit; a couple necking openly, and inconveniently, against the fridge door.

Tom, blond and goofy looking in tweed and spectacles, is pouring out a bottle of champagne. "Here," he says, passing us two glasses, filled almost to the brim. "Impeccable timing. This is the good stuff. And who have we here? Have you been fraternizing with freshers again, Gabe?"

Gabriel has been absorbed into Louisa's second-year crowd of friends; I doubt he spends much time with his year at all. And he clearly hasn't told Tom about me. *Or hasn't told anyone?* Paranoia fizzes and splutters in my gut.

"This is Beth. She had an interview at St Anne's today."

"Welcome, Beth. I like your dress."

We fight our way through a hallway three-deep in bodies to the relative calm of the drawing room, where Gabriel seems to know everyone. He is greeted, kissed on both cheeks, embraced, and backslapped as he introduces me: "This is Beth," he says. "She's down for her interview. We grew up in the same village."

I smile at the Glorias and Claudias and Imogens in their rich-girl twinsets, their ropes of pearls, all the time wondering why he hasn't introduced me as his girlfriend.

"Gabe, you came!"

I'm involved in a conversation with Claudia or Imogen and I can't turn away, although the voice I hear behind me is instantly familiar. Affectionate, American. But I listen, even as I reply to questions about my interview—"mostly we talked about the Romantics"—and my attentive ear picks out the lowered voices.

"You said you couldn't come."

"I think Beth wanted to."

"I hope it's not awkward."

"It's fine, we won't stay long."

"Gabe, about that night—"

"Say that again, Beth, I didn't quite catch it—?" says Claudia-or-Imogen, and I miss the rest of their conversation.

Suddenly I'm being embraced by Louisa, and everything about her—the way she is dressed, the cigarette she smokes in

its black-and-gold holder, her round, black-framed glasses—
glasses—which manage to make her look even more beautiful than I remember—destroys me.

Helen, my talented friend, surprised me with a polka-dot
dress she'd made for me before I left—a Christian Dior rip-
off from his New Look days, copied from a *Vogue* pattern.
Low neck, fitted at the bust, a flouncy circular skirt. I loved
this dress, I felt like a different person in it. Looking at Louisa now, I'd like to rip it to shreds.

Her black top is off the shoulder, revealing satiny golden
skin and a glimpse of cleavage, and she's wearing it with
black-and-white checked pedal pushers which she has cinched
at her waist with a wide gold belt. Perched on the back of her
head is a white-and-gold naval cap. She looks incredible.

"How was your interview. Did it go well?" Louisa asks,
smiling at me with her pretty blue-green eyes.

I'm so bored of the question, so bored of myself.

Actually, it couldn't have gone better. Out of two dons
interviewing, one was a woman and we seemed to click instantly. Within minutes we'd segued from the Wife of Bath
and Shakespearean tragedy to trading poems from our favorite female poets. Professor Gilbert told me to look out
for the modern Americans Anne Sexton and Mary Oliver,
and a young Cambridge scholar she'd just come across
named Sylvia Plath. Escorting me from the room, she'd
said: "We have an active creative writing community. I believe you'll do very well here."

I manage to tell Louisa some of this and she touches my
wrist and says: "Oh, you write too?" She puts one hand
to her bosom, closes her eyes. "The novel Gabe is writing,
it's beautiful. Funny, devastating, brave. What you'd expect
from him, I suppose. You must have read it?"

I manage to smile. "He's quite cagey about his writing.
We both are."

"Talking about me, by any chance?"

Gabriel is smiling as he comes to stand between us.

Louisa's face lights up the moment she sees him. She places a palm against his chest, the gesture jarring in its familiarity.

"I was telling Beth about your wonderful novel," she says, turning back to me.

But I am not looking at Louisa. I'm looking at Gabriel, at the deep flush in his cheeks. He looks uncomfortable. Or guilty. Even after Louisa has removed her hand.

A battle is raging in my head when Gabriel and I leave the party a short while later. I want to rail at him: *Why didn't you tell people I was your girlfriend? And why did you blush when Louisa touched you? Is there something between you? Something I should know about?*

"Most of the restaurants will be closing," Gabriel says, looking at his watch, "but there's an Indian that stays open."

"Do you think I'm a country bumpkin?"

Gabriel frowns. "Of course not. Where's this coming from?"

Oh, I don't know, being in a room full of clipped, upper-class voices, girls in cashmere, boys opening bottles of champagne as if they were lemonade. Money and acceptance and me having neither, the fish out of water with a Dorset intonation.

"Your friend Claudia, or whatever her name was, kept asking me to repeat myself. She seemed to find me hard to understand."

"How bloody absurd." Gabriel pulls me to a stop. Leans forward to kiss my forehead, then my eyes, my nose, my mouth. "I love the way you talk. It's one of the things I miss the most."

I breathe in the Oxford night air, the sight of him, the most beautiful boy on earth.

93

"What do you say we skip the restaurant and go back to my rooms?" he asks.

"I say, thank God."

We stand there in the cool night air, watching each other. Gabriel has this look on his face, one I know from before, where everything shrinks, until it's just him and me. A look that tells me I am enough; more than that, I am everything. All I have to do is keep the faith.

"I wish you could see what I see, Beth. You're worth a thousand of the girls in that room."

1968

"You think you know someone," I say, as we turn onto a long, tree-lined drive and the hotel comes into view. It is a large, redbrick house on the borders of Devon, and Frank has planned our stay as a surprise for my birthday.

"Not every day you turn thirty," he says, pulling up in front of the house.

Everything about the hotel thrills us. The way our shattered blue suitcase is carried up ahead of us into our room. The decanters of whisky and gin waiting for us on a silver tray. The biggest bed either of us have ever seen. When the bellboy has gone, Frank lies across it to demonstrate how its width is the same height as him.

"Come here." He pats the space next to him.

We lie in silence, fingers interlaced, staring up at the ceiling's intricate plasterwork.

"I'm worried this is costing too much, Frank," I blurt out, and my husband frowns.

"I told you you weren't allowed to worry about money. I sold that old trailer we never use, so we've got a bit of extra cash. Not another word now, you promised."

"All right," I say, kissing him. "What are we going to do with ourselves with all this free time?"

Frank smiles. "I can think of a few things."

"Oh yes?" He starts to unbutton my shirt with his strong, efficient fingers. "We won't be needing clothes as such," he says.

Frank takes off my shirt, my skirt, my underwear, and

props himself on one elbow so he can look down at me. "Did I tell you how lovely you are?"

"Not for a while."

"Then I'm an idiot. Because you are. Very."

Frank knows exactly how to touch me. I close my eyes as his fingers begin their expert trail across my flesh. I know how this goes, how Frank likes to take his time, but a sudden yearning takes hold of me. I don't want to wait. I'm unbuckling his belt, yanking at his trousers, and Frank is laughing.

"Slow down. What's the hurry?"

"I need you."

That's all it takes. He pulls off his clothes and leans above me, a palm on either side of my face, easing into me, slow and deep. It is all I want.

"Thank God," he says. "Thank God for you."

Afterward, we don't bother to get dressed but stay in bed for the whole afternoon. Frank rings down for tea and it is delivered by the same bellboy, politely averting his eyes from me in the bed and Frank naked beneath his hotel dressing gown.

"He thinks we're on a dirty weekend," I say, when he's left.

"We are," Frank says, untying his dressing gown and hopping in beside me. "Didn't I tell you?"

We fill the old Victorian bath to its brim and climb in either end, refilling it from the hot tap until our skin is flushed and crinkled. Sometimes we talk but mostly we don't, we just smile at each through the steam. There has been so much tension between us lately, this afternoon I feel it drifting away. For this fragment of time, we are us again.

At dinner, we hold hands across the table drinking an expensive bottle of wine our solemn waiter recommended, both of us too intimidated to ask for something cheaper.

"Who cares?" Frank says, chinking his glass to mine. "It's your birthday."

He orders a steak, and it is cooked just the way he likes it, crisp on the outside and bloody within. I have sole fillets which are soft, buttery, lemony mouthfuls of deliciousness. They come with sautéed potatoes and green beans: simple, beautifully cooked food.

"What does this remind you of?" Frank says.

"Our honeymoon?"

I can see us now, two teenagers with their whole lives ahead, who knew nothing of what the next decade would throw at them. It was the first time either of us had spent the night in a hotel; this is the second.

The expensive wine slips down quickly and when the waiter asks us if we would like another bottle, Frank says yes.

"When do we ever get to do this? I like getting drunk with my wife."

It's probably a mistake, the second bottle.

We begin to reminisce about the good times with Bobby. The toy tractor he had for his fourth birthday, which we had wrapped so carefully in many sheets of paper. Bobby took one look at it and burst into tears. "Why can't I have a real tractor? This one doesn't even go." The day we took his stabilizers off, soon after that birthday, and he cycled around the yard for an hour without stopping. We called him the Lone Biker for a bit. The way Bobby always insisted on going milking on Christmas morning before he would open a single present from his stocking. He'd stuff his pockets full of apples for the cows and biscuits for the sheep. "It's their Christmas too."

Tonight, I can hear his voice exactly, and it's not often I can. My eyes are full of tears, Frank's too. It's a knife-edge we are on, we both know that, but it feels significant, this thing which binds us so closely together and yet we never discuss it. Something about being away from the farm with all its memories has made it possible.

"I wish—" Frank says and then he stops himself, but I see pain rushing into his face.

There are so many things both of us wish about the day Bobby died. So many things that could have made all the difference if we'd done them. But we didn't.

Suddenly, I understand how it is our togetherness that bars us from healing. It's like an exterior vision, as if I'm looking from the outside in, the two of us vacillating back and forth on our shared black rock of grief.

"I do, too," I say. "Everything you wish, I wish. But it won't bring him back. We have to try and let him go."

We reach for each other's hand at the same time.

"Are we going to be all right?" Frank says, and I see how much it costs him to ask it. Frank, who never talks about feelings or failings or anything that comes too close to the bone, and certainly not a question like this, one which might result in the wrong answer.

I'm not sure what to say. Are we going to be all right? Is there a time when we won't both ache for our missing child? When the guilt which lurks in corners, waiting for the right moment to attack us, might diminish into something that is easier to bear?

"I hope so," is the best I can come up with and Frank nods, as if this is what he expected.

"Time," he says, and we laugh a little ruefully because we have a private joke about the people who bandy this cliché about, as if it might actually be insightful.

We are still smiling when the grim-faced waiter comes over to ask if we'd like coffee and perhaps a digestif to go with it; he can particularly recommend the cognac. When we both say "yes" with alacrity, he cracks his first smile of the night.

Before

In the morning, I watch Gabriel dressing for his lecture, throwing on the clothes he discarded yesterday: corduroy trousers, a black jumper with several of my long dark hairs clinging to it, a tweed jacket on top.

"See?" he says, holding out a hair between his thumb and forefinger. "I miss these."

At the door he turns back for one more kiss, runs his hands over my body beneath the sheets. "It's torture leaving you. I will not be thinking about Sir Gawain for the next sixty minutes, that's for sure."

"Can't you skip it? Just this once?"

He holds out several pages of lined paper, covered in his handwriting. "It's my paper this week, unfortunately. Don't move, I won't be long."

After he's gone, I put on one of his shirts and boil the kettle on the little camping stove Gabriel brought with him from Meadowlands. All those mornings by the lake when he brewed coffee and cooked scrambled eggs and bacon, it seems a lifetime ago.

I take a cup of tea to Gabriel's desk with its view of the gardens below. I watch a boy cutting across the lawn, disheveled, harried, late for his nine o'clock lecture, perhaps. Next year, so long as I don't mess up my A levels, it will be me. I revel in the fantasy for a few minutes while I drink my tea. I'll be in my college room at St Anne's, but Gabriel will have his own lodgings by then. I picture us cooking exotic feasts of beef Stroganoff or coq au vin in the evenings for our friends, whom I imagine as a broader mix than the people

I met last night. Poets and scientists and art historians and musicians. Boys and girls from grammar and comprehensive schools who have worked so hard to get here.

His mother was right. I am more comfortable with my own kind. In my own way I can be just as elitist.

A green notebook catches my eye and I reach for it almost without thinking. I'm about to open it when I realize what I'm doing: This is probably Gabriel's novel, the novel Louisa has been allowed to read.

I understand, utterly, the horror of letting someone read your work before it's ready. And also, how it will never be ready unless you put it out there, risking humiliation and failure. Reading someone else's writing is like having direct access to his innermost thoughts. And he chose to reveal that to Louisa, not me.

As soon as I open it I realize this is not Gabriel's novel. It's his diary.

September 25
Missing Beth like an illness, I feel sick with it. There's no one like her here.
September 30
How is it possible to be with someone every day for a whole summer and then never see them? I feel like a part of me is missing. We used to say we shared a brain. Well, half my brain is gone.

I slam the notebook shut. Reading another person's diary is the worst kind of deceit, the lowest, the ugliest. I will not allow myself to do it. Minutes pass, and the temptation to look again burns in my throat. It's no good: I cannot resist. This is how Adam must have felt biting into his apple. One minute there's purity and innocence, the next I am fully immersed in a world I wish I had never entered.

The mentions of me start to dwindle as the weeks pass and are replaced more and more by Louisa, or rather, "L." There are other names too: Richard, Claudia, Nigel, Imogen. Talk of good lectures and indifferent ones, parties and concerts and nights in the pub. Weekend house parties staying, no doubt, at the grand country houses belonging to his friends. I begin to flip the pages, searching only for the name that sears and, sure enough, in the last two weeks, I find what I am looking for.

In late October, Gabriel writes:

Stayed up late talking to L. I told her everything, all the doubts I've been having, how guilty I feel. She was wonderful, as always, don't know what I'd do without her. God, I feel so terrible about this, she ended up spending the night with me. I had to smuggle her out through the back door this morning, I can only pray no one saw her and Beth won't find out.

Then, fatally, an entry four days ago.

Louisa is in love with me. What am I going to do? Beth arrives in three days for her interview. My life is a mess.

How could he have made love to me in the way he did when he had these feelings for her? And these doubts about me? I picture Louisa at the party, the joy in her face when Gabriel came to join us. The way she put her hand to his chest. Unconscious. Intimate. Knowing. As if she had touched him before. And I see Gabriel, reddening as I watched him, the guilty flush of a betrayer.

I read the entries again. The words seem like incontrovertible evidence now.

The magnitude of this, it's too big to comprehend. Gabriel and Louisa. Louisa and Gabriel. She *loves* him. He slept with her. How could I have been so blind, so foolish? And why did I open his diary? Even now, with my world crashing around me, I wish I could turn back the clock to the ignorance of a moment ago.

I walk around his room, unsure what to do with myself. To Gabriel and Louisa I'm just some stupid schoolgirl he once had feelings for and they are counting down the time until I go away again.

I spy a pale pink scarf balled up in the corner. I pick it up, inhale its overpowering flowery scent and throw it to the ground.

It takes no time at all to dress in my own clothes, hurling the offensive spotty dress in my bag. I pause at Gabriel's desk before I leave, heart racing while I consider what to write.

It's over, Gabriel.
I can't see you anymore.
You know why.
Beth

My bus has not yet arrived at the station. There's a cluster of people waiting and I stand amid them, arms wrapped around myself, in shock. My breathing is too loud, too gaspy, and I feel as though I am fighting for air. *Gabriel and Louisa. A perfect coupling. They will look so good together.* Everything I dreaded has come true, as if I wished it into existence.

And then, Gabriel is here, running into the station, frantic.

"What's happened?" he says, when he reaches me. He pulls me into his arms and, for a moment, a blissful, forgotten moment where everything is still as it was, I weep against him, my face pressed to the hard muscles of his chest, his smell—lemons and cedar and cigarette smoke—so intensely familiar and no longer mine.

I jerk myself away. "I know about Louisa," I say.

His face betrays nothing. "What about her?"

"She *loves* you. You slept with her. I read your diary, Gabriel. Don't bother denying it."

"You read my diary? How could you—?" Gabriel is shouting so loudly people turn around. Fury in his eyes I've never seen before.

"I'm glad I did. Because you would never have had the guts to tell me. What were you going to do, string us both along? Your mother warned me about you. She said you use people, and move on when you get bored of them. She warned me you would tire of me as soon as you got to Oxford. I should have listened to her."

It's the worst thing I could have said.

His anger switches into something else: coldness, a look of such intense dislike—of me, of her?

"Gabriel," I say, pleading, knowing I've gone too far but he turns his face away. He can't bear to look at me.

My bus arrives, people get on, the engine starts up. The conductor leans out of the door. "Are you coming, love?"

I look at Gabriel, hoping he'll say something to stop me, hoping there's a way of this not being our end.

"You should go," he says, and still he doesn't look at me. "You're right. This is finished."

Heartbreak is commonplace—a young girl in a tempest of crying surprises no one—but there is concern on every single face as I get on the bus.

"Let's get you safely home, darling," the conductor says.

I do look at Gabriel as the bus leaves the station. His face is expressionless, but I know from the hard set of his mouth, from the fingers that creep beneath his eyes, he is crying too.

It is the last time I will see him for a very long time.

Part Two

Bobby

Before

Bobby is born on the kitchen floor in the midst of a storm. All day the wind has been rattling the farmhouse windows so fiercely, at times I wondered if they might be blown in.

In the final stages of pregnancy, my days were slow and I seemed to achieve so little. Some half-hearted tidying, the leisurely preparation of the family's supper, chores which formerly took minutes could last for hours.

When I first arrived at the farmhouse—a tired, unloved place that housed three diffident men—I was shocked by the state of it, the state of them. They needed me, all three of them, they just hadn't realized it. There was David, Frank's dad, still aching from the loss of his wife. David had done the best he could bringing up his sons without Sonia, but his best was almost nothing. Frank learned to cook because his dad couldn't, and six months of cheese sandwiches began to wear thin. He learned how to wash their clothes, he began supervising Jimmy's homework. He cleaned too, here and there, but when I first came I was shocked by the ingrained grime—years of dust and cobwebs—he had not noticed or cared about.

Domesticity was something I'd never expected to find satisfying. My mother always hated cooking and cleaning when we were growing up, and was fortunate to marry a man who loved her enough to do it instead. What I have discovered is that the transformation of the farmhouse and the men within it has been more rewarding than I would ever have imagined. I thought I was predestined for a life of books: first university, then, with any luck, a career as a poet. I haven't given up on my dream of one day being a writer, but Frank came along at exactly the right moment and swept me into a new and unimagined world where every single day is a different kind of education.

Turning down my place at Oxford hurt, not least because of the way it disappointed my mother. But what choice did I have? Spend two years in the same town as Gabriel and Louisa? Nothing on earth would have induced me to swallow my pride and do that. Soon enough there was Frank, the handsome, uncomplicated boy who had always loved me from afar.

If people were surprised I segued from one love affair to another they did not say. For Frank and I, in a sense, had known each other forever. I fell for him perhaps because he was the exact opposite of Gabriel. I was drawn first by his kindness and his honesty, a more straightforward man you could not meet. He gave me back my self-belief with uncomplicated devotion.

Like most women I have a birth plan: The moment my waters break or I feel the first twinge of pain, I will call my mother at her school. The secretary has been alerted that no matter what my mother is doing she must be interrupted. If she's umpiring a netball match, the game stops. If she's taking an English class it is abandoned, and the pupils must fend for themselves. The journey from her school to the farmhouse is less than fifteen minutes; the hospital, were we to need it quickly, half an hour away. First-time labors, I am told, can last for hours, often a whole day or more, so there will be plenty of time to get to hospital. I have learned the drill. I know how to time my contractions so I can tell how much my cervix has dilated. In an ideal world, we would sit out the first part of labor in the farmhouse and Frank would drive us to hospital for the final hours.

My waters break at three o'clock in the afternoon when I stand up from my chair with the intention of making a cup of tea. It's the strangest sensation. Not a bucket of liquid splashing onto the slate floor, as I'd expected, but a trickle that alarms me initially until I realize what it is. The first contraction comes, in textbook fashion, almost immediately afterward.

It hurts a surprising amount for a first contraction. This is no twinge. And, even worse, just as I'm recovering, realizing labor is not going to be the cinch I'd hoped for, another one comes. That can't be right, can it? Contractions close together? I stagger to the phone—I know the school telephone number off by heart—pick up the receiver, phone to my ear . . . the line is dead, just a crackling sound. I scream into the empty kitchen. How can this be? Only later will I discover a telegraph pole has crashed to the ground in the storm, wiping out phone lines for miles around us and, crucially, blocking the lane to the farmhouse. We cannot get out and no one can get in.

To begin with, I manage to stay calm. I retreat to my armchair, legs splayed in front of me, trying to breathe through the contractions, the way I've been taught. *Imagine you are blowing a table tennis ball across a swimming pool.* It's an absurd phrase. I can picture neither a Ping-Pong ball nor a swimming pool. And the pain is so intense I can scarcely breathe, let alone master these long, gentle exhalations.

Fast labor leaves no room for thought or planning or even comprehension. It takes you. Catapults you from one world to the next, where you are simply a birthing machine, a screaming, writhing, sweating mound of primal woman. I'm disconnected from it to such an extent that, at first, I don't realize the groans, the deep brittle lowing—I've heard cows in labor, it's the exact same thing—is me.

By the time Jimmy arrives home from school, I am on all

fours in the kitchen, sobbing, screaming, trying to prevent my body from doing what it wants to do, which is push the baby out.

"Oh, my God, Beth!" He's across the room in seconds. "Is it the baby?"

"Of course it's the fucking baby."

A word I've never used before, but it feels good. Just right.

"There's a pole down, blocking the lane. No way we can get out. I'll go and find Frank."

"No!" I scream it, a horrifying, bloodcurdling sound. Jimmy looks terrified.

"The baby is coming. Help me."

He becomes calm efficiency straightaway, this schoolboy who is an almost exact copy of his brother. Jimmy, who has been monosyllabic and closed off since the day I first met him. It is as if the urgency switches something on in him.

"Right, right, got it," he says, hurling his blazer across the kitchen floor.

I'm wearing a tent dress, which is a good thing, but my underwear will have to go. "Scissors, Jimmy. You'll have to cut my pants off. I can't reach them."

Crying, but also laughing, at the chronic absurdity of this.

He is back in what feels like one second with scissors and towels and he snips off my underwear, the skirt of my dress flipped onto my back so I am butt naked before him. He doesn't care and nor do I. There's no time for that.

"Right," he says, after he's taken a look. "I can see the head."

"Jesus Christ."

"Yup."

I scream again, in pain, in rage, in fear, but the scream is also the start of my giving in to this immense pressure which feels as if my insides are being squeezed with metal. There is nothing to do now except push, and even the pain—no words for the intensity, like being ripped in two, worse than that—feels good, helpful. My body has taken over.

"You're doing really well," Jimmy says in the soothing, professional tone of a midwife. Later we will laugh about this. "And you don't need to worry. I've birthed loads of lambs and I reckon it's the same thing. We are mammals, after all."

And so it is that I deliver our baby into the waiting hands of my teenage brother-in-law. I don't know how Jimmy understands he has to turn the baby over, this slippery, bloodied creature, and slap its bottom for that first reassuring cry, or whether he ties the umbilical cord then snips it off with scissors still smeared with this morning's bacon, or how he realizes—lambing, I suppose—that two minutes later I'll need to push out the afterbirth and we're not done yet. But before long I am sitting on the floor with my baby boy, wrapped in a towel, in my arms.

"We did it," I say to Jimmy, crying again. But these tears are different.

What can I say about the instant rush of love I feel for the tiny human in my arms? The dear little face I don't yet know but am already addicted to.

"You did it," Jimmy says. "I just helped at the end."

"Is he OK?"

I don't know why I'm asking a schoolboy without a scrap of medical training, but he has become godlike to me in this final hour.

"He's perfect, Beth. Should you try feeding him? I think that side to side thing he's doing with his mouth might mean he's hungry?"

I unbutton the tent dress, push down my bra, direct my nipple toward my baby's mouth, and, like a miracle, he clamps his lips around it and begins to suck. Jimmy and I look at each other and laugh.

Just then, the front door opens and Frank comes in, taking in the scene in an instant. "Oh, my God," he says, hurling himself toward me, his face a fury of anxiety.

"It's all right. Look," I say. "Isn't he lovely?"

"A boy?" He kneels on the floor and places a hand on the baby's cheek.

And I see it, the wave of elation that transforms his face, just as mine must have been when I saw our baby for the first time. There can be no greater intoxication, no purer feeling, than the moment when you meet your child after all the months of wondering and hoping and dreaming.

"I love him," he says.

"I know."

"We're lucky."

"We are."

He is ours, we are his, we are three.

1968

Nina's father insists on marking her engagement to Jimmy with an open bar at the Compasses. I could have told him free drinks on a Friday night would mean bun-fight at best, total carnage at worst, but, as a pub landlord, I suspect he knows that.

To begin with, I enjoy the engagement party. I love watching Nina being hugged and kissed, and even thrown up in the air by one whiskery old farmer. Like Jimmy often says, teasing her—she's a big hit with the over-seventies. In truth, Nina is everyone's favorite. In her bright pink minidress, joy is radiating from her. The men pretend to be jealous—"Lucky bastard, what have you got that we haven't?"—and give Jimmy too many pints, then too many whiskies. The women want to see Nina's ring. An opal surrounded by seed pearls, it used to belong to Jimmy's mother.

There's a fair amount of backslapping and cheek-pinching for Frank too, as he's well loved in the community. Frank donates a whole lamb for the church raffle at Christmas, allows farming friends to graze our fields for free, has been known to leave mystery food parcels on the doorsteps of those who need it. When Bobby was alive Frank was often at the school bleeding radiators and patching up rotten doors as if he were an odd-jobman rather than the time-pressed farmer he is. Every year he won the fathers' race at sports day, a foregone conclusion with his long legs, his fitness and extreme youth, but even so, you'd see the whole crowd screaming his name.

I watch my husband climb up on a barstool which looks

too rickety for his frame but he balances effortlessly, bangs a spoon against his glass. "There's going to be a wedding at Blakely Farm. And you are all invited."

The uproar is intense. Village weddings tend to follow a pattern in Hemston: Everyone comes, everyone provides, the cost and stress shared equally among the families who have lived here forever. The people of Hemston know how to throw a good party. And if these collective weddings feel a bit formulaic sometimes—same faces, same food, once or twice even the same dress, altered a little to fit the new bride—no one cares.

Within an hour we have been offered a marquee, trestle tables, bunting, a live band, barrels of cider and ale from the pub, pigs for a spit-roast, a wedding cake. The ladies who do the church flowers volunteer for the wedding, and a sideline conversation breaks out. What would be best for September—marigolds and white azaleas? A traditional orange-and-white theme, they decide. Helen says she will make Nina's dress. She's still a talented seamstress who, like me, was once top of the class at school and destined for greater things. Life rarely works out the way you expect.

I could watch my brother-in-law all night. He looks so proud as his future wife is embraced by one pair of arms after another. Nina has tried her best to modernize Jimmy, bringing home jeans from London and a rather garish short-sleeved shirt, which he wears tonight, under duress.

"Snazzy outfit," I tell him, and he rolls his eyes.

"I feel like a fool."

"What will you wear for the wedding?"

"Something my fiancée"—he breaks off to grin at me—"doesn't have a say in. She'd have me trussed up in a purple suit, no doubt."

Trays of whisky are circulating through the pub. Jimmy takes two glasses from a passing tray, offers one to me, downs both of them when I refuse. I've never acquired a taste for whisky.

"Oof," he says, turning to me, eyes streaming.

"Horrible?" I ask.

"Actually pretty good."

Helen comes up to us, hugging Jimmy first, then me. "This is the best news. Let me make you a suit, Jimmy. I've been wanting to try my hand at men's tailoring."

"He's thinking purple," I tell her, and Jimmy laughs.

When Jimmy begins another conversation, Helen and I talk in our learned language of glances and half phrases.

"How's Frank?" she says, and we both turn to look at my husband, standing a foot away, surrounded by friends, laughing.

"He's good," I say. "We both are."

Because in this moment, it's true.

With all this festive fever none of us notice how drunk Jimmy is getting until Andy Morris, the local bobby, reaches out and places one palm in the small of his back, keeping him upright. He's a good guy, Andy, we have known him for years. Plenty of times he delivered Jimmy back to us blind drunk in his delinquent, pre-Nina years. He got into fights, was caught drunk driving without a license, and, every single time, Andy let him off with a warning. He understood, like everyone in the village understood, the loss of his mother had hit Jimmy hard.

"Steady on, lad" is all Andy says. "Maybe give the whisky a break?"

"Are you joking?" Jimmy says, spilling a bit of his pint as he throws his arm around Andy's shoulders. "I'm getting married. It's traditional for the bridegroom to get very drunk."

I glance at Frank, raise my eyebrows a fraction, a warning he understands instantly.

He puts his arm around me, murmurs in my ear. "His night, isn't it?"

There is a sudden quiet, voices dipping, a few people turning to stare before I see for myself Gabriel has walked into the pub. It's the first time I've ever seen him in here.

Gabriel has not made any effort with the villagers since he arrived. I don't blame him. He's lived away from home for most of his life, and he always said he didn't fit in here. The people know him without knowing him. It's an uncomfortable dissonance and it makes them wary.

When Gabriel sees me, standing close to the bar, surrounded by family, his face tenses. Quite suddenly, we are in a goldfish bowl.

"What can I get you?" Nina's dad asks him.

"A pint of bitter, please, and a lemonade—?" He turns to me with an apologetic shrug.

"Leo's in the car. I know it's late. Just felt I needed to get out."

"Why don't I go and keep him company and you can drink your pint in peace? You won't be long, will you?"

Before Gabriel can reply Jimmy grabs his arm, spins him around until their faces are inches apart. "You're not welcome in here." He almost spits the words, the scorn in his voice sharp as a blade.

"Is that so? Bluntly put," Gabriel says. "Well, don't worry, I'm leaving the moment I have my drinks."

"Lay off, Jimmy," Frank says, stepping in. "The pub is for everyone."

Gabriel nods at him, that's all. But something about the quiet understanding between the two of them inflames Jimmy—he's on edge anyway, so it doesn't take much.

"Why don't you go back to London or wherever you came from? No one wants you here. Get lost."

None of us see it, the way Jimmy draws back his arm,

fist clenched in sudden anger. None of us but Andy, who moves in, quiet and efficient, encircling Jimmy's chest with his arms. Jimmy flailing and helpless. Andy, soothing, restraining.

"No need for that, lad, on such a happy night," he says, as Jimmy slackens in his arms. "Fresh air is what we need. Come on, fella, let's take a turn outside."

"Why does he do this, Beth?" Nina says beside me. "Why does he get so drunk? Five minutes ago he was happy."

"He shouldn't drink whisky. He's not good with spirits. It's my fault, I gave him mine."

"No. It's my fault," Gabriel says. "It was wrong of me to come. I didn't realize—"

Gabriel doesn't say what it is he has realized and I am left watching him walk away, feeling my husband's eyes upon me, wondering how much longer the three of us can carry on like this before something catastrophic happens.

The Trial

Andy—or DS Morris as the prosecutor is calling him—is on the witness stand today. Not so long ago, we considered him a friend. All that changed the night of the shooting.

I watch him swearing his oath, hand on the Bible, voice steady. He does not glance, even once, at the man in the dock.

"DS Morris, before we move to the night of the shooting, I'd like to ask you about your relationship with the Johnsons. I believe the brothers were friends of yours? You had known them a long time?"

The policeman hesitates. Thinking of the best way to distance himself from our family. "Only in the way all the villagers are friends. We didn't know each other intimately. I saw them here and there in the pub, that's all."

"My understanding, DS Morris, is that you'd had regular dealings with the family over the years. On account of Jimmy Johnson's behavior."

"Yes. That's correct. Jimmy was a bit of a tearaway when he was young. I broke up a few fights. Caught him drink driving more than once. Nothing too serious. Nothing like this."

"Let us move to the night of September the twenty-eighth. When did you first learn of the shooting?"

DS Morris looks down at his notebook. "We received a call at nine thirty-seven that night. We'd had report of a shotgun accident at Blakely Farm. The victim was already deceased."

"Let's pause there for a moment. You were the officer

on duty that night. You drove straight out to the Johnson farm?"

"Yes. The police station is based in the local town, a drive of around eight minutes."

"Can you recall your thoughts on that journey? A man had died in a shotgun accident. One who was well known to you. Did it strike you as strange or sinister in any way? What I'm asking, DS Morris, is whether you had any inkling this might have been murder?"

"Not at that point, no. Farming accidents are fairly common, unfortunately."

"But you changed your mind, once you got there?"

"I did, yes. The facts didn't seem to add up. I've been in this job twenty years, and you have an instinct for when you're being fed a story."

Now Andy looks at the defendant. "Within twenty-four hours, I knew we had a murder investigation on our hands."

Before

If I had begun the process of civilizing the Johnson men, it is the arrival of Bobby that has the biggest impact.

Frank is like a caricature of a doting father: He wants to do everything I do, he'd breastfeed Bobby if he could. When he comes in from the farm each night he holds his arms out, impatient for his turn, holding Bobby so tightly against him our baby's skin is scented with the day's labor—cow dung, tractor oil, and Imperial Leather, the soap Frank uses so frequently throughout the day I have come to think of it as his particular smell.

"I missed you," Frank says, kissing his son's soft cheeks. "And you." He reaches out to grab whichever part of me is nearest.

I always save Bobby's bath-time for Frank, no matter what time he comes in from the farm. I fill up a tub with warm water and Frank lowers him in, swooshing him back and forth, while I dab at his face with a soft flannel. Mostly, the two of us gaze down at him in wonder, cooing occasionally. It's my favorite time of day.

The biggest surprise is the way David falls for Bobby. Frank and Jimmy always mentioned how absent David was in their childhood, out on the farm all hours of the day. Now he is a changed man. In the evenings, he sits with his grandson on his lap, singing to him, songs that come from another age, music hall numbers and lullabies Frank and I have never heard. He reads the newspaper to him, which seems strange at first, but there is something about David's low, gravelly voice that lulls Bobby to sleep. If Bobby is crying, I'll hand him to David and say: "Can you work your magic?" And it is like magic, for the baby settles instantly in his grandfather's solid embrace.

"Will you look at that?" David says, looking up at me, thrilled.

Bobby has humanized him. This stiff, wordless farmer has become a man who laughs and sings and smiles. In bed, at night, Frank and I whisper to one another that our baby is nothing less than a miracle.

The change is apparent in Jimmy too. He's still in trouble at school from time to time, but I have noticed a new confidence in him. Jimmy has grown up, or perhaps it is more that ever since he stepped in and calmly delivered our son, averting disaster without once giving in to panic, I have found myself looking up to him. He is someone who can thrive in a crisis.

When Bobby is a few weeks old I start walking around the farm, baby strapped to me in a sling I fashion from an old blanket. The farm seems vast and unending when you traverse it by foot, it's rare to pass anyone else. Sometimes it feels as if Bobby and I are the last people on earth.

I talk to my sleeping infant as we parade around the land, which is his land, I tell him.

"One day, Bobby, you'll be doing this with your son or daughter."

There are so many species of birds here and David seems to know them all. On warm evenings he'll walk out with us, his fields changing color in the dusk light, a shimmering purple, a deep blue. He teaches me how to recognize lapwings and yellowhammers and chaffinches by sight and by song. Nothing is too small to go unremarked upon. Butterflies are named—marbled white, skipper, meadow brown—and a scurrying vole makes him gaze upward for the predator he always finds. A sudden rustle alerts him to hedgehogs, perfectly camouflaged in nondescript brown, as they hunt for beetles and slugs. When we stumble upon a litter of tumbling fox cubs, David grows still and I do the same. In silence we watch them play while, close by, their mother hunts for food. It feels like a gift catching this.

Through David's eyes, Blakely Farm is coming alive for me.

Before Bobby is a year old, David starts taking him around the farm on his tractor.

"You will be careful?" I say, but David just laughs, driving away with the baby wedged between his knees.

He drives with one arm on the steering wheel, the other draped casually around his grandson. I am glad of the time alone but I never relax until they return to the yard an hour or so later, both beaming.

"You don't need to worry," Frank says, when I tell him of my fears at night, the two of us facing each other in the darkness. "My dad is a safe pair of hands. He grew up on this farm. He would never let anything happen to Bobby."

Look what happened to your mother, I think, although I would never say so. Her accident, being kicked in the head while she was milking, came out of the blue and couldn't have been avoided. A stark reminder, if ever there was one, that you could never be too careful on the farm.

Despite my misgivings, I adore the way Bobby is growing up with his grandfather. Before long he'll be shooting and skinning rabbits himself, he'll fish for pike and carp, he will learn to birth a lamb, he will be able to name every bird and insect on this two-hundred-acre farm; all the wisdom that has been passed through the Johnson men over generations will be his. It is his right. And I want that for him.

1968

In my favorite photograph, Bobby is sitting cross-legged on the kitchen floor, bottle-feeding an orphan lamb. I've looked at it so often it has become incarnate to me now—this is the Bobby I see whenever his name is mentioned, even though I knew him at six, seven, eight, and nine. I used to keep it loose and uncovered in my handbag, transferring it to coat pockets sometimes, until the photograph began to look creased and worn. Frank bought me a little leather holder for it and now the photograph resides permanently in the macramé bag I take everywhere.

It's an unwieldy thing, this bag, crammed with treats for Hero, a library book I have waited months for—*A Wizard of Earthsea* by Ursula K. Le Guin—a clutch of shopping receipts, binoculars, a half-eaten packet of Marie biscuits, and a pair of Leo's balled-up socks from when he walked home barefoot through the long grass.

"You know you could probably just about squeeze the kitchen sink in," Frank says, surveying the detritus laid out on the floor.

I take the bag into the courtyard and shake it out, getting rid of every crumb. The photo is missing. I cry out in dismay.

"What's happened?" Frank is beside me in a moment.

At first, I'm too distressed to answer. I'm turning the bag inside out again, retrieving my book and flicking through the pages, looking, looking.

"The photo. It's gone."

"It can't have."

Frank takes me into his arms but I'm too tense to return the embrace. I hear the note of anguish in his voice as he tries to reassure me. We didn't take enough photos of Bobby, we didn't understand photos would be the only thing we'd have left.

"Let's be methodical about this. Can you remember the last time you saw it?"

I'm embarrassed to tell Frank the truth. I look at it every day. At Meadowlands, whenever Gabriel and Leo are out of the room. When I'm cooking supper. Or filling the bath or hanging out the washing. I see it and, also, I don't. The photo is a kind of talisman, my reminder that Bobby existed.

"Yesterday."

"Then we'll be able to find it. I'll look upstairs."

The doorbell rings while I'm in the middle of emptying a drawer of the dresser, a pointless exercise because not once have I ever kept the photograph in there.

Gabriel and Leo are on the doorstep. My mind is fraught, it's only with effort I manage to be civil. "Hello," I say. "Would you like to come in?"

Gabriel shakes his head as I had known he would. After Jimmy's outburst in the pub, I tried to reassure Gabriel it meant nothing, just a bit of silly drunkenness, that was all, but I don't think he believes me. The line I walk, going between my home and his, grows ever thinner, it seems to me.

"Leo has something to tell you."

"Uh-oh. That sounds ominous." I look at Leo to encourage him but he slides his eyes away, refusing to meet my gaze. "It can't be that bad. Come on, the suspense is killing me."

The two of them look so serious, Gabriel with an expression I can't quite read. I think he might be angry.

Leo shoots his hand out in front of him, uncurls his palm to reveal the little leather photo holder. "I took it from your bag."

He looks ashamed, staring down at the ground but, for a moment, the flood of relief is so great all I can do is clutch the photo to my chest. I feel the weight of tears rising in my throat. "I was going out of my mind. I thought I'd lost it."

"I'm sorry," Leo says.

"Nowhere upstairs," Frank says, then he takes in the scene on the doorstep.

"Ah, you found it? Kind of you to bring it back. It must have fallen out of Beth's bag, she's been so worried. We both have."

I think Gabriel is going to let Leo get away with it and I'm glad—no need to humiliate him any further.

But Leo cries: "It was me! I stole it. I wanted it. I like looking at Bobby."

I see the shock on Frank's face as he takes in what Leo has said. "I see," Frank says. His voice is neutral but he is looking only at me.

"Anyway," I say, hurriedly, "we're making far too much out of this. The photograph is safe, and Leo has apologized."

The minute the door has closed behind Gabriel and Leo, we stand inches apart, looking everywhere but at each other.

"The photo stays here in future. Let's not lose it again," Frank says.

"I'm sorry," I say, not sure what I'm apologizing for. It feels like everything.

"He was our boy," Frank says, his voice breaking. "And he's gone. Why should they have anything to do with him?"

"Frank—" I reach out to grab one of his hands but he shifts away from me.

"You knew what you were doing when you took that job. You refused to listen to me when I said it was a bad idea. How the hell do you think it's going to end?"

Before

The society wedding everyone has been discussing for months takes place on Bobby's third birthday. While I am planning a small picnic beneath the oak tree for our family, an army of vans are unloading their contents at Meadowlands.

There is a running commentary on the decadence unfolding, a narrative that is mostly bitter since none of the villagers have been invited. How wasteful and extravagant are the hothouse flowers—rare blue orchids, first reported by the cleaning lady, and denigrated at length in the village shop. Twenty-four cases of champagne unloaded by the gardener, something French-sounding, he'd said, he couldn't remember what. The marquees—not one, but two—positioned so they have a perfect view of the lake, easily seen from the road. These tents are quite something, I am told. Even Helen, who knows better than most how painful the subject matter, how thin the ice upon which we skate, cannot resist elaborating.

"They've covered them with strings of colored lights. Stunning—like something out of *Arabian Nights*," she says.

My heart does beat a little faster then.

Some of the villagers are employed in the run-up to the wedding—extra cleaners, gardeners, laundry maids—and now there is a deluge of detail. Three hundred guests invited, Hollywood stars rubbing shoulders with English aristocracy, novelists, musicians, and politicians. There is rumor of Elizabeth Taylor and Alec Guinness, Doris Lessing, the Duchess of Argyll. Tessa Wolfe must be in her element.

A wedding dress designed by Norman Hartnell, pictures taken by society photographer Antony Armstrong-Jones. A swing band flying in from the States. A chef from Paris. The wedding of the year—it said so in *Tatler*.

Bobby wakes early on his birthday: It is half-light when I hear his bare feet running along the floorboards and his small, soft body squeezes in between us.

"I'm three," he announces, and I know Frank is thinking the same thing as me when he replies, "Three whole years of you? Wow."

"And there was a storm that day," Bobby says, his prompt for Frank to tell the story of his birth.

He settles his head on his father's chest and Frank curls an arm around him.

"We don't get many storms in the summer but when we do they tend to be big. And this one was colossal. Trees came down, phone lines were cut, people lost electricity. Your mum was all on her own. And the baby was coming—"

Bobby's favorite part is when his uncle Jimmy arrives home in his school uniform and saves the day. Jimmy is Bobby's hero. He believes Jimmy saved his life. And maybe he did.

As it's his birthday, Bobby is allowed to go milking with the men. He's too small to be much more than a hindrance but they always wait patiently while he tries and fails to do what they do. Milking takes a good while longer when Bobby is involved.

I listen to Frank helping Bobby dress in his room, sudden riotous laughter when he puts both feet through one leg hole of his underpants, the discussion about his navy overalls, which Helen made for him—an exact copy of the ones David, Frank, and Jimmy wear.

"Not a baby anymore," Bobby says.

"Clearly," says Frank. "Better start pulling your weight."

They clatter down the stairs and across the yard and I listen to their fading chatter, luxuriating in both my aloneness and the fact they are mine.

We will be celebrating Bobby's birthday later today, after the second milking. My parents and sister are coming, David, Jimmy, Frank, me, and the birthday boy. No one else. I thought about asking Helen, who has a son almost exactly the same age, but the truth is, I have insulated myself within these thick walls of family and it is all I need. Bobby seems content enough surrounded by grandparents and an aunt and uncle who adore him. Why change it?

When Bobby gets back, we spend the rest of the morning preparing a feast. The Wolfes' guests may be dining on oysters and lobster tails, but we have jam tarts and honey-roasted sausages and a pineapple hedgehog with quills of cheddar. When we've finished icing the cake, Bobby's cheeks and nose are smeared in chocolate and I take a picture of him, grinning at me, wild on sugar and excitement as we count down to the main event.

There are still a couple of hours before we'll gather for the picnic. Although I've done my best to drown out the noise around Gabriel's wedding, I know to the last second when it is happening. I see three o'clock arrive on the kitchen clock, think of Gabriel waiting in the village church, his bride about to walk up the aisle with her father. After fifteen minutes, I imagine them exchanging their vows, Gabriel staring into Louisa's eyes how once he looked into mine. I think about my own wedding in the same church with only our families present, my dress of imitation lace, Frank's borrowed suit that was a couple of inches too short. I wouldn't change any of it, I love everything about the new life I have built. But the temptation to look, one final time, rises up in me until I can no longer suppress it.

"Want to go and spy on a wedding in the village, Bobby?"

"Like real spies?"

"Yes. We can hide behind one of the big trees in the graveyard."

"In fact, I would."

"In fact" is a big thing for Bobby: It's a phrase he's just learned.

It's only a five-minute walk to the village, ten at Bobby's pace, but I begin to worry we might have left it too late. And when we get there, I see a line of photographers outside the church, both sides of the road crowded with villagers waiting for a glimpse of the couple, jars of homemade confetti at the ready.

"This is where we need to be proper spies so no one in the village sees us. Think you can do that?"

Bobby puts a finger to his lips, already committing to stealth.

We enter the cemetery from the far side and dart from tree to tree, shielding ourselves behind a tomb while I look for the best vantage spot. When the church bells begin to ring, with an evocative, celebratory peal, I grab Bobby's hand and sprint for a yew tree wide enough to accommodate us, close enough to see.

"Look," Bobby hisses, when the bridegroom walks out in a top hat and tails, pausing in the porch, his tiny bride clinging to his arm.

The official photographer rushes forward to take the first shot, dapper in his narrow black suit, white shirt, and black tie. "If you could look into each other's eyes . . . oh, that's it, absolutely spot-on." His chiseled upper-crust accent floats toward us.

The press photographers form a semicircle around the couple, clicking frantically while Gabriel and Louisa wait and smile, knowing this is part of the game. Their image will be in all the social pages tomorrow.

It is years since I've seen Gabriel. He hasn't changed. Tall and elegant in his fine wedding clothes, a face that will always be more beautiful than handsome. Looking at the two of them, I am filled with a jealousy I have no right to feel.

I watch Bobby watching Gabriel. My son will never know this man, who once meant so much to me. It's unlikely he will ever see him again. He certainly won't think of him. Or remember the day we hid behind a tree and played spies. It's a moment, that's all, when we are suspended in time.

"What do you think of the bridegroom?" I ask.

"Is he a bit—fancy-pants?" Bobby says, shushing me when I laugh out loud, though his dark eyes flash with humor.

"Fancy-pants" is what Frank calls Bobby when my mother has got him ready for bed: hair parted and slicked by a wet comb, pajamas buttoned to the top and tucked in, a face that gleams.

I watch as Louisa turns her head to say something to Gabriel. See how he leans closer to hear her, how he kisses her cheek.

Louisa's mother, Moira, who hasn't aged a day since I last saw her, comes out of the church now, holding the hand of a toddler dressed in head-to-toe white—frilly shirt, knickerbockers, and tights. I'd heard tell of Gabriel and Louisa's son but it's mesmerizing seeing him. I watch as Moira lifts the child into Louisa's arms, as Gabriel stoops to kiss his forehead, as the photographers click away in a frenzy. There's been no judgment in the reporting of their choice to have a child before they wed. I don't know why I expected anything different. The rules never did apply to people like Gabriel and Louisa.

Beside me, my little boy begins to wriggle impatiently, bored now. I feel a rush of love for him: I have all I need right here.

I'm glad for them. They are three, we are three. There's a pleasing symmetry to that. Everything worked out for us both.

"Well, that's it, then, Bobby," I say, turning away.

"Yep," he says, mimicking Frank. "It certainly is."

He throws his hat up in the air, a flatcap like the ones the men wear, a present from David, and catches it on the first attempt.

I pull him into me. "I know it's your birthday and the presents are all for you today, but can I say, you're the best present I've ever had."

1968

I don't bring up Bobby's photograph with Leo because the truth is, I feel responsible. He's a boy who misses his mother and I've managed to make it worse by showing him how much I miss my son. Or that's my reading of it, anyway.

I've been a little selfish, I think, telling Leo about Bobby, just because it was a way of helping me to keep his memory fresh. Trouble is, no one lets me talk about him. Frank can't often bear it because he's so steeped in guilt he manages to carry on only by acting as if Bobby never existed. I worry for Frank. Where will it end, all this unresolved grief that has no place to go? His way of coping is to work himself into the ground so that he falls into an exhausted sleep each night, ready to start over again at sunrise. Jimmy is the same, although he also relies on booze to get him through tough times. But at least he's got Nina and the prospect of their wedding to look forward to and, I hope, a baby of their own soon enough.

I'm about to go home when Gabriel comes into the kitchen. He's been working all afternoon and I haven't yet seen him since the incident with the photo.

"We should talk, don't you think?" he says. "Stay for a glass of wine?" He glances at Leo, doing his homework at the kitchen table. "We could have it in the library?"

It seems more like a command than an invitation and I feel a sudden, stabbing anxiety as I follow him along the corridor. Perhaps he'll ask me to stop looking after Leo. It's not what I want, but it would probably be the best thing for us all.

This room, this beautiful, book-lined room. We once spent a week here, curled together on the sofa as we worked our way through novels with thin, yellowing pages and fancy typography, pausing to read out sentences to one another if they were funny or particularly good.

On the coffee table in front of the sofa, a bottle of white wine is waiting, with two glasses.

"Presumptuous," I say, and Gabriel laughs.

"I could probably manage it on my own if I had to."

The wine is delicious, as I'd known it would be.

"From the cellar?" I ask after my first taste.

He nods. "More down there than I'll ever drink on my own. Some of it has probably turned to vinegar."

In the beat of silence that follows I am wondering if I can distract him with small talk, but my mind is ridged with worry and I cannot find anything to say.

"I need to talk to you about Leo," Gabriel says, at last. "But I don't want to upset you."

I return my wine to the table, sit bolt upright as if I'm being interviewed or, more likely, sacked. "If this isn't working out, I completely understand. There are plenty of people who'd watch Leo after school for you. I could put word around—?"

I see the surprise come into Gabriel's face as he registers what I have said. "No, no, that's the last thing I want. Leo is not a very happy boy; we both know that. He hates school. The only thing he looks forward to is the afternoons with you. Look, this is difficult—"

"Just say it, Gabriel."

"You talk to Leo about Bobby quite a bit, don't you?"

"I suppose I do," I say, as casually as I can.

"And I think Leo has become a bit obsessed with Bobby. I know that must sound very strange to you. I think Leo sees Bobby as this perfect child he can never live up to.

It's because of the divorce, it's messed with his head. Leo misses his mother, he feels displaced here, and suddenly you've come along with this golden boy who died—"

I won't allow myself to cry but I clench my fists together, breathe out one long, shaky exhalation.

"Oh, God." Gabriel looks stricken. "I knew this would hurt you. I'm sorry."

I'm nodding at him, nodding and nodding. "I knew I shouldn't talk about Bobby so much. But Leo was curious about him, he kept asking questions. And no one else asks me about him, ever. It's like Bobby is a ghost everyone has forgotten. And I miss him. I miss him so much. I loved telling Leo about him. Once I started, I just couldn't stop."

"I wish I'd known him," Gabriel says, quietly.

The pain of that. There is nothing I can say. My whole life moving forward will be filled with people who never knew my son.

"What was he like?"

"I'm trying my best to *stop* talking about him, Gabriel." I'm laughing now, calm again.

"But not to me. I'd like to know what sort of boy Bobby was. From the little you've said, he sounds wonderful."

"Really?"

My traitorous heart, always racing.

"Really. Tell me everything."

This is how our friendship begins to change. Slowly, at first, so that I hardly register it. The early evening wine drinking. An hour when I talk about my dead son and Gabriel listens as if I am telling him a story, night after night, while I draw Bobby's character from scratch. And perhaps I am. Where to start, describing the boy he was to a man who will never meet him? With his birth, of course, the day when a violent storm ripped down trees and telephone poles and blocked the road to our farm. A day when a teenage schoolboy delivered his nephew onto the kitchen floor. Pause after the recounting, take the time to taste again the euphoria of that day, when everything was ahead.

When I walk home, I am alive to the memories, the sweet, sweet years, all nine of them, when Bobby was here. I feel excited thinking of stories to tell Gabriel the next day. And frightened when I think how much it would hurt Frank if he knew I was sharing intimacies about our treasured only son.

Before

We have a farm boy who wants nothing more than to be outside from dawn to dusk with his parents, his uncle, his grandpa. The glory of these first five years, did I appreciate it enough? Listening to Frank and Bobby crossing the yard to the dairy each morning, our son's ceaseless, high-pitched chatter. The men back again for a cooked breakfast, Bobby sitting next to his grandpa, raised up on cushions, still talking. He and I weeding, the endless weeding. Bobby's expert detection for rogue plants, small hands that clasp and tug at roots until there is a great pile beside him. Rewarding ourselves with hot chocolate before we venture out again. Sometimes sitting on the iron gate at the bottom of the sheep field while the valley echoes with ewes calling for their lambs and the air hums with insects, a breeze whipping our skin. Drinking it all in, like Frank once did, and David and his dad before him; my boy reaching back to his ancestors through these lumpy green fields, to the sounds and sights, the taste, the touch of a thousand years.

Already Bobby is turning out to be his own person. He can sometimes drive me mad, refusing to come in when he's called. I have a little handbell I ring when he's out playing in the garden—or at least that's where he's supposed to be—and I'll ring it for several minutes before I accept he's wandered off to find Frank or David. I can never stay cross with him for long, none of us can; one disarming grin from Bobby and all is forgiven.

*

All too soon Bobby begins at the primary school. He looks like someone else's child in his shirt and tie, his shiny lace-up shoes.

"I look really weird," he says, inspecting himself in the bathroom mirror as he cleans his teeth.

"Smart, not weird."

"Hmm." He looks unsure. "If you say so."

At the school, my son's confidence amazes me. Most of the new kindergarten children are clinging to their mothers, but Bobby saunters toward his classroom without a backward glance. At the last moment he remembers me, sprinting back to whisper in my ear, "Will you be all right without me?"

No, Bobby. Let's go home. We'll try this another day, I manage not to say.

"I'll be fine. You go and have some fun."

With Bobby gone during the day, I throw myself into working on the farm. David shows me all the things his sons absorbed from childhood. I learn to spot the early signs of mastitis in a heifer, where to look for abscesses in sheep, how to examine their eyes, hooves, the quality of their wool. I can press my hands to their bellies and haunches and know if they need a better grade of grass, if they are fat enough to be taken to market. I learn how to roll fields with the roller looped up to the tractor. David even teaches me to drive the combine harvester. There is something cocoon-like about being high up in the cab, the panorama of our fields stretched before us. I used to love spending time in the combine with Frank, traveling up and down the cornfields at its leisurely, unhurried pace. There was an intimacy, an aloneness that could be hard to find in the farmhouse, and we talked about everything in those long stretches while we reaped and threshed the family corn. I sometimes say, because it makes Frank laugh, we fell in love in a combine harvester.

Perhaps it's for reasons of intimacy—the two of us looking straight ahead rather than at each other—when David asks: "Will you be having another little one soon? What with Bobby at school."

I'm taken aback by the question. It is by far the most personal thing my father-in-law has ever asked me. "Are you trying to get rid of me already, David?" I say, teasing him.

He nods and says no more about it. *Fair enough*, the nod says. *It's your business, not mine.*

It's not that I haven't thought about it. Part of me craves a newborn, that blissful, insular vacuum, coexistence in a sleep-deprived parallel universe, as closely connected as you were when the tiny creature was in your womb. The scent of them, the shape of them, the warm weight cradled in your arms, the delicate sound of their breathing. Second time around it would be different, of course. Now there is Bobby, who expects my full attention when he gets home from school. I picture myself nursing a baby, trapped in my chair for forty-five minutes while Bobby grows more and more impatient waiting for me to finish. But then, the baby needs changing. And now he is crying, and I must walk him up and down, soothing him, no option but to neglect my elder child. I feel Bobby's shock and disappointment that his mother, who has walked each step of the last five years with him, is no longer available for his every whim, even for a few of them. And then his resignation as he accepts the new order of things. The way Bobby would change, the gradual loosening of the bond between us. I'm not ready for that.

Several days later, it's apparent Frank has been talking to David. He gets into bed and asks: "Is your diaphragm in?"

The fact of his asking is unusual.

"Of course."

We have sex most nights, almost without exception.

Frank says it clears his head of the day and helps him get to sleep. For me it's when I feel most connected to Frank, a closeness that is hard to find at any other time of day.

"Why do you ask?"

"I was thinking we could stop using it. Only if you wanted to."

"You've been talking to your dad, haven't you?"

"I have."

"Do you want us to start trying for a baby?"

"It would be nice, wouldn't it? A brother or sister for Bobby."

"It would. It really would."

I think I have injected the right amount of enthusiasm into my voice but I can never fool Frank.

"Why don't you want to?"

I pause for a moment, trying to find the words to help him understand.

"I know it feels like the right time. But I'm not ready to cut ties with Bobby just yet. I'm sure I will be one day, but we're still so young, you and I. And it's different for mothers, so full-time and unrelenting. I wouldn't be able to be with him in the way I am now. Does that make sense?"

This is the thing about Frank: He always gets it. He reaches out an arm and pulls me toward him until my face is pressed against his chest. "Perfect sense. We got the best one. Why risk it with another?"

It's different the way we make love tonight. For a start we never break eye contact, not once. Frank presses himself very deeply inside me and he stays there, not moving, looking down at me, and I feel so turned on by him, running my hands up and down his chest, feeling the hardness of muscle under skin, his broadness, his strength, the heft of him and, also, how much I love him. When he finally starts to move in slow, deep circles, each one draws a gasp of pleasure from my throat, even though we always try to be quiet with the rest of the family just across the corridor. But I'm too taken to stop, my whole body starts to spiral and shake and I'm gripping on to him, crying his name, and he's whispering in the darkness, "It's OK," and it feels violent and tender and like nothing on earth. And then Frank is moving hard and fast now, his breathing hectic and broken, but he still keeps looking at me, as he comes, as I do, and then, instantly, we are holding each other, laughing and laughing at the intensity, the raw madness of it.

Frank whispers: "Christ. What was that?"

And I'm half crying, half laughing, when I whisper back: "I know."

We ease into our sleeping positions, his arm wrapped around me, and his voice is already slippery with drowsiness. "Why would we want to change a thing?"

1968

Leo and I are in the garden at Meadowlands when a black taxi comes rattling up the drive. It's such an unusual sight, here in the depths of Dorset, we stand together and watch to see who it is arriving.

"Do you think that cab's come all the way from London?" Leo says.

"Only if they're a millionaire. No one else would be able to afford it."

"It's my mom, it's my mom!" Leo shrieks, as the passenger in the back seat first comes into view. He's running over to the taxi, trying to open the door before it's even drawn to a halt.

Louisa steps out, her arms held wide, and her son leaps into them.

"Mom. Mom. Mama." He says it over and over, his voice reducing to a whimper, and it is all I can do to stop myself from bursting into tears.

"Why didn't you say you were coming?" Leo says, when they break apart.

"I wanted to surprise you. I did check in with your dad to make sure you'd be here, but I didn't tell him either."

Louisa looks over at me for the first time. A guarded smile. "Beth," she says. "It's nice to see you again. I've heard so much about you in the last few months."

The front door opens, Gabriel comes running down the steps. "My God, Louisa," he says. "I can't believe it."

She looks up at him, a little wary, but he's grinning as he kisses her cheek.

"This is the best surprise, isn't it, Leo? How long can you stay?"

"A few days while my parents look after Marcus. I thought, if it was all right with you, I could take Leo to London. We could stay in a hotel, visit some of our old haunts." She looks down at her son. "Would you like that?"

"I would love it!"

Leo wraps his arms around his mother's waist and the three of them start walking toward the house, father, mother, son. It's an odd sensation watching them, picturing the family they once were. Two parents and one son. Just like Frank and me and Bobby.

At the front door, Gabriel remembers me. "Beth, won't you come in for a cup of tea?"

I shake my head. "Absolutely not," I say. "It's lovely for Leo to have some time alone with both of you. I'll leave you to it."

Later, Frank and I are finishing supper when the phone rings.

"Beth? Is that you?"

The voice is high, nervous, American.

"Louisa."

"Leo and I are going to London first thing, so I won't have a chance to see you again. I wondered—you might think this odd—would you meet me in the pub for a quick drink?"

"You don't have to drop everything the minute that family calls," Frank says, when I put the phone down. "You don't do it for anyone else."

It hasn't gone unnoticed I've been returning from Meadowlands later and later this summer, and sometimes there's the tang of alcohol on my breath. My marriage is in a downward slide and I know, only too well, what needs to be done to halt it. The trouble is, I'm not sure I want to. I've felt happier—if you can call it that—in these past weeks with Leo and Gabriel than I have in years. It's selfish of me to carry on like this when I know how much I am hurting Frank. But I don't seem to be able to stop.

When I arrive at the pub, Louisa is already there, sitting at a small corner table with two gin and tonics in front of her.

"Gin all right?" she says, sliding a glass toward me. Her smile is warm, open. She wants us to be friends.

There was a time when I used to pore over press photos of Louisa and Gabriel. If she was unsmiling in the picture, I'd decide she was cold, haughty. If they looked particularly happy and in love, I would remind myself she had stolen him from me. She was a ruthless American and Gabriel hadn't stood a chance, was the story I told myself.

"Leo was over the moon to see you," I say now. "He hasn't looked like that in all the months I've known him. So radiant. It was wonderful to see."

"He has changed so much. I can hardly believe it. My little boy has gone."

"It must be hard not being with him."

"You have no idea." Louisa places a manicured hand over her heart. Pale pink nails with white tips. Gold bangles jangling on her wrist. She looks so well put together in her spotless white coatdress. Just like her mother. And Tessa Wolfe. Women of a different caliber to anyone I know. It's not just money that sets her apart—Louisa has real style, I think.

"To be honest, Beth, I'm finding it really difficult living away from him. I'm constantly on the brink of saying, 'I can't do this anymore.' I wish he'd come and live in the States with me."

"Deep down, he probably wants to."

"I'm not so sure. He and Gabe are very close. Leo chose to stay here with him."

"And Gabriel would be devastated."

I would be devastated. My little surrogate family ripped apart.

"Which is why I'm trying to see if we can make this work. The problem is Gabe never tells me how Leo is really doing. I guess he doesn't want to worry me. But I sense things aren't great. Will you be honest with me? Is he all right?"

I hesitate for a moment, torn between wanting to do what is best for Leo and feeling whatever I say might inadvertently hurt Gabriel. I don't know Louisa well enough for a cards-on-the-table conversation.

"Please, Beth. I wouldn't ask if I wasn't worried about him."

I nod to show her I understand.

"He does seem very close to his father like you say. Leo is happy when he's at Meadowlands. But he finds school hard, he doesn't seem to have many friends there. He struggles to control his anger, there's been trouble over that. The main thing is, he really misses you."

"What would you do? Would you insist on him coming back to America with you? As a mother—"

Louisa breaks off. Panic flits across her pretty face. "Forgive me. I spoke without thinking."

"It's fine," I say, too crisply. I know my voice hardens when there's a reference to Bobby—it's how I steel myself. "But I can't answer that. I've never been in your situation. If you can find a way to visit more, I'm sure Leo will be fine. Sooner or later, he will begin to settle here."

"Do you really think so?"

"I do. It's early days, he has only been living here for a

few months. By this time next year, I bet he'll be back to his old self."

"You're a nice person, Beth. I'm glad Leo has you in his life."

It's strange how with certain women you can be enemies one minute and intimates the next. By the time we have bought our second drink, I feel Louisa and I could talk about anything.

"What went wrong with you and Gabriel?" I say, looking up at Louisa. "Do you mind me asking? You always looked so happy and in love when I saw your photo in the papers."

"Did we? Just goes to show how deceptive appearances can be. Oh, I loved him, absolutely I did. And Gabe tried to love me back. But we were kidding ourselves."

"Do you think you'd have got married if you hadn't had Leo?"

The words are out before I can stop them. "Sorry, it's none of my business," I say.

But Louisa shakes her head, unfazed. "In all honesty? Probably not. Gabe asked me to marry him the moment I found out I was pregnant. It was me who wanted to wait. Looking back, I was still hoping he'd fall in love with me."

"And Tessa? I can't imagine she was happy about you being pregnant?"

"She didn't care one bit. Just thrilled we were engaged and we were giving her plenty of time to plan the party of her dreams."

I pick up my drink and take a big glug of gin. It is never a good idea talking about Tessa Wolfe. I can hear her scornful tone as if it were yesterday. *Boys like Gabriel don't end up with girls like you.*

"Why did you split up in the end?"

"I was visiting my parents in the States and my father invited Michael—Marcus's father—for dinner. They were working on a movie together. It's a cliché to say it was love at first sight but he was just so smitten with me, so charming and forthright. He said he was completely bowled over by me. And you know, that was something I'd never experienced before. I'm not making excuses, really, I'm not. I will always feel guilty about falling in love with someone else while I was married."

She looks straight at me with a clear, unflinching stare. "You can't imagine how wearing it is, how endlessly demoralizing, knowing your husband loved someone else far more than he would ever love you."

I look down at the table, trying to gather myself. I can't really believe what I am hearing. Once upon a time, the only thing I wanted to know was that Gabriel loved me more than Louisa. It gives me little pleasure to hear it now. I love Frank and the life we built together so painstakingly. There will never be a time when I don't love Frank, when I don't need him. Even having this conversation feels like a betrayal. And yet, I feel it, the unmistakable rush of adrenaline. A knot of excitement in the base of my stomach.

"I don't know what went on between the two of you, but I can tell you it ruined Gabriel for anyone else. I was an obvious rebound, I'd been in love with him from the beginning."

Every word Louisa speaks seems to echo right through me. Beneath the table I clasp my hands together, almost afraid to look up at her.

"Everything has happened the wrong way round, hasn't it?" Louisa says, and I inhale sharply in an effort not to cry.

"Can I say one more thing and then we'll change the subject, I promise. I can see you're upset. I'm sorry, Beth."

Louisa reaches out and takes hold of my hand, just for a moment. Her diamond engagement ring is insultingly large. "It's not too late."

She leaves the rest of the sentence unsaid.

It's not too late for you and Gabriel.

Before

My favorite times are when both families are together, which happens, without fail, on Bobby's birthdays. He is seven today and it's doubly special because tonight Jimmy is introducing us to his new girlfriend, Nina.

They met a couple of weeks ago when she was lost in a maze of identical-looking fields and flagged down his tractor. When he heard she was the new publican's daughter, Jimmy said he'd give her a lift home.

"In that?" Nina said, looking skeptically at the Massey Ferguson with its coating of mud, cow shit, and various other substances.

"Too posh for it, are you?" Jimmy said, riling her before they'd exchanged more than a couple of sentences.

"Hardly," she said, clambering up next to him.

They've been seeing each other ever since and David, Frank, and I are trying our best not to show our relief. The three of us have had plenty of conversations about how best to keep Jimmy on track. Most of the time he's fine, but there are the drinking sprees that come out of nowhere and often end in trouble. We are all hoping Nina is going to be the answer.

My parents and sister arrive first with a carload of presents. Eleanor is down from London, she always takes the day off on Bobby's birthday. She is a hotshot solicitor these days, after fighting her way to the top of the firm she first joined as a secretary. She'll take over one day, I have no doubt about it. She has a flat in Parsons Green, which I have yet to see, and earns more money than Frank and I could dream of, but I wouldn't swap lives with her, nor she with me. We're very different these days, Eleanor and me.

"Where's my favorite boy?" she says, swooping Bobby into her arms.

Her presents are always the best, partly because she can afford it, but mostly because she puts so much thought into choosing them.

When Bobby unwraps her package, he screams: "Oh, my God, Elly!" and Eleanor beats her palms together like a seal; she loves to please him. Inside is a battery-powered record player. Bobby has become obsessed with music in general and Elvis Presley in particular. The farmhouse throbs to the sound of "Hound Dog" and "All Shook Up" turned up so loud, I sometimes wonder if the windows might shatter.

It wouldn't take much: The frames are mostly rotten, the glass thin and cracked in places. Fixing up the farmhouse has always come bottom of the list.

My mother, Eleanor, and I are cooking tonight's feast. We've become rather good at it. My mother hated cooking when we were growing up and mostly left it to my dad, but she's a different woman as a grandmother. She rings up weeks before the big day to "menu plan for our prince," as she jokingly calls him. Tonight it's beef stew followed by pineapple upside-down cake, Bobby's favorite. My dad has brought red wine to go with it and Coca-Cola for the birthday boy.

While we cook, Bobby and my father start work on an Airfix model he has given him, peering in confusion at a bag of plastic parts. I hope Bobby never grows out of Airfix, because my father certainly won't.

One time, watching them together, I asked him if he'd wanted a boy instead of two girls.

"Absolutely not," he said, not missing a beat. "I'm strictly a ladies' man. Can't you tell? But this boy, you would have to admit, is rather special."

The men come in from the farm at five and take it in turns to wash and change, and by six, we are all assembled around the big oak table, Bobby at the head, wearing a white cowboy hat Eleanor brought down from London.

Nina is not like me at all. If I were walking into a house filled with someone else's family, I might feel some trepidation. I remember the first time I met David—he barely looked up from his copy of *Farmers Weekly*. Afterward, Frank told me he had been depressed ever since Sonia died and that was why. But it was a long time before I was able to relax around him, and it wasn't until Bobby was born we finally became close.

Nina walks through the front door, not bothering to knock, and stands before a table of strangers, a parcel in her arms that is wrapped in gold paper and tied with a red ribbon. "I don't suppose there are any Elvis fans here?" she says.

"Me!" Bobby shoots his hand up, as if he's at school.

"Then you'll be needing this." She hands over the parcel.

Inside are a pair of blue suede boots she found in a charity shop, a couple of sizes too big for Bobby but fine with a thick pair of socks.

"I'm never taking them off," he shrieks, parading around the kitchen, showing each of us in turn.

Jimmy scoops up his nephew, lifts him high up onto his shoulders, and runs around the kitchen with Bobby shrieking in delight. And then, of course, it's imperative to play "Blue Suede Shoes" on the new record player and it transpires that, as well as giving perfect presents, Nina also knows how to dance. She teaches Bobby to shimmy his shoulders and rotate his hips, Elvis style, the two of them snaking across the kitchen floor in their socked feet, while the rest of us look on, laughing.

I will always say afterward that Jimmy fell in love when Bobby was seven years old—and Bobby did too. For the rest of the evening, he watches Nina with eagle-eyed devotion. I can see the thoughts running through his mind: *Who is this firecracker and how long can we keep her for?*

Dinner with my loved ones follows a familiar pattern. The more wine we drink, the louder we become. There is constant laughter and the odd tense moment when the conversation veers toward politics. When Eleanor becomes heated, slating the Tories, whom David vehemently supports, my mother steps in with a neat subject change.

"Actually we've got some news. I've been offered a head teachership. But I can't decide whether or not to take it."

"Of course you should," Eleanor says. "High time you had a promotion."

My mother pauses and I notice how my father is fiddling with his wineglass, twirling it between his fingers.

"It's in Cork," she says.

"You mean Ireland?" I can't keep the shock from my voice. They have a grandson now. How could they consider living anywhere other than Hemston?

"That's fantastic," Eleanor cries. "It's always been Dad's dream to live in Ireland." She fixes me with her stern big-sister stare and I offer my reassurances.

"Of course you must go."

"Really?" my father says, looking up at me.

He knows me so well.

"Absolutely," I say, firmly. "Time you did something for yourselves."

"It won't be forever," my mother says. "Just a few years. An adventure while we're young enough to enjoy it."

She glances at Bobby. "But we will miss this young man so much."

As the evening wears on, I see how Jimmy and Nina touch one another constantly, her palm resting on his knee beneath the table, his hand sneaking out to tuck a strand of hair behind her ear. I catch their secret smiles and hand-holds, read their longing to be on their own. Nina hasn't stayed at the farmhouse yet and I doubt her parents would welcome an overnight visit from Jimmy—the affair has been a strictly outdoors, rural one, just like Frank's and mine at the beginning.

We are all of us transfixed by the new lovers, especially Bobby.

"Are you in love?" Bobby asks Nina.

"Yes," she says, confidently. "I am."

Jimmy flushes and looks as if he might erupt with joy.

"Do you think you'll get married?" Bobby says.

"What is this, twenty questions?" Nina laughs. "We've only known each other a few weeks."

"My mum and dad got married when they were young. They hardly knew each other."

"Not true," Frank says. "I'd been ogling your mum on the school bus for years."

A look of satisfaction passes over my father's face. He couldn't bear my heartbreak over Gabriel, seemed almost as devastated as me. At the time, my sister and mother were quick to denigrate him. Understandable, but not what I wanted to hear.

"He was completely wrong for you," Eleanor said.

My mother told me it was a lucky escape. "Now you know what he is capable of, you're better off without him."

But my dad, who'd watched me crash full pelt into my first love affair, without care or caution, the way I always was back then, didn't criticize Gabriel once.

"People make mistakes, particularly when they are young," he said. "I believe Gabriel will come to regret it."

It wasn't long before Frank began calling for me at the cottage. Our love affair was sweetly old-fashioned in comparison and my parents adored Frank from the outset. When I discovered I was pregnant, I was worried my parents would think it was too much, too soon. Frank and I hadn't been together very long. But they were elated we were providing them with a grandchild years before they expected one and, as soon as he was born, Bobby became their new favorite person.

Bobby has changed us all.

"Is it normal to love one person your whole life like you and Daddy?" Bobby asks me, out of the blue. "Or can you love other people first?"

As his sweet, innocent voice carries across the table, the other conversations fade away. I feel it, a shimmer of awkwardness in the room, see Nina's look of perplexity as she picks up on something she doesn't understand. No one moves to speak, and it is left to me to answer him.

"It's simplest when you do," I say. "But the only thing that matters is finding the right person to spend the rest of your life with. However you get there."

"I'll drink to that," Frank says, holding my gaze until I smile and look away.

1968

Jimmy's stag night, such as it is, takes place exactly one week before the wedding. He and Frank disappear off to the Compasses in high spirits: Every male in the village, young and old, has gathered to celebrate his last days as a bachelor.

"Watch out for him, won't you?" I whisper to Frank as they leave, and he rolls his eyes.

"Obviously," he says, kissing me to make up for his impatient tone. "When do I ever not?"

An evening alone. So many jobs I should be getting on with, sauces and puddings to make for the wedding, a house that always needs cleaning, a laundry basket in need of emptying.

Instead, I build a fire in the grate, even though it's a warm night, and I sit in front of it staring into the flames. Thinking.

Over and over I replay the conversation I had with Louisa in the pub. Her suggestion Gabriel had always loved me and perhaps still does. "It's not too late," she said. Although, of course, it is.

Nothing has happened with Gabriel and nor will it. I love Frank, we belong to each other. But there's no denying Gabriel and I have drawn closer in the past weeks.

It's that glass of wine we have most evenings—often the highlight of my day—when he encourages me to talk about Bobby. Gabriel is curious, he asks questions that make me pause and consider. I find myself searching my memory for Bobby's favorite food—honey-roasted sausages—or the name of his best friend: He didn't have one, as he was friends with everyone. Each time, a new piece of Bobby comes back. It feels like a small miracle, this remembering.

What I feel in this hour with Gabriel at the end of the day, an hour when Leo is watching television in another room, and we sit side by side on the sofa, talking and quite often just being, is something close to happiness.

I am asleep when Frank comes back from the pub, waking as the front door closes behind him. I hear his quiet tread on the stairs, then the sound of him undressing in the dark. He gets in beside me but leaves a gap between us.

"Are you awake?" he says, eventually.

He must know from my breathing, my stillness that I am.

"How was it?"

For a moment he says nothing. Then: "As you'd expect, I suppose."

His voice is bleak, sober.

"Did something happen?"

"Oh, God, Beth, I don't know. Not really. He's in bed now, anyhow. Snoring his head off. Don't think he'll be up to the cows in the morning, that's for sure."

"Then I'll help you. What's wrong, Frank? Was there a fight?"

"It was worse than that. He was so drunk, he couldn't stand. I know we've been here before. Countless times."

"It was always going to get messy. Jimmy's stag."

"Yeah."

"It's me," I say, reaching for his hand. Which is not something I've ever needed to say to Frank before. "You can tell me."

"On the drive home, he started crying. And I know it's because he was out of his mind, beer tears or whatever you call it, but he said this thing—" He stops talking.

"What did he say?"

"He said—"

At last I understand that Frank, who never cries, is fighting tears himself.

"He said he didn't think he was any good at living. Sometimes he thought we'd be better off without him. We would. Nina would. He causes us too much trouble. That's what he said. It all goes back to Bobby. Jimmy's never been right since he died."

"Oh, Frank." For a moment I struggle to speak. None of us have been right since Bobby, but it's rare for Frank to acknowledge it. "I know you're upset he said those things. But I don't believe he meant them. It's just the drink talking. Think how happy he's been recently, him and Nina. They've got everything to look forward to. You know they have."

We reach out for each other at the same time and it's us again, me and Frank, the scent of him so familiar, his warm, hard body pressed against mine.

We don't make love, it's not like that. We hold on to each other and I whisper reassurances—he'll be fine, it's drunken nonsense, he won't even remember it tomorrow—pressing my lips to his skin until at last the steady in and out of his breathing tells me Frank has fallen asleep.

Before

At the end of the summer holidays, when Bobby is nine, we invite the whole of his class for an afternoon at Blakely Farm. Bobby is in charge of events and he plans it like a military operation: First the children will meet his favorite animals, before a picnic tea beneath the oak tree, and then target shooting.

We begin with a tour of the farm. Bobby shows the kids how the milking machine works, demonstrating how he fits the teats to the cow's udders, how it is suction that keeps them on. He can do it in seconds, just like the men.

In the sheep field, Bobby hands out biscuits so the children can feed our ewes.

"Wow, Bobby," says Hazel, a gorgeously pretty child with bright blond Rapunzel plaits. "Are you allowed to do this every single day? You are so lucky."

This was a good idea, I think, as we begin our picnic beneath the old oak tree. The children are getting to see Bobby for who he really is. I know, because the teachers tell me, that Bobby spends his classroom hours gazing out of the window, like a prisoner who pines for the outside world, missing the sensation of sunlight warming his skin. Well, he does pine. Being inside is a torture to him.

One time, he let himself out of the playground at break time and arrived home in the middle of the day. I was about to take him back when Frank stopped me.

"Let him have this just this once," he said. "What good is school to him, really? Everything he needs is here."

Frank was exactly the same as a boy, Jimmy too. They are men of the earth.

The oak tree has more meaning for us than any other on the farm. It is where Frank asked me to marry him. Not on bended knee or with a ring or champagne. He said, simply: "I don't want a life without you in it. I never did."

I could tell from the way he was looking at me, in a blaze of love, he meant something significant by the words.

"Frank. What are you saying?"

He picked me up and carried me around the oak tree, as if we were performing some bizarre pagan ritual. "To marry me, you silly woman. Wasn't it obvious?"

While the children eat, I find myself watching a boy called William. I know William, of course. There are only twelve in the class and the children have been together for four years now. William's homelife must be lonely. A strict, older father, a timid, devoutly Christian mother, neither of whom seem to have much time for William and none for the other parents at school. William is never invited to the other children's houses and, as far as I know, none of them have ever visited him at home either.

More than anything, it's his clothes that set William apart. In his smart white shirt, corduroy shorts, and Fair Isle pullover he looks like a wartime child, one of the evacuees you saw in photographs sitting disconsolately on their suitcases, clutching a stuffed toy. William is wearing a felt trilby and he cannot stop playing with it. He picks it up in one hand and twirls it on a finger, he throws it in the air and catches it, before putting it back on his head. The hat is a statement of some kind, perhaps his attempt to stand out, but the other children don't seem to notice. There's something rather sad about William.

Finally, with tea cleared away, it is time for the target shooting. All the children are excited about it, even the girls, who I imagined might be bored at the idea of firing guns. We line them up in front of two hand-painted targets: red, white, and blue rings with a small black bull's-eye at the center.

David demonstrates how to hold the air rifle, wedging it into his armpit, so the weight of the gun rests on his chest. "It's heavy," he says. "You need to get used to it before you start looking through the sights. Take your time, there's no rush. Everyone will get a turn."

He is stern as he talks to them about gun safety and the rules which must be obeyed before a shot is taken.

"Is your pathway clear? Look left to right and behind you to make sure no one is in the way. Always wait for the word 'clear' before you fire. Do you understand?" The children stare at him, transfixed. Yes, they say, nodding their heads. Outlining the risks simply feeds their excitement.

David stands beside each shooter, stamping out any silliness before it can begin. Jimmy and Frank are the reloaders, taking each gun as soon as it has been fired and slotting in the next pellet. The boys can hold the guns themselves and most of them hit or get close to the bull's-eye; with the girls, Frank and Jimmy hold the gun in position, while they get used to the sights, fingers on the trigger, David's sharp "Clear!" like a shot of adrenaline.

It is when William comes up for his turn that the atmosphere changes. William, I realize too late, is an attention seeker. He stands beside David, squirming and jiggling on the spot, swiveling to grin at the kids behind him.

"Keep still," David snaps. "Or you won't see the target."

I sense it, before it happens. Something repressed in the child, a simmering frustration. He lines up his shot, David shouts "Clear!" and, like a nightmare, William spins a half circle, pointing the gun at the other children, who freeze in shock as he yells: "Take that, suckers!"

David smacks the rifle from his hand with such force it smashes onto William's sandaled foot and he howls in pain.

David yells, "What were you thinking, you bloody little fool?" and William bursts into tears. There's something odd about his crying, even then. He's shocked, embarrassed, his toe is probably bruised and possibly broken, but the way he cries, a tearless, earsplitting wail, feels put on. I catch the bemused glance that passes between Jimmy and Frank.

"Do you have any idea how dangerous that was?" I say, crouching down to examine William's foot.

His big toe is bright red, the nail already beginning to discolor—it will bloom from maroon to black in no time.

"It was only a joke, it was meant to be funny," William says, but David snaps at him.

"Your finger was on the trigger. You could have killed someone. There is nothing funny about murder."

William buries his face in my chest and I force myself to put an arm around him as we walk back to the farmhouse.

Alison, William's mother, is waiting in the yard with the other parents. As soon as he sees her, William starts up with the deafening wail, his limp exaggerated.

"Stop that!" Alison says to him. And then to me: "What's wrong with William's foot?"

"He's bruised his toe—" I begin, but David steps out in front of me. I hadn't realized he was following so closely behind.

"I'll explain, Beth. I'd like to get across the severity of what just happened. Your son did something so unbelievably stupid and dangerous this afternoon he could have killed someone. The kids were target shooting with air rifles—heavily supervised, I might add, we were rigorous in our safety instructions—but, somehow, William got it into his head it would be funny to swing around and point his gun at the other children. I knocked it out of his hand and that's how he came to bruise his toe. All I can say is we are very lucky the injury is such a small one. It could have been so much worse."

"William, shut up!" Alison snaps, silencing her son's caterwauling in a heartbeat. "Am I to understand the children were playing with *guns* at the party?"

"Air rifles, Alison," I say. "Target shooting. It was written on the invitation."

"What kind of person invites a class of nine-year-olds over to play with guns?"

I see the other mothers watching intently, not sure which camp they should belong to. They all knew about the shooting activity.

"What you really need to be asking yourself," David says, "is what kind of child, despite repeated instructions about safety, would turn his gun on his classmates? Whether or not he intended to shoot, I didn't wait to find out."

I notice how far apart Alison and William are standing, how she hasn't looked at him or tried to comfort him once, how he cowers as he watches her. I thought she was meek and timid, but this woman is all steel and cold, suppressed anger.

"I should never have let him come. You don't take enough care. Everyone knows what your family is like."

"Do tell," David says. "What are we like?"

"Reckless." Alison spits the word out, a bad fairy come to ruin the party. "Sooner or later something bad will happen and, when it does, it will be your own fault."

The Trial

Robert Miles, our barrister, has given us a full list of the witnesses appearing in court but it's still a shock to see Alison Jacobs on the stand. She could not look more mousy and unprepossessing with her limp hair and pallid skin; the shapeless, unalluring costume she favors. Beneath lies a heart of ice.

"Mrs. Jacobs," Donald Glossop, the Crown prosecutor, begins, "you were late to come forward as a witness. May I ask what prompted you to do so?"

"I was in two minds about it. But, after talking with various people in the village, I realized I had relevant information which would shed light on the characters living at Blakely Farm. And that could be helpful for the jury."

The account Alison relays is heavily embellished, so much so at one point I cry out and my sister, who is next to me in the public gallery, takes hold of my hand. Alison tells the court her son William and the rest of his class were invited out to the farm in the school holidays. All the parents were wary, she says, knowing what the Johnson family were like. "We used to worry about Bobby and the way he was being brought up."

"Why was that?"

"The Johnsons don't live by a normal code of conduct. They're a bit feral. I'll give you an example: Bobby saw a new-born calf being shot in the head with a pistol when he was five years old. Such brutality. Quite unnecessary for a small boy to see it. Next day he came in and told his class about it. Some of them had nightmares for weeks afterwards."

A ripple of disgust passes through the courtroom.

"We all knew the Johnsons didn't take enough care. Sonia Johnson was killed when she was milking because she put her head right up close to the cow's rear. Surely she should have known better?"

"Is that everything, Mrs. Jacobs?" Mr. Glossop asks, and I can hear even a note of disdain in his voice.

Good. I hope everyone in this court sees Alison for what she is: a sneak, a troublemaker, a gossip. A predator, feeding on new flesh.

"The afternoon our children were invited out to the farm was a fiasco," she says. "Quite frankly, my son was lucky to come out of it alive."

I see how she glances at the dock before she delivers her final bullet of hate. "Afterwards, we said we'd never again let our children go to Blakely Farm. There will be a fatality at that place, sooner or later, we said. Sadly, it came sooner than any of us expected."

1968

Weddings are joyful by nature: the public celebration of love and togetherness, the carefully curated festivity, the music, the dancing, the indulgent eating and jubilant drinking. Today at Blakely Farm that joy feels heightened, and it's not only the collective pleasure at seeing Jimmy and Nina finally tie the knot. Our family has seen too many storms and today, all resentments and disagreements have been cast aside, the village out in force to witness this change in our fortunes.

Nina and Jimmy opted for a quick registry office wedding with only Frank and me in attendance, followed by a proper ceremony at the farm. It's being held in a barn we have scrubbed and polished and painted until it looks as good as any church. Chairs borrowed from various houses in the village are lined up in rows, homespun and mismatched and all the better for it, a wedding forged by a whole community. The church ladies have excelled themselves with six-foot-tall flower displays, and we even have a roll of red carpet for Nina and her father to walk down.

Every face turns as they come into the barn, "You Can't Hurry Love" playing from speakers in the corner. I could look at Nina forever, so slender and lovely in her pale gold dress, and scarcely changed from the girl we first met five years ago.

When Jimmy and Nina exchange their vows, Frank reaches for my hand. This wedding means more to him than it does to anyone else.

After the ceremony there is nothing left for us, the family, to do except enjoy ourselves, our friends from the village have taken care of everything. Trestle tables are covered with food, far too much of it, a gift from each family. Dishes of coronation chicken, cold joints of beef and ham, great bowls of coleslaw and potato salad, and two pigs roasting on spits outside. There is a bar serving cider and ale, wine, gin, brandy, whisky, more booze than we can possibly drink, almost all of it donated.

For the first hour I am busy talking to guests, the same conversation, over and over. How beautiful the bride is, how lucky the bridegroom, they took their time, didn't they? I can respond on autopilot, which is just as well, for beneath everything, is one pervasive thought. *When will I have a chance to talk to Gabriel?*

The decision to invite Gabriel and Leo was last minute. Jimmy has never tried to hide his dislike of Gabriel, plenty of villagers can bear witness to that. Frank said—and I agreed, for reasons of my own—it might be awkward having them at the wedding. Then Leo came out to the farm in the summer holidays and struck up a friendship with Nina. Together they whitewashed the barn, radio blaring, Nina teaching him dance steps as she once taught Bobby. Leo was lovestruck just like my son—Nina tends to have that effect on people.

"What shall I wear to your wedding?" Leo asked, out of the blue, one day.

After a pause, Nina said, "Something fun. Surprise me," and shrugged at me in apology.

They come up to greet me the first moment I am alone; Gabriel must have been watching me too. There are two hundred people crowded into this tent and I have not turned in Gabriel's direction once, but I've always known exactly where to find him.

Leo has taken Nina at her word, dressed in a fringed

cowboy shirt and a Stetson sent over from the States by his mother.

"Has Nina seen you yet?" I say, hugging him. "You'll be walking off with Best Dressed Male, no competition, and that includes the bridegroom in his fancy new suit."

"Is there a prize?"

"If there isn't, there should be."

"I like your dress," Gabriel says, and I turn to look at him.

It is a mistake. For I know this look, this gaze, I remember it from before, from the days when we were free to show all that we felt in our faces.

"My friend Helen made it for me," I say, the rush of color staining my cheeks.

It is a fabulous dress, the boldest thing I have ever worn: a sleeveless A-line shape which stops short of the knee. It is white with bright pink-and-yellow flowers splashed across it. I feel nothing like a farmer's wife tonight.

I'm startled by the sight of Gabriel, clean-shaven in a dark suit. Even as a teenager, I loved how he looked in a suit. Perhaps because he wears one so often, he looks as relaxed in it as he does a pair of jeans, or because Gabriel's suits, with their fine wool and elegant, narrow fit, are clearly handmade.

I force myself to turn away and find Frank standing a yard or so away, watching. He is holding two glasses of wine in his hands.

"You could have said hello to them," I say, walking over and taking a glass from him.

Frank looks at me, expressionless, and says only: "Speeches are about to start, are you ready?"

I've heard most of Frank's best man's speech already but it's a different thing seeing him stand up in front of a whole village. These people are his friends, his extended family, he has known them all his life. Frank hits all the right notes, the funny stories from boyhood, the challenging teenage years, the sudden transformation when an exquisite blonde flagged down Jimmy in his tractor. Overnight, he shaved off his beard and requested money for aftershave.

"That was five years ago and since then, as you all know, this family has been through difficult times. Nina has walked every step of the way with Jimmy. She is his rock, his soulmate. He would be lost without her and so would we."

Jimmy and Nina have chosen "Can't Help Falling in Love" for their first dance. Nina asked if we'd rather they didn't play Elvis, but Frank and I felt the same: It was what Bobby would have wanted. They dance the first bars of the song alone, then Nina stretches out an arm toward me and Frank, beckoning with one finger. Frank takes me into his arms and we turn a slow circle, the two brothers and their wives on the dance floor with the village watching.

"You're crying," Frank says.

"The song. You. Me. Him."

The *him* I mean is Bobby. But that's not how Frank takes it, his mind is somewhere else. "I suppose it was a mistake having him here."

For a second, I don't understand what he means. And then I do. "I wasn't talking about Gabriel."

"Beth—" Frank says, then he stops himself. "Let's not do this now. It's their day. I won't ruin it."

Instead, I bury my face in Frank's chest for the remainder of the song. To everyone else we must look like the thing we used to be, a couple who were devoted to one another, who once had everything and lost it, foolishly, devastatingly, but still managed to cling together.

The dance floor floods with other couples and for the next hour or so Frank and I are in demand. I dance with Helen's husband, Martin; with David's best friend, Brian; with Jimmy; with a whole sequence of village men whom I have known since they were little boys beginning primary school. People I have known my entire life. We dance to the Beatles, the Byrds, the Supremes. When Frankie Valli starts crooning "Can't Take My Eyes Off You," Nina and Jimmy happen to be dancing together and the crowd forms a spontaneous circle around them. Nina dances with her train swept up over one arm, hips keeping perfect time with the beat, shimmying her shoulders back and forth at Jimmy while he mimes the words of the song to her. I think, look-ing at Nina, she's always been a performer, she knows what people want and how to give it to them, it's why she is so good at her job. There could be no better bride.

Nina and I dance with Leo after that. We teach him how to twist, and he spirals up and down like a corkscrew, his cheeks flushed, eyes glowing. For a second or two, it's like being with Bobby, my son who loved to dance, particularly with Nina. I can't allow myself to go there. He'd be twelve now, a different proposition altogether. Who knows if he would have even liked dancing anymore?

Across the marquee Gabriel is watching. I've known where he's been, of course, but this time when I catch his gaze, our eyes linger on each other for a beat too long. He tilts his head, almost imperceptibly, and walks out of the tent. My heart begins to thump painfully in my chest. I glance at Frank and see him talking to Helen and Martin in a corner; I have a moment, but that is all.

Gabriel is waiting for me outside.

"We can't talk here," I say, and he follows me to the elm trees at the edge of the field.

"There's something I need to tell you," Gabriel says.

But for a moment or two he says nothing, we just watch each other in the shadows.

"You were wrong all those years ago about me and Louisa."

"Let's not do this. It was all such a long time ago."

"I need you to know the truth. I didn't sleep with Louisa while you and I were together. She stayed in my room, it's true, and I felt guilty because I knew it would hurt you if you found out. But nothing happened between us."

"Gabriel." My voice is a wail, too loud, a little demented. The alcohol I have drunk is rushing through my veins. I'm drunk on wine, cider, on him, on the terrifying possibility of truth. "Why are you doing this?"

"You must know why. Tell me you know. Tell me you feel it too."

I can't look at him, to look will be fatal. Instead, I stare at the ground. "You told Louisa you had doubts about me. You can't deny that."

"Not you, Oxford. I was thinking of dropping out to become a full-time writer. Louisa talked me out of it."

"It's too late for this," I say, desperately.

"Is it?" His voice is soft, tempting me to look at him.

"Why wouldn't you have told me the truth? You knew I thought you'd been unfaithful to me."

"I was so angry, Beth. You believed what my mother told you. You said I used people and threw them away afterwards. That hurt me so much."

"I'm sorry."

"No, it's me who should be sorry. I was a bloody fool. Too proud to beg you to come back."

"Why would your mother tell me you were with Louisa if you weren't?"

"Wishful thinking?"

"Or worse."

I always knew Gabriel's mother would find a way to stop our being together, even if I hadn't managed to sabotage it myself first.

"How stupid and stubborn we were. Such a waste," I say,

and this time there's no mistaking Gabriel's tone when he says: "Is it?"

I look up at him and he looks back at me. A stare that feels dangerous, intimate, intoxicating. Every bit of resistance crashing down.

What I want, more than anything, is to reach out and touch him. I'd like to place my palm against his cheek. Or his heart, to see if it's beating as wildly as my own.

There have been too many thresholds like this one, chances missed, turns not taken, and always the question burning between us, me and Gabriel, Gabriel and me, the life we might have had.

"What are we going to do?" Gabriel asks.

The music pouring from the tent is loud and yet, in this sudden stillness, I hear only us. Our breathing. The blood pounding through my head, my pulse or his?

"This," I say, standing on tiptoe to kiss him.

Finally.

My mouth against his.

A kiss that feels like everything all at once. Unhinged. Tender. Too much, too much, nowhere near enough. Teeth snagging lips, hands caught in hair, every second of every year we've been apart in this kiss.

The record changes and the party continues, and it feels as if we are the only two people here, the only two people in the world.

Before

The oak tree is pronounced dead in early June, first by David, then by Frank, then by a tree surgeon friend who can take it down for us, but it's a big job and will have to wait until he's free later in the summer.

"You can't cut it down," Bobby says. "It has to stay forever."

He is bereft at the thought of losing the oak, we all are, it has always been the most magical spot on the farm.

David says: "But, Bobby, it's too dangerous to leave it. If one of its branches came down in a gale it could kill you."

"I won't go near it in a gale, Grandpa."

David stoops to put his face closer to Bobby's. "Maybe the tree wants to be taken down. It's old and sick and exhausted. It's given us, and so many people before us, the best years of its life."

Bobby nods at him. "All right, Grandpa," he says.

The tree felling is planned for Saturday, the men will take care of it themselves.

When Saturday comes, Bobby is excited. While David and Frank and Jimmy make plans and read over the instructions left by the tree surgeon, he slides around the kitchen asking questions.

"Will it be noisy when it comes down?"

"Very," David says. "It will make a crack like thunder."

"Wow. Do you think it will make a huge gash in the earth?"

"I reckon so," Frank says, looking up from the instructions to smile at his son.

"But, Bobby," I say, "I don't think you should go and watch. Because I'm not going to be there and the men will be too busy to keep an eye on you."

I try to hug Bobby, but he pushes me off. "Why are you so mean?"

I see the look that passes between David and his sons: weariness, impatience. My fretting around safety irritates them.

"It will be fine," David says, curtly.

"Frank? Have you forgotten I'm meeting Helen this morning?"

"For goodness' sake, one of us will watch him."

"Maybe I should cancel Helen," I say.

"Don't be silly," Frank says. He crosses the room and takes me into his arms.

"What a worrywart you're turning into in your old age."

"Promise you won't let him out of your sight? You know how he runs off."

"Yes, woman. Go and have fun with your friend. Leave these noble foresters to get on with their work."

Bobby whoops in delight.

Later, when I return to the farm, I go up to the field to visit our poor old oak, which I'm expecting to see lying on its side. I'm surprised to see the tree is still standing. It must have been a much harder job than they thought. The crown has already come down, and it saddens me to see it, this beautiful tree that has been such a big part of my life, of all our lives, now a vast trunk with butchered stumps. No wonder Bobby felt so upset.

I watch as David, Frank, and Jimmy step back from the tree to inspect their work. I can't see Bobby anywhere—he must have got bored waiting and wandered off to see his sheep. I think about going to find him, then realize there's no time.

There's a great crack, just as David predicted, and the trunk begins to tip, almost in slow motion, it seems to me.

And now I do see Bobby, running right in front of its path, screaming first in joy, then in fear. A long, long, anguished scream, his, mine, me running toward him like a wild woman, as the film speeds up, just a flash of red shorts, pale legs, dark hair, before the oak crashes to the ground, turning everything black.

Frank and David and Jimmy start running. They've heard Bobby's scream, seen the shrieking demon hurling herself toward her child but there's no sign of Bobby. The trunk is so vast it has swallowed him whole.

I will never forget Frank's face when he looks at me, the terror on it. He is frightened—of me. But I am not looking at Frank. Or David. Or Jimmy. My eyes are on the tree, slain like a vast mammal on its side.

"I am here, Bobby, I am here." I scream it over and over again. Ten times. Twenty. It's the only thing I can think of, if he can hear me, and please, God, may that be true, he needs to know I am here.

Frank is roaring, "Get it off him," and trying, hopelessly, to raise it with his bare hands before his father stops him.

"I'll get the towropes, son," he says. "Call an ambulance."

"I'm sorry, I'm sorry." I hear Frank's exhaustive apology but I can't connect to it, my mind is whirring with invented science and medical trivia as I try to hold on to hope. People survive the strangest things, they say that. We can't hear him but that's because he's been knocked unconscious, a good thing. Perhaps he'll have some broken limbs, we can cope with that.

"We told him to stay in the tractor," Frank says. "He promised."

"He was nine."

Was. I said *was*.

I start to scream and Frank comes toward me but I hold up both hands to stop him. "Don't touch me. Please."

I just say it, I don't even know why. Perhaps that I can't bear to be held, I'm far too tense. Perhaps that, even now, before we know the outcome, I blame my husband for this needless accident.

He promised me he would watch Bobby. He promised he'd keep him safe.

And so we are apart when David drives the tractor forward, winching its colossal load, the dead tree rising inch by painful inch.

When the tree is a foot in the air, I see the first flash of red cotton and the sound that comes from me has no human in it, spirit shriek, ancient, guttural cry.

An ambulance has come through the gate and two paramedics are racing across the field with a stretcher, but I get to him first. My boy, my lovely boy, skull smashed, limbs broken and bloodied, but still him. Still mine. I lie down next to him as close as I can. He was right, the tree did make a huge gash in the earth.

I am here. I say it silently now. A pledge that has come too late, but I hope my words will find a way to reach him.

Bobby, I am here.

Part Three

Jimmy

The Trial

My mother, sister, and I are in the front row of the public gallery when my father takes the stand. There are many things I will never forgive myself for and here is one of the worst—the impact the trial has had on my parents. I've seen my father several times since the shooting but today, I am shocked by how much he has aged. Eleanor sees it too, for she gasps and grabs my hand. His hair has been thinning for a while but, from our bird's-eye view, I see how the sparse strands he carefully sweeps over disguise an almost naked pate. His face is deeply lined, his neck has become craggy without any of us noticing, and his hands are shaking. For his court appearance, my dad is in his best suit, the one he used to wear to weddings and now gets out for funerals. A landslide of grief none of us were prepared for.

Once he begins talking—confirming his name, address, profession, and relationship to the defendant—my father's nerves seem to disappear. This is his calm, confident teacher voice, a man who has spent three decades holding his pupils' attention. We were advised to choose a professional person as a character witness, a doctor, a lawyer, a teacher, someone of high standing in their community. No one with better credentials than my father. Do I feel guilty about his testifying in court knowing, as I do, he does not have the full set of facts before him? Yes, I feel sick with it. If he finds out, there is every possibility he may never forgive me. But what else could I do? There are three of us bound by this lie and far too much at stake to risk telling anyone, even my dad, the truth.

The examination with our barrister passes easily enough. No difficult questions to trip my father up, plenty of opportunity for him to provide a glowing reference for the defendant. Beside me, my mother begins to relax. She even manages to turn to me at one point and smile.

But, all too soon, the Crown prosecutor Donald Glossop is standing for his turn.

His voice is gentle at the start, but I have seen enough of his cat-and-mouse tactics to dread what lies beneath.

"How long have you known the Johnson family, Mr. Kennedy?" he asks.

"I've known them many years. David Johnson, Frank and Jimmy's father, was initially an acquaintance, I would say, rather than a friend. Hemston is not a big village and we all knew each other to varying degrees. Once my daughter married into the family, I came to know the Johnsons much better."

"And in that time, did you see much friction between the two brothers? Can you think of an incident, perhaps an argument that got out of hand, an explosive row, say, or indeed any sort of conflict?"

"Absolutely not."

I catch my mother's half smile as my father leans forward with intent. She knows exactly what he is about to say; the two of them must have rehearsed his witness statement a dozen times.

"The brothers were closer than any siblings I have ever seen. They looked out for one another. Frank was a devoted older brother. He worried about Jimmy constantly and always tried to keep him on track. A good man, a kind man, he went the extra mile not just for Jimmy but for everyone in the village. And Jimmy was the same. A sweet boy, troubled at times, but with a big heart."

"But, latterly, you were aware of the conflict between them?"

My father hesitates. For him, not telling the truth is an impossibility.

"Things became tense at the farmhouse in the days leading up to"—he stumbles, for the first time—"the tragedy. Jimmy became very volatile I am told. He was drinking heavily, and I believe it clouded his judgement. The brothers disagreed on how certain matters should be handled."

It is unbearable, my father tying himself in knots as he tries to navigate the perilous task of saying enough, yet not too much.

"You're referring to your daughter's affair with Gabriel Wolfe?"

"I am not here to comment on my daughter's private life. I am here for the sole purpose of providing character evidence for the defendant. Which I hope I have done."

"I understand that, Mr. Kennedy. Nevertheless, I believe it is in the jury's interest if I ask you how long you have known Mr. Wolfe."

My father hesitates again. "I knew him as a young man, briefly."

"When his relationship with your daughter began the first time?"

"Yes."

"How long did that first love affair last, Mr. Kennedy?"

"Not long. One summer and perhaps a month or so after that."

"And quite soon after it ended, she started a relationship with Frank Johnson?"

"Yes."

"They married young, didn't they?"

"They did, yes."

I feel it, a new alertness in the room. We are all of us—the judge, the jury, the journalists on the press bench, the members of the public who queue up day after day to ensure their place in the gallery—attuned to the changing nuances of Donald Glossop's tone. A softening in his timbre does not signal empathy, quite often the reverse.

"One might think your daughter, Beth, had not fully recovered from this first, most passionate love affair."

My father says nothing. His hands are not visible but I know he will be clasping them together—*Here's the church, here's the steeple, open the door and see all the people.* How many times did he chant the rhyme with Bobby? A hundred? Five hundred?

The prosecutor's voice grows forceful. "It is my belief Frank Johnson harbored a ferocious jealousy of Gabriel Wolfe from the very beginning of his marriage."

"No."

"No? He wasn't jealous of the man your daughter was in love with as a girl? And he wasn't jealous many years later when the affair started up again, right under his nose?"

"Frank is not jealous. That isn't his temperament."

"Are you an honest man, Mr. Kennedy?"

My mother frowns and Eleanor sucks in a long, jagged breath as she tries not to cry. My father is the most honest man you could ever meet.

"I am."

"Then allow me to ask one final question. Do you genuinely believe your son-in-law felt no jealousy whatsoever while the woman he loved was spending her daylight hours in bed with another man?"

So heartless to draw that picture for my father in the witness stand, my mother beside me in the gallery. You'd think I'd be macerating in shame, but the truth is, I've been ashamed for so long now it is my background noise, my everyday wallpaper, the emotion so familiar I feel little else. Our love triangle—the farmer, his wife, and the famous author—has been prodded and picked over and sensationalized out of all proportion in Fleet Street. A blizzard of headlines pointing the finger of blame—and shame—at me. You grow inured to it after a while. None of it matters, anyway.

"Frank understood my daughter's reasons for the affair," my father says. "If he felt jealous, then he was extremely good at hiding it."

Donald Glossop allows himself a tiny smile of satisfaction. "Thank you, Mr. Kennedy. No further questions, my lord."

Sunday

"Are you and Frank all right?" asks yesterday's bride, as we stand shoulder to shoulder at the sink facing a landslide of washing-up.

I wonder what Nina means. It could be anything. When we finally got to bed around three this morning, Frank fell asleep straightaway. Several hours later, when he rose to milk the cows, I was so exhausted I didn't hear him leave. We have not had a chance to speak since the wedding, but last night I caught him watching me across the tent from time to time. He looked so sad. And it eats away at me, that sadness. It's rare for a person to be purely good. I'm not. Gabriel isn't. Nor Jimmy or probably even Nina, not all the time. But Frank has kindness running through him. Injuring him feels doubly cruel, like torture.

And all the while, my mind is a rash of conflicting thoughts. *I love Gabriel, I won't leave Frank. I love Frank, what am I going to do about Gabriel?* No, Nina, we are not all right.

"I said to Jimmy last night, it was selfish of us to choose Elvis for our wedding dance. You were crying, weren't you? I saw you."

"Oh," I say, although the "oh" is more a gasp of pain as Bobby swims into the room.

Bobby. In some ways so present, but mostly, just horribly absent. The ache of missing him never really goes. Not for long.

"Shit," Nina says, curving a soapy hand around my neck, pulling me close. "And now I've made you sad."

I can feel the cool strip of her new wedding ring on the back of my neck.

"Just the hangover," I say.

"God, this hangover. Why did we drink so much?" When Nina laughs a beam of light catches her eyes, turning them from green to gold.

The day fills with villagers coming to collect their things, then staying to help. Cups of tea and slices of wedding cake. Stories from the night before. Helen's husband woke up fully clad in his suit and tie, even his boots. Someone else reversed their back wheels into a ditch and abandoned the car. The violinist who played "Ave Maria" during the ceremony hitched a ride home in a Land Rover and stood, head and shoulders through the open sunroof, serenading the lanes with "Hey Jude." I wish I had seen that.

There is talk of inappropriate kissing and at this my heart slows, although I am sure no one saw Gabriel and me leaving the tent, nor returning to it a short while later.

All afternoon, beneath the gossip and laughter, that kiss hums through my blood, a secret that sustains me, confuses me, makes me long for more.

Monday

On Monday it feels as if nothing has changed and everything has. The marquee is down, the farmhouse is back to normal, the men are out on the farm. Nina is at the Compasses, getting ready for the lunchtime shift.

And I am alone, marooned in the endless cycle of thoughts.

At one o'clock, I snatch up my car keys and drive to Meadowlands before I can change my mind. Park outside the house, ring the doorbell, wait. Gabriel's face when he sees me holds everything I am feeling myself. Relief, fear, longing.

He pulls me inside, slams the door behind us. "I'm so glad you came. I've been going out of my mind." He takes my face between his hands. "I love you. I never stopped."

This kiss is different, it is a kiss from before. I can feel my whole body relaxing, as if it remembers the learned patterns of long ago, when this was our normal. Gabriel and me.

We are in a vortex, one that is dragging us back through the years until there is only this. Somehow we end up in the library and that's familiar too. There is no time to question any of it, the heat rips through us like lava obliterating everything in its path. We are naked, enfolding each other, bones mapping bones, curves meeting hollows, bodies that sigh in relief. Every thrust is like fire. He says my name with the note of wonder I feel myself.

It feels so good, so right, this locking of our bodies, this giving in to the ache. At last. After all this time. It's more than sex, more than love, the two of us are consumed, flesh and bones and wild hearts, as we drive ourselves harder, faster until we reach white blindness, until I cry out, until he does, all these months of secret longing finally realized.

Afterward we lie on the sofa in shocked silence, my face against his chest, which is damp with sweat and smells the same, of citrusy soap and the aftershave Gabriel has never stopped wearing. The muscles on his chest, the line of black hair running down his stomach, the same. His legs entwined with mine, the scratch of his stubble against my cheek, the same. A time capsule of before, if we could just keep the rest of the world out for a little longer.

"Good thing the dog wasn't in here," Gabriel says. "God knows what he'd have made of it."

I start to laugh and then, suddenly, I'm crying.

I am sick with regret as if, only now, while the heat fades, can I process the cost of this.

I'm going to lose Frank.

"What have we done?" I cry.

"The only thing we could," Gabriel says, but his voice is gentle and he uses both thumbs to brush away the tears beneath my eyes. "But no one needs to know. And it doesn't need to happen again."

"I want it to happen again."

"So do I. So much."

I watch Gabriel as he gathers up our scattered clothes. His body has changed in the intervening years, he is broader, the skinniness I remember from before has gone. He passes me each garment in turn, waits while I put them on. Only when I am fully dressed does he turn to his own clothes.

"Do you think," Gabriel says, "if we are careful, we could have this for a little while? Because, what we had before, you and I, it was more than most people ever have, wasn't it? And we threw it away. In my wildest dreams I never thought we'd have a chance to get it back."

I know how this village works. The snooping, the chatter, a whispering undercurrent that blows through the lanes and the churchyard, the school, the shop, filters beneath doors, behind windows. I know how the people watch, how they talk and conspire. Secrets are not safe here. They are harbored and chewed over until the people decide to release them, splintering lives with a perfectly timed, needlepoint precision.

All this I know. But it isn't enough to stop me. I walk into our love affair with my eyes wide open.

Monday Night

In bed, Frank's voice cuts out from the darkness. "I saw you."

The sickening rise of my blood, my pulse. White noise rushing in my ears. I wait a moment before turning the lamp on. "Saw me when?" I say, trying to sound relaxed on this, my first ever day of infidelity.

"At the wedding. You and him."

"Gabriel?"

"Obviously."

"Saw me with him, when? I hardly spoke to him."

"At the beginning, before the speeches."

"With Leo, you mean?"

He nods.

"And?" My voice is calm, I am too good at this. Already I can pretend, effortlessly.

"You know what."

"I don't, Frank. I can't read your mind."

"You used to be able to."

I hate his inverted smile, the corners of his mouth turned down. We were always so good at communicating without words. It meant we could leave parties early with nothing more than a raised eyebrow or a glance at the door.

"You're annoyed with me for talking to Gabriel and Leo at the wedding, is that it?"

"I saw how you looked at him. Sorry if that makes me sound like a jealous freak."

Frank smiles a little, his old self.

"Maybe. But you're my jealous freak," I say.

"Hope so."

"You know so."

And then we're kissing and it doesn't even feel wrong, kissing one man, and then another. They are different things.

This is a love story with too many beginnings. I refuse to think about how it is going to end.

Tuesday

When Bobby died, I left Frank for a while. My parents were living in Ireland by then and I went over for a visit.

As soon as I got there, I realized I didn't want to come back.

"It's helping me to be here," I told Frank on the phone, soon after I'd arrived.

"Then you should stay," Frank said, as I had known he would. "I want you to stay."

The weeks ticked by. Our phone calls dwindled to almost nothing, Frank has never liked talking on the phone. I convinced myself this was a good thing, the only way for us to recover from what had happened was to stay apart. Frank didn't have to wake up next to me every morning, knowing part of me would always blame him for not watching over Bobby. And I didn't have to pretend I believed the story we told everyone, that it was an accident, accidents were an unfortunate, sometimes tragic part of farm life. Just look what happened to Frank's mother. Instead, we could lick our wounds in private.

I came home because of Jimmy.

Nina traveled all the way to Cork to tell me how far things had fallen since I'd left. Jimmy had started drinking heavily again, she said. He was asked to leave the pub almost every night for picking fights and being obnoxious, as she put it. He had been found wandering through the village in the middle of the night, talking to himself. It felt as if he were losing his mind.

"Why, though?" my mother had asked her, not understanding. Bobby was our child, mine and Frank's. There was no reason for Jimmy to fall apart.

"Isn't it obvious? Jimmy has always blamed himself for what happened to Bobby. He thinks he should have watched over him. And he needs to know Frank hasn't lost his wife as well as his son," Nina said.

Even now, Jimmy still needs reassurance our shrunken family will stay the same. And that's impossible to give. For the truth is, I'm not thinking about Frank, not if I can help it. I'm thinking about Gabriel.

The first time we made love was frantic and fevered, driven by our bodies more than our minds. Our minds, until then, had been trying to say no. It is different today.

We undress slowly and stand naked before each other. Anticipation that is exquisite, almost painful. An uprush of feeling, as if all our senses are magnified. I take my time to kiss the parts of him I have been noticing these past months, remembering how I loved them: his nose, his cheekbones, his prominent Adam's apple. I know he is doing the same when he traces my profile with his forefinger, pausing at the channel above my top lip, which he used to say was exactly the right shape and size for his fingertip.

We move to the bed but continue our gentle rediscovery of one another. It feels dreamlike, this touching and kissing, we are suspended between fact and fantasy in our own perfect no-man's-land.

When Gabriel is inside me, raised up on his hands, pressing into me with the same slow, deep rhythm of long ago, it is almost more than I can bear. I am so immersed in the sensation of this, in the familiarity of our two bodies being together once more. Perhaps he sees pain on my face for Gabriel asks: "What's wrong?"

The only thing I can find to explain is: "I remember."

There is such feeling in his voice when Gabriel says: "I remember."

And there's no need to say anything else.

I was right, our lovemaking is more than sex, more than love, it is pure, unadulterated nostalgia and there is nothing more intoxicating than that. I wonder if it is always like this when you sleep with someone you once loved long ago. The knowledge of that first time is hardwired into your physiology. It feels raw and right and so real, everything else fades, just the two of us in high relief. In bed I feel more myself with Gabriel, or rather, more like the carefree young woman I was before heartbreak altered me, and tragedy molded me into someone I never wanted to be. It's addictive, this temporary shedding of skin, this glimpse of the person Gabriel remembers.

With him, for a few hours, I get to be unbroken.

Afterward, we lie in each other's arms until it's time for me to collect Leo. We keep the bedroom curtains closed, existing in a lamplit glow like creatures of night. And we talk. We talk about everything.

I ask him about his first book deal, what it felt like being published at twenty-four.

"For a long time, I felt like an impostor. That I hadn't earned it. Emperor's new clothes kind of thing."

"And now?"

He smiles. "Good days and bad days. You think that the second and third will be easier. Not in my experience. If anything, they get harder." He pauses. Looks at me. "Why aren't you writing poetry?"

"How do you know I'm not?"

"I just know."

His voice when he says this—quiet, considered, compassionate—takes me right back. Gabriel understands what it feels like to want something so badly and be afraid you'll never get it. The undertow that pulses beneath the dream, the voice of doubt—*What if I'm not good enough?* The temptation to give up before you have had time to find out. It was once the thing that bound us together.

"It's not that I don't want to" is the only thing I can find to say.

I associate poetry with moments of great happiness in my life: As a young woman who loved to daydream, then during that first passionate love affair with Gabriel, and even, in snatched moments, as a young mother when I'd scribble lines down, here and there.

If I were to answer Gabriel properly I would say: *Because I'm scared. Because when I open up a blank page I think I'm only going to see one thing. Bobby.*

Gabriel takes my hand. "It's there for you waiting, whenever you're ready. It never really goes away."

He tells me about Louisa and the guilt he feels over their failed marriage, even though she was the one who fell in love with someone else. "It is an awful thing," he says, "when the love between you is uneven. I pretended, of course, but Louisa wasn't fooled. I know I hurt her."

We talk about Leo, his struggle to fit in at the village school. How we need to find a way of changing that.

I say out loud the thing I most dread. "Do you think you should move to the States? So Leo can be close to his mother?"

Gabriel looks at me in shock. "How can you say that? After this?"

"Because it scares me."

"It's not going to happen. Not now."

"You promise?"

"I do."

It is only the second day of our affair and we are filled with hope and optimism.

*

How quickly I have become used to my double life. Yesterday, walking into the playground, I worried the guilt must be written on my face; this afternoon, I'm already at ease. Greeting Leo with a quick hug, not caring about the eyes of the other waiting mothers whose scrutiny I always feel, no matter how much they try to hide it. I hear the question that buzzes between them in my absence—what must it be like spending time with a child, day after day, who is not your own? A boy not so far off in age from the one you lost?

It is not a question I could easily answer. Leo is very different to Bobby. For one thing, he seems young for his age, whereas Bobby, who spent so much of his time helping the men on the farm, often seemed older than his years. In the brief time I have with Leo after school each day, my concern is only that I should make his life a little more enjoyable. Curb the missing of his mother, for a short while, if I can.

We are in the kitchen waiting for a shepherd's pie to cook when Gabriel comes in. He spies a bag of sweets on the kitchen table between us and snatches it up.

"You might have said," he says, popping a humbug into his mouth.

Leo grins up at him, he loves it when Gabriel is around. "Sorry, Dad. We went to the shop after school."

"What are you playing?"

Leo and I are midway through a card game, writing down our scores on a piece of paper.

"Rummy."

"I used to love that." He pulls out a chair and sits down opposite us. "Room for a third?"

"More the merrier," I say, and I don't know who is more elated—me or Leo.

Is it wrong, the surge of contentment I feel as I shuffle the pack and deal out cards to Gabriel, to Leo, to me? The sweet simplicity of us as a three, two adults, one child, engaged in a game I once played with my own parents.

Every day can be like this. Every day can be me and my borrowed family.

Tuesday Evening

I'm guessing Frank is in the pub with Jimmy for the second night in a row and hasn't bothered to leave a note. This is new terrain for us. Has he sensed what is happening between me and Gabriel? Frank, who has been attuned to my every mood, who hears the words I don't say just as much as the ones I do. He must have noticed I no longer mention Gabriel at all. I try to, knowing my failure to do so might make Frank suspicious, but his name stays stuck in my throat.

It is strange, being home alone with our hallmarks of familiarity—Frank's muddy boots waiting by the front door, his wax jacket flung over the back of a chair, unopened post on the table—all the same, and me wholly changed. I wonder if Gabriel feels like this, walking through his house at night, when Leo is in bed. Replaying the day, the conversations, the kissing, the touching, the electrifying sex. Or if it's different for me as I try to fit myself back into my duplicitous life. A woman who loves two men and, perhaps, always did.

I wish I could talk to someone. But who? Not Eleanor, who never bothered to hide her distrust of Gabriel on the basis of his being " . . . let's face it, a bit of an entitled prat." After we broke up, she couldn't help saying, "Didn't I tell you this would happen? Boys like him cannot be trusted." Even if she found out the truth about our ending and the lies that drove it, I don't think Eleanor would change her mind about Gabriel. Aside from anything, she's very close to Frank. I certainly can't tell my parents, who have openly

197

adored Frank from the start. My dad, my God, I hate to think what it would do to him if he knew. Or Helen, whose husband, Martin, is Frank's closest friend—he's probably having a beer with him right now. Or the whole damned village, come to that. I can't think of a single person who doesn't love Frank. Frank Johnson, our Hemston hero, beloved of grannies and farmers and church ladies alike.

The night has grown dark without my noticing and it is a shock when Nina bursts through the front door. "Why are you sitting in the dark?" She starts switching lamps on, talking all the while. "Boys are on the lash tonight, by the looks of things. I thought we'd have our own party, you and me. I think my husband's"—she turns to make sure I've caught the word, her marriage is four days old—"bad habits might be rubbing off on yours. Since when does Frank drink whisky on a weeknight? Or any night, come to think of it."

Frank, I think, as a soft glow begins to spread through the room. *What have I done to you?* Frank, who has always been moderate in his drinking, mostly preferring a cup of tea made with fresh milk from our cows. Not so long ago, trips to the pub were something we did together on a Friday.

"Shall we have a fire, at least?"

I watch my sister-in-law peering into the log basket, fingers wavering as she seeks out the best kindling: strips of bark from our silver birches, pine cones, a fistful of bone-dry twigs. She rips out pages from a copy of *Farmers Weekly* and begins placing tight little paper scrunches in the grate. On top goes a pyramid of kindling, then the perfect positioning of the smallest logs; we burn oak, ash, and elm mostly, cedar is my favorite for the smell. Nina and I are good at fires, you'd have to be, living in a house as decrepit and cold as this one.

Within minutes we are warming our faces in front of a glorious blaze.

"What's our booze situation?" Nina asks.

"Plentiful. Still loads of wine in the fridge."

"Leave it with me." Nina half dances, half struts into the kitchen. She is so happy.

We sit cross-legged on the floor with full glasses of wine and a plate of cheese and biscuits.

"How much longer before we finish off the leftovers?" I ask.

"The cheese will be walking out of here before we do. There's so much left."

"You should have had a honeymoon."

This is not a new conversation, Nina and I have had it most days since they first decided to get married. Frank insisted he could look after the farm on his own for a few days, but Jimmy wouldn't hear of it. "Remind me," he said, teasing, "where did you two go again? Was it Paris? Or Rome?"

Pain rushing in. Our twenty-four-hour honeymoon in Dorchester. Frank carrying me over the threshold of the hotel we stayed in, a present from David. I see us, baby-faced amid a dining room of septuagenarians, struggling to contain our laughter.

"Well, at some point you could have one."

Nina waves a dismissive hand. Holidays are for other people, not farming folk.

"Guess what?" Her face in the firelight glows with excitement. "I am a woman without birth control."

It takes a moment for her words to sink in. When they do, I suck my breath in too sharply, wounded instantly though I have no right to be.

Nina reaches out to take my hand.

Another child at Blakely Farm, not ours but theirs. It is the thing we both hoped for, above everything else. Neither of us have felt ready, after Bobby, to try again. But sometimes I long and crave for a baby, one I could borrow, a sweet, uncomplicated newborn who belongs to the people I love most in the world.

"I'm so happy for you," I say, half laughing. "I know it doesn't look like it. But it's the thing Frank and I have been hoping for."

"Really?"

"Absolutely."

We embrace and I think of all the other men and women who must have sat beside this ancient hearth, sharing their good news. The centuries pass but the hope and optimism that accompanies each new family at its beginning is the same. What else is there in life, really, of such significance? This momentary pause in which everything changes.

"When did you decide?"

"We've been talking about it for a while. We're both ready. Well—" Nina breaks off to laugh. "Jimmy is as ready as he's ever going to be. I'm hoping a baby might help him get his act together, you know?"

"It will. Don't forget how amazing he was the day Bobby was born. That man has hidden depths. I can hardly wait. I'm going to be the world's best auntie. Oh, my God, Frank an uncle. Imagine what he'll be like."

My face must fall when I think of Frank.

"Beth?" Nina asks, quietly. She waits until I'm looking at her. "Is something wrong?"

If only I could tell her. I've done something so bad, so wrong, and I can never undo it. And the problem is, I'm not sure I even want to. How is it that infidelity, a line you think you will never cross, becomes almost commonplace after a while? Tomorrow, when I have finished all my chores at home and on the farm, I will sneak off to Meadowlands to see my lover. We'll go straight to bed and for those precious hours I won't allow myself to think of Frank. It takes a certain mindset to exist within two parallel spheres. I never imagined myself as the kind of woman who would have it. But it turns out I am.

"No. Nothing's wrong."

"Good," Nina says, leaning forward to kiss my cheek. "Because it's still my wedding week and I want to keep celebrating. Here's my honeymoon, Beth. You and me and, with any luck, the return of our drunken husbands sooner or later, to keep the party going. Right now, that's all that matters."

Wednesday

The front door at Meadowlands is always unlocked and I decide to creep in and surprise Gabriel. He will be at his desk, snatching a few minutes of writing time before I arrive. In my head I'm thinking I will discard a trail of clothes in the hall and be fully naked by the time I reach his study. I feel deranged, no other word to describe it, possessed by eroticism, by this fierce, rapid rekindling of love.

From the hall, I hear voices; Gabriel is talking to someone. A woman. My mind reels in shock. What if it's someone I know? Someone who might mention to Frank they happened to run into me at Meadowlands during the day, no Leo in tow. I've thought about this scenario, we both have, deciding if anyone asked, we'd say I was doing some cooking for Gabriel. What am I doing coming here day after day with no thought to the consequences? It is as if I'm in free fall, waiting to crash-land, or to be caught.

I retrace my steps, hoping I can get in the car and drive away before anyone sees me, when Gabriel comes into the hall.

"Hey," he says, in a voice that denotes the presence of a stranger. "Please don't go. I won't be long. I'd forgotten a journalist from *The Times* was coming today."

"I can come back."

"No, don't. Come through, we're almost done. I've made coffee."

A young woman is sitting at the kitchen table, a spiral notebook open in front of her. She smiles when I walk in.

"Beth, this is Flora Hughes, she's writing a feature for the color supplement. Beth is an old friend of mine."

I feel a confusing stab of envy looking at Flora, a fledgling journalist with her whole career ahead and already writing for a national newspaper. She is wearing a navy minidress with white, knee-length platform boots, her hair cut into a fashionable low fringe that hovers just above her eyes. She seems intimidatingly "London."

Gabriel passes me a mug of coffee, smiling fractionally when his fingers touch mine. *Not long*, his look says.

"You've got a few more questions?" he says to Flora. And to me: "Flora tells me she's writing a piece about a new wave of young authors tearing up British publishing, along-side her interview with me, the has-been. I'm officially the old guard at thirty-one."

Gabriel laughs. Flora doesn't.

"That's not what I meant at all," she says. "Please don't think—"

"Flora. I'm joking."

When Gabriel smiles at her, she blushes.

It's an odd sensation, witnessing this. I've always known Gabriel was widely regarded as a pinup, particularly when his first couple of books came out. Various breathy articles were written by female magazine journalists who seemed to spend almost as long on what he was wearing and the fragrance of his aftershave as the content of his novels. It wasn't just his good looks. The sex scenes he wrote, which were more explicit than anything encountered in publishing before, had brought him readers in their thousands. He left D. H. Lawrence, with his daring carnal references, in the dust.

I sit at the other end of the table with my coffee and Gabriel's copy of *The Daily Telegraph* open at the crossword, where he has begun filling out answers in his elegant loopy handwriting. I find myself gazing at his writing, remembering letters he sent me from Oxford, so passionate in the beginning. After we broke up, I burned them, but I read those letters so often I can still recall the things he wrote. *How can it be right for two people who lived inside each other the way we did, almost as if we became the same person, to be separated like this?*

It seems unfathomable now, knowing what I do, that we allowed ourselves to fall into disillusionment without at least trying to understand what had happened. Was it youth and naivete that made us behave like that? If I'd called him, if he'd sent one of those letters he has told me he wrote and ripped up, if his mother hadn't been so obstructive . . . what then? This life I might have had, the one I'm half living right now, in some strange, inverted fantasy where nothing is quite as it should be.

Flora is asking Gabriel about his latest novel and, it strikes me as I listen, I have never asked him what it is about. I might say, "How's the writing going?" or "Where are you up to in this draft?" but not once has he talked about the subject matter. I feel myself stiffen as I take in the words.

"This novel is a return to an idea I had many years before I was even published. It centers around a young woman who is sexually adventurous at a time when double standards were even worse than they are now. We are living through a sexual revolution, according to the newspapers. And yet, some of the reporting I read about women, even in more respectable papers like your own, makes me uneasy. For me, writing is a way to make sense of the anxiety I feel in my subconscious. I don't always know why I'm writing a novel at the beginning, it only becomes clear to me after a while."

"And is the idea of gender equality something you've found easy to embrace as a man?" Flora asks.

Ah, I think. *This is why Flora has won her place on a national.*

She's unafraid, she asks the right questions. She's happy to show her claws.

Gabriel laughs but I can hear his irritation. "I'd hardly be writing the novel if I hadn't." He pauses and, fatally, looks at me. "Beth and I used to talk about this when we were young. Do you remember, Beth?"

"What was that?" I say, looking up as nonchalantly as I can.

"Those conversations we used to have about inequality. You used to point out all the things I took for granted that women couldn't do. Like opening a bank account. Or sitting in a pub on their own."

It is an innocent reference—after all, Gabriel introduced me to Flora as an old friend. But I find myself blushing. There is a tense moment of silence when I say nothing and Gabriel, registering my discomfort, looks away.

Flora is watching with naked curiosity. "How did you say you two knew each other?"

"I didn't. We both grew up here in Hemston."

"I'm sensing some sort of history between you . . . ?"

Flora's voice is light and teasing but Gabriel slaps her down. "You're wrong. And it's hardly relevant to the piece. I trust you have everything you need now?"

When the journalist has gone, Gabriel and I go upstairs to bed, curtains drawn to the outside world. We have sex, then we talk, and the afternoon unfolds as the others before it, but I cannot truly relax. My fear of being discovered by someone I know does not leave me. I can't shake it off. The intrusion of Flora Hughes into our lives, a young writer looking for sensationalism, has unnerved me and this temporary universe we have created no longer feels sacred. No longer feels safe.

Wednesday Evening

"It's the pub every night now, is it?" I say, trying to keep my voice light when Frank gets up from the table the moment our supper is finished.

"So it would seem." He's trying to sound lighthearted, too, but I pick out the tension in his voice, and the sadness.

Frank does not ask me if I want to go with him as he might have done even a week ago. We ate our cheesy baked potatoes in near silence, me hating myself for every attempt at conversation. There is nothing in my head except, "Are we going to be all right?" "Please don't hate me," and, endlessly, "I'm sorry, I'm so sorry." From time to time, I caught him watching me, but it was impossible to know what he was thinking.

"Frank—" I say, as he's about to go out the front door.

He turns around. Waits. "Yes?" he asks, when I can think of nothing to say.

Nothing and everything.

"Have a good time" is all I manage, cursing myself silently for the inanity of this.

"Good night, Beth," he says.

Already we are becoming strangers.

Alone now, I walk around the kitchen, unable to quell the storm of thoughts. What should I do? Please, someone, anyone, tell me what to do. There is no one I can turn to, no one who could offer advice without chastising me with their words or their eyes, their judgment. How is it you continue to hurt your husband like this? A man who has loved you from the very beginning? It's because I am innately bad, all the way through. I must be, for how else would I be able to betray Frank like this, not once, but day after day? How is it that even now, with the blackest of hearts, I will go to bed longing for the morning to come. For in the morning there is Gabriel again.

Thursday

Will there be a time when I see Gabriel's face and don't feel this lurching vertigo at how beautiful he is or, at least, how beautiful he is to me? When he doesn't rush into the hall at the sound of the front door closing behind me? Doesn't take me into his arms and kiss me as if we've parted for months rather than just one night? When I don't feel so choked with love, with lust, I am unable to speak? When will our passion, which has been so fierce in its reigniting, begin to diminish?

We seize each other, on this our fourth day as lovers, and do not even make it upstairs, clothes strewn on the parquet floor, the chandelier dazzling above me, our lovemaking fast and reckless this time. Afterward I show Gabriel the red mark where the edge of the bottom stair had pressed into my lower back so painfully I almost had to stop. Almost but not quite. Gabriel reaches down to kiss the mark, which will bloom to a bruise in a day or so.

"Why didn't you say?"

"It wasn't like that."

He laughs. "No, it wasn't. But I never want to hurt you. So you have to tell me."

It is warm today and we decide to spend our free hours at the lake. It is foolish to risk being seen outside with Gabriel in broad daylight, particularly after yesterday's intrusion from the journalist, but I do it anyway. I wonder if I take these risks because I long for it to be over, whatever that might mean. But, perhaps, it is simply that we are chasing the ghosts of before, the girl and boy who once spent a whole summer by this lake.

We spread out the old blue picnic rug, the same one from the day I met Gabriel.

"Do you remember that first afternoon?" I ask.

"Of course I do. I thought you were the rudest, most infuriating, completely dazzling girl I'd ever met."

"You were the one who was rude. You told me to get off your land."

"God, I was insufferable. And dressed like an old-age pensioner. No wonder you loathed me on sight."

"You managed to win me around pretty quickly."

We smile at each other, remembering. I realize it's the first time I've been able to look back to those days without pain. That's what the love affair has done, it's softened our beginning into the thing it actually was, a giddying, vertiginous melding of two selves. For a short while, we understood what it was like to be each other. We could read a silence with forensic expertise, always asking the right next question so there was never a need for secrets. Nothing that could not be shared. No wonder neither of us could fully recover from it. No wonder we had to return.

For a few hours we have no one to please but ourselves. And we have this lake, this enchanting picture-book lake, where once upon a time, it all began.

We are both watching when a skylark soars above the water in a perfect, show-off vertical. And I know our thoughts are running as one, the way they always used to, when Gabriel says: "I'd happily take this as my forever."

When it's time for me to fetch Leo, Gabriel says he will do it instead. "Stay here, enjoy the sun," he says, leaning over to kiss me. "I don't pick him up from school often enough."

We both know there is no question we could risk being seen in the playground together.

While Gabriel is gone I sit up and stare out at our lake,

my mind transported to another time. As a teenage girl I did nothing but daydream. Now I find myself immersed once more as I imagine the life we might have had if our relationship had not foundered.

See us here in Oxford, a pair of clever undergraduates with the world at their feet. Walking hand in hand through moonlit streets, pausing to kiss in a cobbled alley. Punting on the river, Gabriel in a straw boater, me trailing my hand through the water. Writing papers side by side in the Bodleian Library. At night, Gabriel reading from his novel, waiting anxiously for my opinion. Me showing him my poems. The writer's life I craved once upon a time, and secretly still do. Gabriel's first novel being published, the two of us drinking champagne, dazed with joy and incredulous that the thing he had always wanted had actually happened. Later, an anthology of poems for me, Gabriel looking on as I read aloud to an enraptured audience. The two of us as parents, do I dare imagine that? Gabriel and me with our own little boy. My heart throbs at the vision of the family we might have been and, when Leo calls my name and I turn to see father and son walking toward me, I am shocked. As if I have dreamed them into existence.

"We are having a picnic," Leo says, placing a wicker basket next to me on the rug. "You've got wine, I'm having Ribena."

"Pretty much the same thing," I tell him, and Leo laughs.

He begins to unpack the basket. Sliced ham, cheese, lettuce, tomatoes, a little jam jar of French dressing. Echoes of that first moonlit dinner long ago.

"Leo suggested it. Good idea, wasn't it?" Gabriel says, smiling at me.

I nod and quickly look away, worried Leo will pick up on something if we gaze at each other for too long. Every day it becomes harder to detach from my lover and shrug back into the role of Leo's carer.

Gabriel uncorks the wine and pours it into two glasses, another wineglass for Leo's Ribena that they have diluted at home.

"Cheers," Leo says, raising his glass and taking enthusiastic gulps of his drink.

We smile at him, Gabriel and I, like a pair of indulgent parents.

It is a perfect afternoon, the sun still hot beneath a cloudless sky. We take off our shoes and socks and sit at the edge of the lake cooling our feet in its silvery shadows.

Leo lists the birds he can recognize by sound—lapwing, swallow, blackbird, and then, faintly from the woods, an owl announcing the fading of our afternoon.

"Can you teach me?" Gabriel says.

I sit there, face upturned to the sun, opening my eyes from time to time to check on father and son as they listen intently to the cries of wildlife, dark heads bent toward each other. "I love it when you're not working, Dad," Leo says, and Gabriel wraps an arm around his shoulder.

"So do I. We should do this more often."

"It's the best," Leo says, swiveling his head from Gabriel to me. "Isn't it?"

"It is," Gabriel says, with more feeling than should really be allowed.

"It is," I say, quietly.

Friday Morning

Nina turns up just as I am about to leave for Meadowlands.

"Time for a cup of tea?" she says.

We take it outside to the little table in the back garden. Autumn is coming, our hedge is burgeoning with blackberries, rose hips, elderberries, and sloes. Time was, Bobby would have been out here, lips stained purple, standing on tiptoe to grasp the fattest cluster of fruit.

As soon as we sit down, Nina says: "Gabriel had a journalist at his place the other day, didn't he?"

"Did he? I wouldn't know."

Nina looks at me, irritation in her pretty face. "Well, you would know, because you were there. And I want to know why."

"Why what?" I say, stalling.

"Why you were at Meadowlands in the middle of the day when Leo was at school. Why some hack is snooping around in the pub asking questions about you."

Oh, I want to tell her. I do. Unleash a stream of angst and joy and confusion, a snapshot of the myriad emotions switching through me from moment to moment. Nina and I are close, but she is also married to my husband's brother. She is the last person on earth I can tell.

"Tell me what the journalist wanted with me. And I'll explain what I was doing at Meadowlands."

"All right." Nina picks up her mug, takes a sip. "She was very young, very confident—well, you met her. She came in at lunchtime, the first time. Ordered a lemonade. Stuck out like a sore thumb. I was curious about her, so I asked her where she'd got her white boots from. A 'little boutique in Carnaby Street,' she said." Nina carries off Flora's clipped London accent perfectly. "We got chatting and she told me she'd been interviewing 'the famous author' Gabriel Wolfe. Said she was hoping for some background from the villagers who'd known him, what he was like as a boy, blah-blah. I told her the Wolfe family never came in the pub, preferring to drink their own champagne at home, no doubt. As far as I know they didn't go to church either, so no one really saw much of them. Then she said an old friend of his was at the house. Beth. They seemed pretty close. She asked me where she could find you."

I do not flush beneath my sister-in-law's hard gaze. Even as the panic rises in my chest, I am thinking of a story, a half-truth which might work. This is who I have become, a practiced, efficient liar.

"Nosy cow," I say, but Nina doesn't even smile.

"So? Why were you there?"

"If I tell you, you'll have to promise not to say anything to Jimmy. Or Frank. Not until I've had time to tell them myself."

She nods, impatient.

"Gabriel's new novel is a revamp of an old idea, a love story he was working on when we first knew each other as teenagers."

"Don't tell me he's writing about your *love affair*?"

The expression in her voice is almost comical. A vocal recoil. Nina knows very little about the time Gabriel and I were first together—it was long before we knew her and is not exactly a topic anyone likes to discuss at Blakely Farm.

"No, nothing like that. But getting to know me again reminded him of the conversations we used to have. We talked about writing a lot back then, it was something we had in common. And, because he was stuck with this draft, he started talking to me about it. We've been brainstorming the plot, what might happen next, and I think he has found it helpful. That's all."

"I see."

I don't like the way Nina is looking at me. Or how her voice sounds: odd, suspicious.

"Well, you should know the journalist came back in the evening. Probably been snooping around the village all afternoon. She sat at the bar and had a Campari and lemonade. Frank and Jimmy were there."

"What? No."

"She started asking questions again. Your name came up. I'd told her I couldn't reveal the whereabouts of any of the villagers and she told me, gleefully, 'I've found Beth Johnson. She lives at Blakely Farm.' Well, Frank caught that, and he said, 'What do you want with my wife?'"

I'm listening to Nina with my hands pressed to my mouth. "What did she say?"

"Exactly what she'd told me. She was writing a color piece—whatever that is—about Gabriel Wolfe and she wanted to talk to the people closest to him."

"Oh, my God. Why didn't he tell me?"

"Frank was so angry, Beth. He told her to piss off. He said, 'If you bother my wife at the farm, I'll report you to the police for trespassing.' He was wildly overreacting, and you could see her taking it all in. I don't know what's going on with you and Gabriel, but whatever it is, I'd say Frank has a good idea of it."

When Nina has gone, I pace around the kitchen, talking to myself. What does this mean? Does Frank know? Is this it? The end of me and Gabriel? The end of me and Frank?

I pick up the phone and call Gabriel, dialing his number with shaking hands. There is nothing risky about this, the farmhouse is empty, but I still find myself whispering guiltily into the phone as I repeat the conversation I have just had with Nina.

"Obviously I can't risk coming over. Not today, not until I've seen Frank."

"But how was Frank last night? Wouldn't he have said something?"

"I barely saw him. He didn't bother having supper, he went straight out to the pub."

This, more than anything else, tells the truth. My husband is avoiding me because he knows. He has always known. We have been stuck in this triangle for more than a decade and, even in our best years, Frank feared being cast out. He didn't ever say so, he didn't need to.

"What are you going to do?" Gabriel says, quietly.

You, not *we.* This is my dilemma, not his. Gabriel can love whomever he chooses. It's unfortunate he has chosen a woman who is not supposed to love him back.

"I don't know. I need to talk to Frank."

"Are you going to be all right?"

I hear the words he doesn't say: *Are* we *going to be all right?*

"I'm scared."

"What are you scared of? What Frank will do if he finds out?"

"No, not that."

Frank won't get angry. I've never seen him lose his temper. Or perhaps, I haven't seen him lose it yet. Nina sounded shocked when she described Frank yelling at the journalist. Like me, she has only ever seen gentle, calming Frank, an expert in soothing his brother, who is often quick to rise. When we had Bobby, I was glad I married a man who never raised his voice at his child. You'd see it all the time, fathers yelling at their children, lashing out with a quick slap or a cuff. Not Frank. In all of Bobby's nine years, I did not see Frank shout at him once.

"I'm scared of the hurt Frank must be feeling. And of losing you."

"Yes. I'm terrified of that."

For a long minute neither of us says anything, breathing together in silence. I am thinking how impossible it will be to say goodbye to Gabriel. Hoping I don't have to, that whatever it is between us, this crazy, burning obsession, will find its end. And maybe that our ending is not an ending.

"I love you," Gabriel says. "If this is it, you know I understand. I want you to do whatever is right for you. But—can I say this? These last days with you have made me realize what a fool I was to let you go last time. I always knew that, but now I *really* know. We were meant to be together. I just hope we get a second chance."

Friday Afternoon

I see the smoke, great gray twisting boulders of it, as soon as I leave the house but, at first, I can't work out where it is coming from. I stand in the yard, confused, as the smoke slants in curls across the sky. My thought process is too slow. We set fire to the fields a month ago, straight after harvest, burned the stubble to a crisp. There's no other reason for a fire.

When the realization comes it is as if I've been punched in the gut.

I run through our fields like a madwoman. Hedgerows blaze with their glorious autumn colors and I barely notice streaks of red and purple blurring past. Over stiles I scarcely see or feel and will not remember climbing. Gates I wrench open and do not bother to close. Several acres of long grass with hidden holes to stumble upon.

Bobby's tree is burning. I know it before I see it, before I stand at the edge of the field and watch flames curling up its stump and a line of fire streaking across the grass toward the trees. Frank has his back turned but I see the tins of paraffin lying at his feet.

"Frank!" I scream his name, but he doesn't turn at first. Perhaps he doesn't hear me, perhaps he doesn't want to. Perhaps he is so focused on the fire within and without, he has room for nothing else. I can read his mood from here, the fierce governance driving him to destroy the stump with its colossal width, its implied weight, his desperation to burn away a loss that is at the heart of everything.

So much has changed since that fateful day. We have

passed through autumn, once, twice, and now almost three times. I have picked fruit and turned it into jam and crumbles and pies, just as I always did, before Bobby, with Bobby, without him. He wasn't there when our lambs were born, he did not hear the nightingales sing or the cuckoo that always marks the arrival of spring. We brought in the harvest without him. We plowed, we scattered, we sowed. For Frank and me everything changed when Bobby died but the farm stayed the same, season by season. And through all of it, through snow, through rain and scorching sun, the stump remained to remind us.

I have reached Frank now. My eyes sting, the smoke is bitter in the back of my throat. "What about the birds, Frank? He loved the birds."

How many times did we bring the binoculars to this field to see which birds we could spot? Buzzards and sparrow hawks and blackbirds. Woodpeckers, great tits. Robins and wagtails and the rooks that circled their nests at dusk, cawing at one another like socialites at a drinks party. He loved them all.

"His birds are long gone."

Frank still hasn't looked at me.

"There might be some nesting. The smoke will kill them."

"It'll burn itself out soon enough. Wood's damp."

"You can't just set fire to things."

"Why not? It's my land. I own it. I can kill it if I want to."

"Why, though?"

Frank does turn to look at me then. "It's over."

His voice is flat, face expressionless. There's so little of the man I know, no way to reach him.

"What's over, Frank? The tree? Bobby? You and me?"

"All of it."

I'm crying now. "I'm sorry—"

He raises a hand to silence me. "It was always him."

"That's not true."

"I was your second best."

"No. You were different. You were better. You rescued me, remember?"

"None of that matters anymore. It's too late."

"How did you know?"

"I've known since the wedding. It was the way you looked at him. Like you wanted him. People are talking. It'll be all over the village soon enough."

"I still love you."

"And him. Do you love him?"

I hesitate a moment too long. I want to lie, to protect Frank, to save us if that's possible, or at least have a chance of saving us. But the one thing we have always had between us is the truth.

"Yes."

Even now, his face doesn't change but I know him, I see the air go out of him—or perhaps the fight.

"Then you can have this. I won't stand in your way. Or his. You know why."

Frank picks up the paraffin cans and starts to walk off across the field, and I stare after him until he is a small mark on the horizon.

Friday Night

Frank and I are asleep, or at least pretending to be, when we hear a commotion downstairs. The front door is slammed, the strike of boots on the slate floor, a chair tipped over.

"What the hell?" Frank says, as the boots come thundering up the stairs and into our bedroom.

"Did you know?" Jimmy yells.

"Sod off, Jimmy, we're asleep." Frank leans across me to switch on the lamp. His sleeve brushes against my face. Frank, who has never worn anything in bed, not even in the coldest winters, is still half-dressed in a T-shirt and underpants.

The room snaps into light and we both take in the sight of Jimmy, red-faced from anger or beer, perhaps both.

"Tell me it isn't true, Beth."

I can't find a single thing to tell him, can't be what he wants, his big sister, his brother's wife, defender, nurturer. Instead, we stare at each other, Jimmy and I, while the rage roars up inside him. He swivels to look at Frank, his face twisted with scorn.

"So that's it, is it? You're going to allow her to screw that creep and get into bed with you afterwards, as if nothing's happened?"

"Shut up. Don't be disgusting." Frank is out of bed, snatching up his jeans from the floor, pushing his brother from the room. At the doorway he looks back at me. "Stay there, I'll deal with him. You don't have to listen to this."

But I do have to listen. This is it, my moment of reckoning, and in some ways I long for it.

In the kitchen, the brothers face each other, inches apart. Frank's feet are bare, the belt on his jeans still unbuckled. On the table, a half-drunk bottle of whisky glares at us.

"How can you put up with this?" Jimmy asks Frank, while I stand a foot or so away.

Frank glances at me. Then shrugs.

What I have done to him, this man who has been my soulmate, my best friend, the father of my child for almost half my lifetime.

"You cow, you selfish bloody cow," Jimmy says, and Frank grabs him hard, by the top of his arm. So hard, Jimmy yelps.

"Don't talk about my wife like that. I won't have it."

"Is she still your wife? You sure about that?"

"Yes. Not that it's your business."

Jimmy turns to face me. "How could you, Beth? After everything our family have been through. After Bobby—" He whispers his nephew's name with such reverence, as if even the memory of Bobby is too pure to be in the midst of all this. "We need each other. Don't we? And Frank loves you, more than anyone ever could."

When Frank and I say nothing—for what is there to say—Jimmy starts to rant.

He is far far drunker than I had realized.

"So, what? This is allowed to carry on? You do know, don't you, Beth, the whole village is onto you and your dirty little secret? It was all anyone could talk about in the pub. Did you think no one would notice you sneaking out to your love nest, while your husband worked his fingers to the bone?"

"I told you, Jimmy, leave her alone. This is for me and Beth to work out. No one else."

Jimmy starts crying. He looks so lost and all I want is to reach out and hug him, as I would have done every single day of the years gone by. But not now.

"And what about *him*? You going to let him get away with it?"

Frank shrugs. "I reckon," he says.

"Well, bully for you. Because I'm going to smash his face in. Teach him a lesson."

Jimmy swoops for the whisky bottle but Frank is too quick for him. He picks it up, hurls it to the floor, where the glass splinters into a hundred tiny fragments. The only outward sign of the devastation I know is eating him up.

Jimmy slumps against his brother in defeat and Frank wraps both arms around him, as if he's holding a child. He looks at me above his head, darts his eyes to the staircase. "Go," he mouths, wanting to spare me even now.

I have never deserved his kindness less.

Saturday Morning

I spend the morning moving around the kitchen, trying to remember what I used to do with myself on a Saturday before our lives collapsed. I cooked and cleaned and did the laundry, I helped the men on the farm. If I surprised them at the dairy, Frank was always thrilled, his whole face lighting up with pleasure. Such a small and easy thing, I wish I had done it more often.

I half expected to see Nina again today, but she has stayed away from the farm. I have betrayed all of them. Nina, who said the first time she met me: "Can I be you when I grow up, Beth?" I had everything back then, a husband I was in love with, the sweetest, funniest child ever to walk the earth, two hundred acres of blood, sweat, and tears that was also our private paradise. I felt so lucky. For so many years, I felt lucky.

I know I will never forgive myself for what I have done to Frank, the man who gave me all of that. But today it is Jimmy I am most worried about. It's never been quite right, the way he reacts—or rather overreacts—to sudden change. Or how he depends upon Frank, even now as a married man who will soon have children of his own. When Jimmy becomes a father, will he still behave like a child when things go wrong? Will he stamp his feet, will he fight his own child, locked into a playground dispute until Nina intervenes?

I can't stop thinking about how lost Jimmy looked. How Frank held him in his arms like a child. Frank always understood instinctively what happened to Jimmy when their mother died. How he got stuck, unable to mature. He never blamed him when Jimmy resorted to alcohol and occasional violence, anesthetizing his pain in the only way he knew. David used to get so angry with Jimmy, but Frank never did.

I hate myself for the way my family is unraveling, but I see now it was inevitable for both me and Gabriel; that, at some point, we'd find our way back to one another. Our story was incomplete, it still is. There were too many questions, too many pieces that didn't fit. Too much unresolved longing. A lust that was always there in the background, simmering, even as the years passed. One strike of the match, that was all it took. If Bobby had lived, I would have continued in my little enclave of good fortune. But Bobby died. Everything fell apart. And then, soon enough, Gabriel appeared.

I am too pent up to sit down for long. I make a cup of tea that cools untouched, half-heartedly scrub at some overalls waiting for me on the scrubbing board but soon abandon them, assailed by thoughts I have no control over. How much longer will I be doing Frank's and Jimmy's washing? Or cooking the evening meal? Or helping them out on the farm? Is this the end of the life we built together, not just me and Frank, but Jimmy, too, over so many years?

I walk around the ground floor of the farmhouse—just one big room really—the kitchen and a little corridor leading to the stairs. In a windowsill opposite the staircase I spy our wedding photo, the only one we have, covered in dust since the last time I looked. There were no photographers at our wedding, no guests other than my parents and David, Jimmy, and Eleanor.

It was perfect. Just Frank and I staring at each other in shock as we uttered those iconic "I dos" with only our families to bear witness. Afterward, my father took us all for lunch at the County Hotel in Shaftesbury. We ate roast beef and drank little thimbles of sherry and Frank and I were beside ourselves, the formalities over, us a brand-new man and wife. We couldn't believe we'd pulled it off so effortlessly. If my mother had wished for a different kind of wedding—me in a flouncy dress with a veil and train, all their friends invited to a party afterward—she did not say. My parents had taken to Frank almost instantly. Partly, I think, because they'd hated seeing me hurt by Gabriel, but mostly because Frank turned out to be everything they wanted in a son-in-law—he was kind, funny, self-sufficient. And they trusted him.

I take the photograph in its dusty wooden frame into the kitchen, wipe it with a damp cloth. Look at the pair of us for a long time. We look preposterously young it seems to me now, little more than children.

Saturday, Late Afternoon

Frank comes into the kitchen at dusk. I haven't cooked or cleaned or washed clothes or done any of the things that needed doing, just walked whole miles within our cluttered kitchen while my mind exploded with all that had gone before and all that was to come.

Here it is, I think, when I first see Frank. He is ready for the conversation we have both been dreading, the question neither of us has wanted to ask. Should Frank and I stagger from the wreckage of our marriage and see if there is anything left to rebuild? Or should we cut one another free: Go, mend yourself, forget about me. Part of me has always believed it was impossible for Frank and me to heal while we stayed together.

But Frank has other things on his mind.

"Has Jimmy been in?" His voice is odd, distracted.

"Has something happened?"

"He's missing. Can't find him anywhere."

"When did you last see him?"

"This morning, at the dairy. Still pissed out of his head, must have had another bottle somewhere. Still angry. Making stupid bloody threats."

"You think it's different to the other times he's gone AWOL?"

"Honestly, he seemed unwell. Like something had snapped in him. All the time I watch out for him, don't I? Too much, you sometimes say. But now I'm wondering, Was I looking properly? Did I really see what was going on with him? He's not quite right. But we all carry on pretending he is."

"Pubs open again any minute, that's where he'll be."

"There's something else. One of the shotguns is missing." We stare at one another while his words sink in. "He's not gone hunting. Wasn't in a fit state for that. Well, not hunting game anyway."

"Frank?"

"I'm worried he'll turn up at Meadowlands. The things Jimmy was saying about Gabriel, I couldn't even tell you . . . he seemed crazy enough to want to kill him. Well, harm him."

"Oh, my God, Frank. We have to call the police."

I start to move for the phone, but Frank grabs my wrist, pulls me back. "And say what? Jimmy is drunk and armed and dangerous? He wants to hurt his brother's wife's lover? Think about it."

The way he looks at me when he says this. Flat. No feeling left. In Frank's head we are already over.

"No. We deal with this ourselves. Call Gabriel and warn him Jimmy might turn up. I'm going out to look for him."

Saturday, Early Evening

I suppose I wasn't thinking straight when I decided to walk over to Meadowlands and tell Gabriel myself. I'd picked up the phone to call him and his line was busy and I was too distressed to wait.

When Gabriel answers the door and sees it is me, I realize I have made a mistake. His smile is instant, euphoric. His whole face flooded with happiness. Gabriel thinks I have broken up with Frank. He thinks this is me, announcing the beginning of our new lives together.

"Beth," he says, his voice lifting in pleasure.

I shake my head quickly. "It's a crisis. Jimmy's missing. Frank thinks he might come here."

"Oh." I watch as Gabriel's face passes through disappointment, confusion, resignation.

"I see."

"Jimmy knows about us. He's angry. Drunk. Making threats. Frank wouldn't tell me exactly what other than Jimmy has got it in for you. Frank's out looking for him now. He said I should warn you."

"I'm sure it will be fine. I wouldn't worry." Gabriel's voice is nonchalant. Unconcerned.

"Please, Gabriel. Listen to what I am telling you. Jimmy took one of the guns and he's out of his mind with drink. I think he means to kill you. Or hurt you, at least."

We hear a scream behind us. Leo has been standing in the hall, listening the whole time. He must have heard everything.

"Dad," he cries. "Is Jimmy going to kill you?"

Gabriel opens his arms and Leo runs into them. "It's all

right," he says, soothing him, kissing his head. "It's not what you think, I promise. Beth. Come inside. Let's lock the door."

At first, Leo refuses to let go of Gabriel, clinging to his waist, making it impossible for him to move.

"Leo?" I wait until he looks up at me. "I know you're scared. But can I say something? I've known Jimmy most of his life. He doesn't mean it. He would never hurt anyone, trust me." Even as I'm saying this, I'm remembering the times Jimmy started arguments in the pub. How they occasionally spilled over into physical fights. The night Andy brought him home, spread-eagled in the back of his police car, and warned us Jimmy needed to learn how to hold his booze or quit drinking altogether. And Frank is right, we've all chosen to turn a blind eye.

We sit together at the kitchen table, Gabriel, Leo, and me. I try, but fail, to begin a conversation. Anything to lighten the atmosphere, which feels too tense, the three of us waiting. I think of us playing cards here a few days ago, no sense of what was to come. I am thinking about Nina, wondering if Frank has told her Jimmy is missing. Presumably the Compasses would have been the first place he looked.

"Is the back door locked?" I say to Gabriel, trying to keep my voice casual.

"I don't think so. Shall I go and—"

A loud bang makes all of us scream. The window cracks into a web of splinters with a fist-sized hole at its center.

Right outside it, staring in, is Jimmy, cradling his shotgun.

"Jimmy, for God's sake, what are you doing?"

Jimmy's expression doesn't change as I yell at him. It's as if he doesn't understand me. We watch in horror as he takes a cartridge from his jeans pocket and reloads the gun.

"Down!" Gabriel yanks Leo to the ground and shoves him under the kitchen table. "You too, Beth."

"I'm going out to talk to him," I say. "I've spent years dealing with Jimmy. He'll listen to me."

Gabriel rests a palm against my cheek for a second, that's all. "I won't have you in danger," he says. "I'll go."

At the sound of the gun being fired again, Gabriel and I fall to our knees, crouching beneath the window.

The second gunshot has changed everything. It's not my brother-in-law out there, we are dealing with a madman.

I feel a hand grabbing my ankle.

"Beth," Leo hisses at me. "Please come. I'm so scared."

I crawl in next to him. The two of us sheltering beneath the table.

"Can I hold your hand?"

"Of course."

Leo crushes my fingers with his own. His body is trembling.

Think, think. What comes next? Do I make a dash for the phone? Would Jimmy fire at me? Somehow, I don't think so. I am his brother's wife and he thinks of me as his sister, has told me so many times.

"Gabriel!" I yell, coming to my senses. "Don't go out there. It's dangerous."

Too late. I hear Gabriel's boots running along the hall, a bolt being unlatched, the front door opening.

Sometimes you get a chance, mere seconds, perhaps, when you can avert a tragedy before it happens. This is mine. My moment. My chance. But I don't take it. I don't run after Gabriel and throw myself at Jimmy's mercy, begging him to put down the gun before any blood can be shed. Instead, I make a foolish choice, one that will turn all our lives into a horror show and keep me awake night after night with an endless parade of "if onlys."

I decide to stay where I am, cowering beneath the table with Leo.

"Jimmy's going to kill him, isn't he?" Leo whimpers, and then I feel it, the seep of warm liquid pooling beneath me as he lets go of his bladder. Poor boy. Poor baby. He's far too young for all of this.

"I'm sorry," he says, weeping now, and I pull him into me, the scent of his urine sharp in my nostrils.

"We'll be all right, I promise."

Why do adults do this? Why do they promise things they have no way of being able to deliver?

"Your dad will talk to Jimmy and make him see sense. Trust me, Jimmy is not a killer."

"He is, Beth. He killed my dog."

"Oh, Leo," I say, resting my forehead against his for a second.

The dog shooting that began it all. It feels like a lifetime ago.

Part Four

Frank

1968

Everyone in Hemston had their own view about what happened that night: How the young farmer lost his life. Some thought Frank Johnson had finally flipped and shot his brother after an argument. God knows, they said, pausing to chat as they collected their milk and papers from the village shop, he'd had more put upon him in the last few years than any man could be reasonably expected to take.

The first story, broken the next morning by the *Daily Express*, had caused shock waves in the village with its stark headline: "Novelist's Love Tryst Ends in Death."

To think, people said, putting the kettle on for another Nescafé, lingering over their Rice Krispies and Weetabix, their hot buttered toast, something so *menacing* had happened right on their doorstep. It was more lurid and shocking than one of Gabriel Wolfe's novels.

Back then, only the sparest facts were known. Frank Johnson had been arrested for the murder of his brother, Jimmy. Jimmy, known to be unstable, had gone on a ten-hour drinking spree and threatened to kill Beth Johnson's lover, Gabriel. How it ended up that Jimmy was the one who got shot, was anyone's guess.

And guess was what the villagers most liked to do.

As the weeks passed, more details emerged. Frank Johnson pleaded not guilty to the dual charges of murder or manslaughter and was released on bail while he awaited trial. He and his wife kept to themselves in the intervening months, never seen in the village, although Frank could be spied on his tractor from time to time. Stories kept appearing in the press. Every paper, be it broadsheet or tabloid, wanted a piece of Gabriel Wolfe's fall from grace. A former pupil at the Immaculate Conception Convent told *The Daily Telegraph* about the licentious love affair which began when Gabriel and Beth were teenagers. The *Mirror* ran a piece about their open-air "sexploits" alongside a photograph of the lake at Meadowlands. Neither Beth Johnson nor Gabriel Wolfe was available for comment.

As the date for the murder trial drew closer, the villagers were buzzing with excitement. It would be at the Central Criminal Court, in London, and many of them planned to go along and watch. Frank Johnson in the dock, Gabriel Wolfe called to testify as a witness; it was their very own Hemston soap opera.

Days before the trial was due to begin came a further shock.

Frank Johnson had broken his bail conditions and was now awaiting trial in Wandsworth Prison.

The Trial

My former lover is on the witness stand, dressed in a charcoal-gray suit, the same one he wore to Jimmy and Nina's wedding. Opposite him in the dock is my husband, also in his navy wedding suit, the only one he owns. If only we could turn the clock back to that night, to the foolish conversation Gabriel and I had behind our shield of elm trees. Or wind it further, to the day a lurcher tore into our field and slaughtered our lambs.

I have sat opposite Frank at our kitchen table day in, day out for so many years, I know every centimeter of his face, his body. But this man looks almost a stranger viewed from above. I gaze at him until my eyes hurt from looking, until my heart can no longer take it.

It is my first sighting of the jury: The men and women who hold my husband's fate in their hands. Will they hear how Frank was a parent to Jimmy as much as a brother, his friend, his guide, and realize he would never have hurt him, let alone murdered him?

My sister, Eleanor, has been here in the public gallery every day since the trial first began. She points out the press bench, overflowing with journalists. "Twice as many today, of course," she whispers, with a quick eye roll.

A man has died. Frank's brother, Nina's husband, the boy who once delivered my baby. But you wouldn't think it to read the endless rash of stories in the press about the "playboy" author Gabriel Wolfe and his love affair with a lowly "farmer's wife."

"Mr. Wolfe," the Crown prosecutor says, "I'd like to

begin at the beginning, if I may? Can you tell me how you first met Beth Johnson?"

I feel, oh, inescapably sad when Gabriel starts to recount our initial meeting. Our trespassing story. Our connection over books and writing. Our mutual boredom, a girl and boy looking to fill a whole summer. The passion that started slowly but soon engulfed us until there was room for nothing and no one else.

"It sounds very powerful the way you describe it. You were in love?"

"We loved each other, yes."

Gabriel stares back at Donald Glossop, QC, never once dropping his gaze. Gabriel has the clear, well-spoken voice of his kind, unfazed by the scrutiny, a sea of faces turned to examine him. He might be on the witness stand, his private life about to be ripped apart, but they are equals, the barrister and him, that's what his look says.

"But the relationship ended. Why was that?"

I find myself watching Gabriel intently now, holding my breath as I wait for him to speak.

"It ended for no good reason at all. Miscommunication."

"A false ending, in a sense?"

Gabriel pauses, as if the words have winded him. "Yes," he says, quieter now. "That's exactly right, a false ending."

"And when you met Beth Johnson again all those years later, you still had feelings for each other?"

I see how Gabriel glances at the dock. He doesn't know of my daily confessions to Frank in the months before he went to prison. If he was to love me again, I said, then he needed to know everything I had done. There were times he didn't want to listen and begged me to stop, but I would always carry on in the end. No secrets, we said. Nothing hidden, all of it shared. Frank knows all there is to know about Gabriel and me, from our very beginning to our savage end.

Gabriel says: "Deep down, yes. Although neither of us wanted to admit it. Beth was happily married. I knew she loved her husband."

"And yet, you began an affair with her?"

You can feel it, a new alertness in the gallery—this is what the people came for.

"Yes, I knew it was wrong. And I deeply regret it. But I loved her . . . I always had."

I bow my head for a moment, look down at my knees. *Oh, Gabriel*, I think, as the inevitable sadness rushes through me. There's no point wishing things had turned out differently, but I do it all the same.

"When did the affair start?"

"Last September. Immediately after Jimmy and Nina Johnson's wedding."

Disapproval crackles through the court as this fact sinks in. That we would so callously begin an affair after a joyous family celebration. That the bridegroom would be dead within a week.

"I'd like to move now to September the twenty-eighth of last year. The night of the shooting. Beth Johnson came to your house, I believe, to warn you Jimmy was missing and armed with a shotgun."

Every minute of this trial matters, it matters so much. Nothing has ever mattered more. So why is it I cannot concentrate on Gabriel's voice as he begins to tell the court his version of events on that fateful night? I am thinking of all the twenty-eighths of September that had gone before it, days of sunshine, laughter, lovemaking or arguing, milking cows or feeding sheep, cooking, cleaning, changing sheets, days when Bobby was alive and days when he wasn't, stretches of time that gave no hint of what this date would come to mean. I am thinking of the absurdity of the entire case, that Frank, who loved his brother as much as you could ever love anyone, and then some more, would be accused of killing him. I am thinking the wrong man is in the dock and I should never have allowed it to get this far.

"How did Beth seem when you first saw her?" the prosecutor asks.

"She was worried. Frank had told her Jimmy wanted to punish me for the affair. He was out for blood, she said. I didn't take it seriously at first. It seemed rather far-fetched. But Beth seemed to think Jimmy might turn up at the house. Within minutes, he did."

I listen to Gabriel describing his son's terror when Jimmy fired at the kitchen window. The glass shattering. The three of us screaming in shock. A great gap in the window with my brother-in-law standing just outside it, loading another cartridge into his shotgun.

"Why would you risk going outside? Were you not afraid?" Mr. Glossop asks.

"I wanted to protect my son." Gabriel lowers his voice. "And Beth. I wanted to keep them safe. I needed Jimmy off the premises. That's all I was thinking about."

"I'm skeptical, Mr. Wolfe, as to why Jimmy, who had shot at you through the kitchen window, would happily get into a car with you, meek as a lamb."

"Hardly meek. I told Jimmy I was going to drive him home and he told me to get lost. He was still brandishing his shotgun, drunk out of his mind. It was terrifying. I had to think of something to persuade him into the car. So I told him it was over between me and Beth. That we had ended the affair."

"Was that true?"

"Not then, no."

"You're saying you lied, Mr. Wolfe?"

"Yes," Gabriel snaps. "On the spur of the moment. It was a stressful situation. I was thinking on my feet."

Donald Glossop nods but says nothing, allowing Gabriel's admission to sink in.

"Why didn't Beth Johnson come in the car with you? Wouldn't that have made more sense? I would have thought she would have been more able to calm him down."

"One of us needed to stay behind with my son. He was traumatized, he believed I was going to be killed."

"What happened when you arrived at Blakely Farm?"

"Frank was in the yard as we drove in, and he came straight over to the car and helped Jimmy into the farmhouse. That was the last time I saw him."

"If we could pause there for a moment. This was the first time you had seen Frank Johnson since he had learned of your affair with his wife? Is that right?"

"Yes."

"He must have been very angry with you . . . ?"

"If he was, he didn't show it. If anything, Frank seemed grateful I'd brought Jimmy home"—Gabriel falters, then recovers himself—"in one piece. He thanked me."

"He *thanked* you."

When Donald Glossop was announced as Crown counsel my sister spent a day in the British Library reading up on the cases he had won. "He's a performer," she told me. "He acts up for the jury and gets them onside. He amuses them, makes them laugh, lulls them into a false sense of security. Then delivers his bombshell. It's his trademark."

"I'm not sure I'd be *thanking* you in the same situation, Mr. Wolfe. If it were my wife, my vocabulary would be rather more colorful."

There is a ripple of laughter in court, several jurors smile. The woman with gray hair and electric-blue spectacles. I'd already registered the flamboyant glasses, wondered what they were meant to signal. The man in pinstripe, whom I think of as "City Gent," puts his hand to his mouth, trying to conceal his grin.

"Frank Johnson has never shown me any anger, not once, despite the obvious provocation of me sleeping with his wife," Gabriel says, evenly. "Jimmy was volatile and prone to bursts of violence. But not Frank, not in my experience."

The man under discussion looks blankly ahead, as he has all morning. If Frank were a poker player, he'd win every hand. His face is inscrutable, devoid of feeling. I know, better than anyone, how he pines for his brother, how he mourned him, the harrowing sobs that would rise from his chest in the middle of the night, try as he might to disguise them. Frank, who barely cried in all my years of knowing him, has wept a lake of tears for Jimmy. But the jury doesn't know that.

"You are paying Frank Johnson's legal costs, are you not?"

Gabriel hesitates, wrong-footed now. None of us expected this to come out in the trial.

"Should I repeat the question?"

Gabriel shakes his head, irritated.

"I can afford it. And the Johnsons can't."

"Most generous, I am sure," Mr. Glossop says in his honey-like tone. He turns once more to the jury. "I hear these legal bills can be cripplingly expensive."

More laughter, the jury are enjoying themselves. It is a moment's reprieve from the grim reality of a murder trial.

"I wonder, is there not another motivation for doing so? You have told the court you loved Beth Johnson, the defendant's wife, and always had. Is it fair to say you have her best interests at heart?"

"Yes. No. Not in the way you mean."

"I don't believe you have any idea what kind of man Frank

Johnson is, as you barely knew him. Your relationship was with his *wife*. A very *intimate* relationship. It seems unlikely Frank Johnson would have wanted to spend a single second in *your* company."

The jury is smirking again, ready for more sarcasm, more performance. But Donald Glossop does the volte-face for which he is famous, his voice raised to a pitch just below a shout.

"I suggest it is *guilt* that has brought you here today, Mr. Wolfe. Guilt your love affair with Beth Johnson was an unfortunate catalyst in Jimmy Johnson's death."

"I fail to see how my feelings about my relationship with Beth have any relevance to this case? I was called to testify because I was one of the last people to see Jimmy Johnson alive."

Gabriel's voice is terse as he says this. To the courtroom he probably sounds impatient. A man trying to keep his irritation under control. But all I hear is Gabriel's desolation, the quiet change in his voice when he says my name.

"Quite so. And it is your viability as a witness I now call into question. A few moments ago, you readily admitted to being a liar. I don't believe we can trust a word you are saying."

He allows one final, significant pause, before he delivers his dismissal in a bored and weary tone as if Gabriel is nothing but a waste of time. "I have no further questions for this witness, my lord."

1968

When the date for the trial was set, Eleanor came to stay with us at the farm. As a solicitor she had been in court hundreds of times, she knew the drill. Night after night, we sat by the fire while Eleanor explained what would happen. She told us who everyone was and showed us where each would sit, drawing a diagram of the court with crosses to mark each person's place. "The court clerk sits here," she'd say, brandishing her felt-tip. "This is the press bench, it's going to be packed when Gabriel testifies." I remember staring at her sketch of the prisoner's dock, with its bleak labeling—FRANK—and thinking, *This cannot be happening. Not to us.*

Eleanor grilled Frank on the events of that night, taking him through it, minute by minute, until he begged for a break. She was relentless. "I know it hurts to think about it, Frank. But it's going to hurt a lot more when you're facing Donald Glossop in court. Believe me, he's as vicious as a rabid dog. You've got to be watertight."

How many times did she make him go over that final fateful scene? Jimmy wild with drink, abusing Frank while he tried to wrest the shotgun from him. A tussle between the brothers which ended in death.

The essence of the case is this: Did Frank, following those last moments of goading from Jimmy, intend to cause serious harm, which would then make Jimmy's death murder? Or was it, as Frank claims, an act of self-defense that ended in devastating tragedy?

Robert Miles, our defense barrister, was young to take

silk. He is in his early forties, slim and fresh-faced, an almost exact antithesis of his opponent. I picture Robert running along the Thames at sunrise while Donald Glossop sleeps off another big night of port and Stilton. Robert is graceful, elegant, courteous; the Crown prosecutor has the bulk of a rugby player, the attitude that goes with it.

Before he hired Robert, Gabriel spoke to everyone he knew in the legal world and quite a few people he didn't, friends of friends, fathers of friends, uncles, boyfriends, brothers. Robert's was the name that came up most frequently.

Gabriel is visibly relaxed as he awaits cross-examination. Robert is on the payroll, after all. And Gabriel's ordeal is almost at an end.

"I see no reason to rake over the details of your relationship with Mrs. Johnson again," Robert says. "I'm much more interested to hear about Jimmy's state of mind in the time you spent with him, both in your garden at home and in the car journey to the farm."

"He was aggressive. Full of vitriol. But also, at the stage of drunkenness where he was not making a great deal of sense."

"But you felt threatened by him?"

Gabriel pauses and Robert quickly adds: "An inebriated, vengeful man in charge of a shotgun could pose quite a serious threat, I imagine?"

He might as well have said: *This is your chance to set up the self-defense scenario, remember?*

"Yes, I felt we were in a very dangerous situation. Jimmy shot our kitchen window out. Any one of us might have been wounded. That's why I wanted him and his shotgun off my property. I needed to keep my son safe. Any father would feel the same."

"Initially, you were able to calm Jimmy down by telling

him your relationship with Beth was over. Was he still in a calm state when you delivered him home?"

This time, Gabriel quickly takes the bait. "Initially, yes. He seemed completely worn out by it all. But as we neared the farm, it was as if he had forgotten what I told him about me and Beth. He started making the same threats. He was in a violent mood again, no question."

I look at Frank in the dock, see the pain flash across his face, though I doubt anyone else would notice. Jimmy was a necessary sacrifice to make our story stick.

"Sounds an explosive mix for Frank to deal with once he got his brother inside?" Robert asks but, before Gabriel can answer, Donald Glossop leaps to his feet.

"My lord, conjecture? Mr. Wolfe cannot have known what went on inside the farmhouse or indeed Jimmy Johnson's temperament in those final moments."

Judge Miskin raises a hand in weary acknowledgment. It must be tiring, the constant wrangling between counsel, like overseeing a playground fight with no end in sight.

Robert apologizes to the judge.

"Mr. Wolfe," he continues. "You were the last person to see Jimmy Johnson alive other than his brother. Did you believe him to be a danger to himself and others on the night of September the twenty-eighth?"

"Absolutely I did. He was drunk in charge of a lethal weapon and in a mind to cause harm."

Gabriel is a leading witness, and one of the conditions of Frank's bail was that the two of them must not meet in the months leading up to the trial. But in those first, awful early days it felt impossible that Gabriel and I should never see one another again. So much between us had been left unsaid. One morning, when Frank was out on the farm, I called him and asked if we could meet.

"But where?" he said. "If anyone sees us . . . "

I told him of a place where Bobby and I used to play hide-and-seek, a field that was halfway between Meadowlands and Blakely Farm and had a huge sweet chestnut tree at one end. We loved that tree, Bobby and I, almost as much as the old oak on the farm. When he was small I used to take storybooks and a little picnic and we'd spend a few hours there, reading about Peter Rabbit or digging for worms, one of Bobby's top pursuits.

I arrived at the tree before Gabriel and waited for him to come. It was a clear blue day, cold, with sharp sunshine. I wished I were anyone but me. And Gabriel was anyone but him. I couldn't tell if the anxiety humming through my bloodstream was because I was seeing him again or because of the things I must tell him.

"There you are," he said, appearing around the tree, a few minutes later.

It was like a miniature heart attack just looking at him.

He had lost weight, there were deep hollows in his cheeks and dark rings beneath his eyes. But still the beautiful boy I fell for long ago.

"Beth," he said.

Nothing else for a minute, just my name. Then he joined me, his back against the tree, the two of us staring out at the long stretch of sodden grass. It was early November by then, weeks since we'd seen each other, since that terrible night.

I asked Gabriel about Leo and he told me he was having nightmares, another arrow of guilt to poison myself with. I thought of him trembling beside me as we sheltered beneath the table, the scent of his raw fear in my nostrils. A young boy who believed his father was about to get shot. We had so much to blame ourselves for, Gabriel and I.

"How's Frank?" Gabriel said.

How could I possibly describe the walking wreckage that was my husband?

"He's so bad," I whispered.

Gabriel took hold of my hand. "I'm so sorry. Sorry for everything."

"I know you are. I'm so sorry too. I blame myself for all of it."

"I'd tell you not to except I'm doing exactly the same thing. I always will."

We spent a minute in silence thinking our own thoughts. I was thinking about Gabriel and how he was one of the only people I knew who always acknowledged when things were wrong or bad, without trying to make it better or shift the blame. That's rare, I think. Most people rush in to assuage your guilt with meaningless platitudes and it doesn't help.

What helps, I have learned, years too late, is to accept responsibility for the things I have done. To be accountable, I suppose.

"I regret what happened so much and I wish, more than anything, I could change it," I say. "But I will never forget the time you and I had together."

"It sounds so final when you say it like that."

"I'll always love you, Gabriel."

"Actually, please don't say any more. I'm not sure I need to hear this."

"I need to say it, though. For myself. For Frank. I'm sorry." I felt bad for making Gabriel listen. But this was my way now. "I've loved you for so long and I know that if certain things hadn't gone wrong back then we would still be together now. Being with you has meant everything to me. I fell in love with you, all over again. People say you can't love two people at the same time, but you can, and I do. I love you. And I love Frank. But it's Frank I have to be with. Even if Jimmy hadn't died, I would still need to be with Frank. It's our history. Everything we've been through together. Frank needs me. And I need Frank. I know you will find that with someone else in time. I'm so sad it can't be me. You're a good man, Gabriel. You really are."

I squeeze Gabriel's hand. Both of us staring straight ahead.

"You think I can move on from you that easily? I don't know how to be without you. I never did."

"It will get easier. In time. You and I know this."

"I wish we'd had longer. I wish you were still with me."

"You deserve someone so much better."

"I'll be the judge of that." There was lightness in his voice now and we turned to look at each other properly for the first time. We smiled.

"I think I'm going to go," he said.

"All right."

Gabriel let go of my hand and without his warm clasp it dangled limp and cold by my side.

"I'm not saying goodbye," he said.

"Let's agree never to say that."

I stayed there, leaning against the old chestnut tree, eyes closed to the bright winter sun, listening to the sound of his footsteps walking away toward the road.

Eleanor had warned me to expect a crowd outside the courthouse but, even so, it's a shock to see how many photographers are waiting for Gabriel. Twenty, thirty? They seem to be three-deep, jostling and straining for a closer shot; any moment, one of them will surely fall over.

"Beth! Beth! Over here."

"Don't look," Eleanor hisses under her breath. "Stare straight ahead."

But ahead is where Gabriel is, perhaps no more than a

yard or two between us. I could reach out and touch him, if I wanted to. And in some ways, I do want to. I long for the chance to say, *Thank you. You have done everything you could. I know you did it for me.*

"Gabriel, look, Beth's right behind you."

Instinctively, Gabriel turns.

It is a moment, five seconds, perhaps ten, before he comes to his senses. He and I, no one else—the rest of the world, the clamor, the flashbulbs, the shouting, my sister at my side—it all just drops away.

For this tiny flash of time, I drink in the sight of him. And I think he does the same. No smile or nod of recognition, there's no need. Our eyes say it for us. *It's you.*

When Gabriel turns back, a reporter presses right up against him. He is tall, like Gabriel, their faces are only inches apart. Gabriel shoves his chest with the flat of his hand and the man stumbles. "Back off. I said, no comment."

His voice is pure rage, I've never heard it in him before.

"Do you still love her?" someone shouts, but Gabriel has spotted a vacant cab on the other side of the road.

I watch as he darts across the street, one hand out as he flags it down. Wrenching open the door, leaping inside. And he is gone.

"Worst I've ever seen it," Eleanor says as we turn the corner walking, so fast I'm breathless. "But they didn't get anything. Don't worry."

She's wrong, of course. They are good at their jobs, these photographers, poised to act fast. The photo that will make every paper in the morning is the one fleeting moment when Gabriel and I looked at each other.

I thought we were expressionless, both of us, but that is not how it looks in the pictures.

"The Look of Love?" is the *Mirror*'s headline. *The Sun*

more accurate with its single word, "Heartbreak." Even *The Daily Telegraph* puts its own spin on our love story, quoting from Gabriel's testimony: "I knew it was wrong . . . But I loved her . . . I always had."

The cameras have picked up on something I didn't even register myself feeling, but it's plainly there in my eyes: I look so happy to see him. Is that surprising? We are involved in this case in exactly the same way, the shame I feel mirrors his, we are the ones who know what it is like to feel responsible for a death. Not Frank, the man in the dock.

Gabriel's expression is different to mine. All you see as he gazes at me, exposed for a handful of seconds, is his unutterable sadness.

Eleanor and I have developed a ritual for when we return to her airy, light-filled flat in Parsons Green at the end of each day. We wrench off our shoes, collapse on the sofa, and argue about whose turn it is to make tea. If I close my eyes, the years drop away, and I can picture almost exactly the girls we once were.

As teenagers we'd arrive home from school before either of our parents was back from work. We'd make a pot of tea and several rounds of hot buttered toast—which we invariably burned under the grill—and we would play our favorite record on the gramophone. Our obsessions changed monthly—Little Richard, Bing Crosby, Doris Day, Frank Sinatra, we loved them all. I only have to hear "Sisters" by Rosemary Clooney to be transported back to the innocence of those days. Eleanor and I were word-perfect in that song, we'd ham it up for our parents when they got home, twirling our hair and executing synchronized spins while we sang of sisterly devotion.

Now we drink our tea in silence, feeling the weight of

the day slip from us. Often, I feel too exhausted to speak. I picture Frank in his prison cell, lying on a thin mattress staring up at the ceiling. He wouldn't let me visit him in prison, said he would bear it better if he knew I hadn't seen him there.

Eleanor went once without warning him she was coming. "What's it like?" I asked her.

I knew she wouldn't try to soften the truth, it's not her way.

"How you imagine," she said, "but ten times worse."

"And Frank? How is he?"

"How you imagine, but ten times worse. Stoic. Broken."

Tomorrow Frank is in the witness box. A gentle start with Robert leading the questioning, but even so, I can't think of anything else. The days go past without my being able to talk to him, touch him, tell him I love him, reassure him that no matter what happens we will be all right. Is that even true? Neither Frank nor I wanted to dwell on the possibility of his being found guilty. If the jury settles upon murder, it could carry a life sentence of up to thirty years and he is unlikely to be allowed to apply for parole for at least ten years. Frank existing in a tiny prison cell for years, his only exercise a daily stroll around the yard. A man who has spent his whole life outside in vastness. What would it do to him? How would he cope? How would I?

"Even though the Crown is gunning for murder, the manslaughter option in the indictment makes their case look weak," Eleanor tells me. "They are hedging their bets."

"Bottom line, they do not have enough to put Frank away."

Every night she will tell me the same thing.

"Keep the faith. It's going to be all right."

Every night I try my hardest to believe her.

*

I've seen plenty of swearing-in over the past days but it's a different thing when your husband is on the stand. I watch Frank place his hand on the Bible, listen to the timbre and pitch of his voice as he promises to tell the whole truth and nothing but. He sounds confident. Robert has been preparing him for the defense hearing for the past two weeks; Frank knows there will be no surprise questions. It is the cross-examination we need to worry about.

"Mr. Johnson, could you outline for the court the events that led up to the fatal shooting of your brother, Jimmy, on the night of September twenty-eighth?"

"My brother had a drink problem," Frank begins, and for a second the room swims.

It is something I would never have expected him to say. This is the new Frank, the person he has become during his months of reflection.

"It wasn't constant. He could stay on an even keel for ages and then something would trigger him. I sensed it had got bad again, but I ignored it. I think I was trying to kid myself Jimmy was all right. The night he found out my wife, Beth, was having an affair he'd been in the pub. He came raging back to the farmhouse and got Beth and me out of bed. Was it true? he wanted to know. I told him it was and Jimmy was shattered by it."

No matter how many times I hear this, it never gets any easier to bear. Jimmy is dead and it is my fault and nothing will ever change that.

"Jimmy wanted to know what I was going to do about it. How was I going to get even with Gabriel? I told him I wasn't going to do anything. As far as I was concerned, Beth and Gabriel could carry on. That was the thing that set him off."

"Why did you feel like that, Mr. Johnson? Your wife was having an affair and you were content to let it continue?"

"If it made her happy, I wanted her to have it. Because I felt I'd ruined her life. I'd taken away the one person she loved more than anyone else. And, without him, her life had become too hard."

Robert's voice is low, gentle. "You are talking about your son, Bobby, aren't you, Mr. Johnson? Who died in a tree-felling accident three years ago."

Frank's face is drawn with pain now. "Yes. Beth made me promise I'd watch Bobby and keep him safe when the oak came down." His voice peters out, he is unable to carry on.

There's not a breath of sound in the courtroom, not a cough or a crackle of paper, all eyes on the man fighting his emotion in the witness stand.

"I knew it was dangerous and I still didn't watch him. I was too caught up in the work, you see. I told him to stay put in a safe spot, but he didn't listen. Well, he was nine. And when the tree came down he—Bobby—got in the way."

I see several of the female jurors surreptitiously wiping beneath their eyes. Perhaps they are mothers themselves. They can picture, all too clearly, the excruciating loss, the burden of Frank's guilt. How it would destroy a marriage, a life. Our marriage, our life.

Robert allows a lengthy pause, time for Frank to recover, before he begins speaking again. "Mr. Johnson, if we could move now to the shooting. I must ask you this because my learned friend will make much of it in cross-examination. You contest the accident happened in a moment of self-defense. You were trying to protect yourself, and indeed your brother, from injury."

"Yes. My brother was far too drunk to be handling the gun. I wanted to get it off him."

"Initially, you told police both you and Jimmy were holding the gun in a sort of tussle and that's when it went off. Is that right?"

"Yes."

"And you thought it fired at very close range?"

"I thought so, yes. But the whole thing happened so quickly, I couldn't be sure."

"The pathology report determined Jimmy had been shot at from a distance. At this point, you told police both of you had staggered backwards as the gun went off. It might appear you changed your story to fit the new evidence."

"It all happened in a split second. I was in total shock. My brother was bleeding on the floor and I was kneeling next to him, pressing my hand against his wound, trying to stop the blood . . . but I knew, even then . . . "

Frank is openly crying now. My heart breaks as I watch him. One time I asked him, in the depth of night when neither of us could sleep: *Is it worth it?* I didn't need to say any more, he knew what I meant. Was there any point in the two of us carrying on? Why should we bother? We had lost all the people we loved the most.

Frank had thought for a long time before he answered me. "We're guardians, you and me, of something even bigger than family. We have to preserve the land for the future. What would happen to it if we weren't here?"

Judge Miskin leans forward. "Do you need a break, Mr. Johnson? The court understands this is hard for you."

Frank shakes his head. "I'd like to carry on please, my lord. To answer the question, if I got my facts wrong, it's because my mind blanked in the moment, and afterwards it was hard to remember exactly how it happened."

Robert says: "In your police statement you said your brother had been provoking you. He called your wife some pretty unpalatable names which we need not repeat here. I must ask you, did that make you angry?"

"Not really. I knew he didn't mean it. Wouldn't remember it in the morning, anyway. I knew how much Jimmy loved Beth, he thought of her as his sister."

"Did you mean to harm your brother that night, Mr. Johnson?"

"No. I was trying to save both of us from injury. My whole life, I have only ever wanted to keep my brother safe."

At last, we have reached the crux of the trial—the prosecution's cross-examination of the defendant. My husband under attack, no way of helping him. The jury watching intently for any change in his voice, his expression. All too soon he will be found guilty or acquitted. And these minutes matter more than any others.

"Mr. Johnson." Donald Glossop begins in a light, conversational tone. "When did you first learn to shoot?"

I can tell from the way he hesitates Frank is thrown by the question. He glances at Robert on the counsel bench, trying to work out how best to answer.

"Allow me to simplify that for you. Growing up on a farm, I assume you learned to hunt at a young age?"

"Around six or seven, I think."

"And this was a skill you passed on to your son?"

"My father taught Bobby to shoot."

"At a similar age, six or seven?"

"Yes."

"It would be fair to say, then, guns were part and parcel of life on the farm?"

"Yes."

Frank's "yes" is cautious. He knows there is a sting coming, but he can't tell what it is.

"Guns left loaded in the porch, guns lying around in the

kitchen, guns in the dairy, guns in the lambing sheds. An entire arsenal of guns, in fact, and none of it kept locked up for safety."

Robert leaps to his feet, but before he can interject, the judge says: "We are not here to talk about the safekeeping of weapons, Mr. Glossop. Your point?"

"Just trying to paint a picture, my lord. Mr. Johnson, how many times have you fired a gun in your lifetime, do you think? Five thousand? Ten thousand? Let us say innumerable times. How is it, then, you did not know whose finger was on the trigger when the gun you were holding killed your brother?"

For a second Frank doesn't react, uncertain from Donald Glossop's delivery if he is asking a question.

"I know I grabbed hold of the barrel. I believe in wrenching it too forcefully the gun misfired."

"Are you a liar, Mr. Johnson?"

"No. I am not."

"Yet you changed your story, didn't you, once the pathology report came in? You *came up with* a scenario in which you might possibly have staggered."

I hate this man. For his silky-smooth sarcasm, for the inverted commas you hear within his speech.

"The two of us were holding the gun, that's what I remember. And then it went off."

"Yes, yes." The prosecutor is dismissive now. "So we have heard. You were angry with your brother, weren't you?"

"No."

"He had humiliated you."

"No."

"He knew where your Achilles' heel was, didn't he?" Donald Glossop turns to the jury. He is facing away from me, but I hear the smile in his voice. "Our siblings know us best, don't they? They know exactly how to hit where it hurts." He swings back around to face Frank. "Your brother insulted you that night, didn't he, Mr. Johnson?"

"Jimmy was drunk. He said a lot of nonsense. I took no notice of it."

"You love your wife, don't you?"

Frank looks confused, as I am, by the change of tack. "Yes."

"You've loved her a long time. How long, in fact?"

"Since I was thirteen."

"*Thirteen.*" Donald Glossop has softened his voice, he is lulling, cajoling. It doesn't fool me. "And you carried on loving her through some pretty tough times, as the court has heard. The son you lost in an accident for which your wife blamed you. Her subsequent affair with Gabriel Wolfe. But nothing swayed your love for her, is that right?"

"Yes."

Frank's voice is quiet. He is bracing himself. He has seen enough of Donald Glossop's performance, the rapid switches from light to dark, to know something vicious is coming.

"When Jimmy insulted Beth, you saw red, didn't you?"

"No."

"He abused her and you got angry."

"No."

"He wasn't abusive?" Donald Glossop glances down at the notes in his hand, but I can tell it's an affectation. He doesn't take time to read them. "According to the statement you gave to the police, he called her a slut. I would call that pretty abusive language, wouldn't you?"

The shocking term rings out, reverberating around Court Seven.

I watch the jury closely as Donald Glossop warms up for his kill. The woman with electric-blue specs clamps her lips into a thin line of disapproval. City Gent frowns at the offensive word. Even the young man in the front row, with his long, hippy hair and flowing shirt, looks shocked.

"He called your wife a *slut* and you lost it, didn't you?"

"No."

"You were in a rage when you grabbed the gun, weren't you?"

"No. That's not how it happened."

"You grabbed the gun and shot your brother, didn't you, Mr. Johnson? It was your finger on the trigger, wasn't it? A huntsman's instinct, all those years of firing guns at defenseless creatures. You did it without thinking."

"No."

Donald Glossop raises his voice to a theatrical shout. "You killed your brother, didn't you, Mr. Johnson? You were in a wild rage, and you shot him."

"No. No, for the last time, NO." Frank's voice is too loud, too stressed, a man provoked. Exactly as the prosecution intended.

I see the jury watch Frank, drinking in this first crack in his armor, a glimmer of the rage that lies beneath. Donald Glossop returns to the bench, leaving a stunned silence and the residue of accusation behind him.

This trial has been about performance, not facts. Donald Glossop is as rousing as any Shakespearean actor—he is Hamlet, Macbeth, and King Lear all at once—manipulating his audience into a frenzied, adrenaline-pumped acceptance of his speech.

I knew he was good. But, in cross-examination, he is brilliant. I fear he is unbeatable.

We are back in court, my parents, sister, and I, waiting for the closing speeches to begin. My mother, Eleanor, and I had sat through my father's mauling in the witness box as he stood up to defend Frank's character. I have never felt prouder of him, or more devastated. He tells me it was the least he could do, he says it was nothing. That's not how it looked. It felt as if he'd had his heart ripped out of him by the time the prosecution was finished.

The judge makes an announcement. "The defense has asked permission to bring one final character witness to court and I have decided to grant it."

"That's odd," Eleanor whispers. "Must have been really last minute or Robert would have said something yesterday."

Eleanor and Robert talk on the phone every evening. He tells her how Frank is doing—"Very well, all things considered"—and what he makes of the day's hearings.

"It's feeling good," he said last night. "That was a tough day for Frank, but it was always going to be. He handled it well."

I am watching Frank in the dock when Judge Miskin says: "Are you ready to call your witness, Mr. Miles?"

And it is his face I see crumpling when Nina walks up to the witness stand. The last time I saw Nina was at Jimmy's funeral, where we didn't exchange a single word, not even a glance. Her parents let it be known Nina wanted nothing more to do with me—or Frank, by association. It was fair enough, what I expected, what I deserved, but how I have missed her. How much strength it has taken to respect that wish, not to call her and say sorry, sorry, sorry. All the sorrys in the world would never be enough, I know that.

I stare at her hungrily as she swears her oath and when I glance again at Frank, I see he, too, is rapt, immersing himself in the sight of her, this woman we both loved so much from the first day we met her.

"Mrs. Johnson," Robert begins, and it stuns me. Her married name, the same as mine. The Johnson women we were meant to be. Oh, if only.

"You decided to come forward as a character witness for the defendant last night. Why was that?"

I watch Nina dart her eyes toward Frank in the dock, a second or two, no more. I doubt she really sees him. "I've been following the trial in the papers. And I felt strongly, in a way I could no longer ignore—" Nina has begun with confidence, her voice clear and strong. Now she pauses to collect herself. "I felt that Jimmy, my husband, would have wanted me to speak on behalf of his brother. In fact, I know he would. And I couldn't live with myself if I didn't."

"Thank you, Mrs. Johnson. May I commend you on your bravery. It can't have been an easy decision."

Nina gives Robert a sharp little nod of acknowledgment.

"What was Jimmy like in the days leading up to the shooting? Did you have any idea he would unravel in the way that has been described in court?"

She sighs. "In some ways, no. We were deliriously happy. We'd had the most wonderful wedding. We were trying for a baby. Everything was ahead. But Jimmy was very vulnerable and I was worried about him. I'd smelt alcohol on his breath when there was no reason for him to have been drinking."

"Was your husband unstable, Mrs. Johnson?"

I see how the question jars Nina, how she steels herself to answer. "Yes, he was. At times very."

"What was his reaction to learning of his sister-in-law's affair with Gabriel Wolfe?"

"He was brokenhearted. He didn't want to believe it was true, at first. Neither of us did. Beth and Frank meant everything to us."

I look down at the spots of tears dripping onto my knees and my father's hand placed on top of them. There's nothing new in this daily dose of shame. It's a very particular pain, learning the different ways in which I managed to hurt each member of my family.

"Was he angry?" Robert asks.

"Yes. He was beside himself. Mostly with Gabriel. I suppose it was easiest to hit out at him. But he was angry with Frank, too, once he realized he wasn't going to do anything about it. Jimmy couldn't understand Frank being so accepting of it."

"On the morning of the shooting, what was Jimmy's state of mind then?"

"Very hungover. Probably still drunk. He'd drunk almost an entire bottle of whisky—I found it later on, hidden behind the fridge. We didn't talk much, it was very early. But he was obsessing over Gabriel, how someone needed to teach him a lesson."

"That was the last time you saw him?"

"Yes." Her voice sounds small and bleak in the courtroom.

"I know this is painful, Mrs. Johnson. I won't keep you much longer. Can you tell the court how you learned of your husband's death?"

"Beth rang the pub."

"She told you Jimmy was dead?"

"She was crying so much I couldn't understand her. But she kept saying, 'Jimmy, Jimmy' . . . so I knew. She said there had been an accident at the farm. And Jimmy had been wounded."

"Those were her words? There had been an accident?"

"Yes."

"Were you surprised when you realized it was a shotgun accident?"

"Not really. Beth used to worry about the guns left lying around but that was when Bobby was alive. I was used to it."

"When you heard Frank Johnson had been arrested for murder, what did you think then?"

"It was absurd. The most far-fetched thing I'd ever heard. There isn't a person in the world who loved Jimmy more than Frank, not even me."

Finally, Nina turns to look at Frank. They gaze at one another for the first time in eight months, a gaze that feels as if it goes on and on, a ribbon of raw emotion flowing back and forth from the witness stand to the dock.

"Do you believe Frank Johnson intentionally shot your husband, Mrs. Johnson?"

Nina lifts her head. "I know he didn't. There is no way that would ever have happened."

When the phone in Eleanor's flat rings dead-on seven, as arranged, I snatch up the receiver on the first ring.

"Waiting by the phone, were you?" Frank is laughing.

"Frank—" I'm crying, even though I promised myself I wouldn't.

"Don't. Please don't."

"I miss you." I gasp out the words.

"Same."

"I love you."

"Same. You know I do."

There's so much I want to say to him: *Are you OK? What if we don't get the result we want? How will I manage? How will you?* But I know it's not what he needs from me tonight. We are expecting a verdict tomorrow, both of us need to stay strong.

We have only a few minutes for the call, the seconds are ticking by in silence. But it's a silence filled with us.

"Nina," he says, eventually.

"I know. So good of her."

"To see her, though."

"Incredible. She was so strong."

"He'd—be so proud of her."

"He would. He really would. And of you."

"Don't."

"He would be, though."

I listen to Frank trying to catch his breath and wonder how many men in prison cry when they phone their loved ones. Most of them, probably.

"Frank—"

"Yeah?"

I hesitate. There's something I want to tell him, something I have a suspicion about, but what if I am wrong?

A few months ago, I made a pretty momentous decision to throw away my diaphragm. I had ended things with Gabriel by then and Frank and I were trying to rebuild ourselves, piece by piece. We'd told each other everything, all the bad things, as if to say, this is me, in my worst, most ugly state, are you sure it's what you want? When we finally made love, reaching for each other tentatively in the darkness, it was almost like the first time. The surprising pleasure of it in those darkest of days, it became a tiny fragment of light, of hope. But, as each month passed, and my period arrived, I began to despair. I'd set my heart on another baby, for Frank even more than myself, and I started to think I had left it too late.

The last few days I've felt something, a nausea that isn't linked to the constant feeling of dread, a revulsion for certain tastes and smells, which reminds me of before. But what if I'm imagining it? I couldn't bear to raise Frank's hopes, then dash them. Not now, when the two of us are hanging on by a thread.

"I love you."

Frank laughs. "You said that already."

"I'm scared."

"I know. Me too."

"What if they find—" The beeps begin, perfect timing.

"The money's run out. I love you."

"Tomorrow," I say.

"Tomorrow."

The line goes dead, and I stand, for a long time, the phone pressed to my ear as if Frank is still there on the other end.

The Verdict

"All parties in the Crown versus Frank Johnson trial to Court Seven."

We have been waiting for a verdict for almost twenty-four hours. Yesterday, Judge Miskin summarized the essence of the case for the jury. The Crown contests Frank Johnson was provoked into shooting his brother in a flash of white-hot rage. The defense claims it was self-defense: Frank was trying to protect himself and his brother. To be convicted of murder, Judge Miskin said, the jury must believe, beyond reasonable doubt, that Frank Johnson intended to cause his brother serious harm when the gun was fired. For a manslaughter conviction, the jury must agree an unlawful act took place, namely the unlawful use of the weapon which killed him. If they believed Frank was holding the gun, with his finger on the trigger when it unintentionally went off, that would amount to manslaughter.

"Please take as long as you need to consider the evidence," he told them. "And I must urge you, once again, to disregard the press coverage which has accompanied this case."

Robert told us juries can come to a decision within an hour. Often a good sign when they do, he said. As the afternoon dragged by without a verdict, we felt more and more despondent. We were exhausted by waiting and the days of tension leading up to it; I just wanted it over and done with.

Now, with the decision upon us, my body freezes in rebellion. My limbs refuse to move. Blood-rush in my brain. All the fear and anxiety I have tried to suppress rising up to crush me.

"I can't do it." I gasp the words.

"Yes, you can." My father puts an arm around my shoulders. "Frank needs you there, now more than ever."

My mother, on my other side, urges me to look at her.

"Remember, my love, we are here, every step of the way. And we always will be. You are not alone."

"Frank's not guilty. He'll be walking out of here a free man," Eleanor says, in a confident tone that doesn't fool me. "You'll see."

There is a sickening quiet within court today, the air thick with expectation. No one seems to be talking, not the journalists on the press bench, nor counsel, nor the people who have queued for their spot in the gallery since eight o'clock this morning for the final day of this trial. I look at the faces around me and wonder what it is that brings them here. This snippet of human drama, a husband and wife whose lives have been wrecked not once, but twice, by death. A well-known author in the mix. A secret love affair which became a national talking point. When the trial is over, they will return to their lives and forget all about us.

The jury files in, one by one, and I am so tense it is all I can do not to scream. I examine their faces as they take their seats. Do they look grimmer than usual? They are dressed smartly for their last, and most significant, day in court. A day when all the power lies with them. Even the young hippy has put on a jacket and tie. City Gent, who has been elected foreman, is wearing a striped shirt with a white collar. Electric-Blue Specs is wearing a dress with a big floppy bow on each shoulder.

Not a single one glances at Frank in the dock. It feels sinister to me, as if they cannot bear to look at the man they are about to find guilty. Then again, they have scarcely looked at him throughout the whole trial, apart from when he was on the witness stand.

The foreman stands up. My heart folds in on itself.

"Members of the jury," the court clerk says. "Have you reached a verdict upon which you are all agreed?"

"Yes," the foreman answers.

"Do you find the defendant guilty or not guilty of count one, the charge of murder?"

The pause can last no more than a second. But you don't know how long a second can feel when your husband stands accused of murder.

"Not guilty."

I must have been holding my breath. It rushes out of me, an outpouring of relief. Beside me, Eleanor shouts, "Yes," and my father turns to me and says: "Thank God, thank God, thank God."

It sounds like an incantation the way he says it.

A buzz of conversation rises from the press bench.

"May we have quiet in the court, please," the judge says. The clerk waits for the noise to settle before he speaks again.

"Do you find the defendant guilty or not guilty of count two, the charge of manslaughter?"

Another fragment of time passes. There are lifetimes, whole worlds within it.

"Guilty."

The word is a pistol fired in the courtroom.

"No! Noooooo!" My cool, collected sister is screaming into the silence.

There is the roar of shock around me, from Eleanor, from my father, from my mother, and from all these people for whom the verdict does not matter at all.

I'm on my feet, crying his name, batting away my parents and sister, who are trying to drag me back to my seat. I lean over the balcony, my father still tugging at my wrist and, at last, Frank looks up at me. He is already standing, two prison officers on either side of him, but he holds my gaze for as long as he can. He even smiles—how does he manage to do that?—and gives me a single nod before he is led away.

September 28, 1968

Leo and I are still cowering beneath the table when we hear the front door opening and footsteps running along the hall.

Gabriel's or Jimmy's?

"Beth!" Leo shrieks in terror, and I pull him more tightly against me.

"It's all right," Gabriel says, coming into the kitchen. "You can come out, Leo. It's going to be OK."

In the bright light of the kitchen, the three of us stand for a moment, looking at each other.

"Thank God," I say, meaning, *You're alive*, and Gabriel reaches out, as he did before, to touch my face.

"I'm going to drive Jimmy back to the farm, but he'll only go if you come too. I think he wants to make sure you're back with Frank."

"No way," Leo says, clamping himself to my side. "You're not leaving me."

"Leo," Gabriel says, "listen. I won't be long. You'll be safe here, I'll lock the door."

"No. No. No."

Leo has his eyes squeezed shut and he shakes his head back and forth, back and forth. He is visibly trembling.

"Leo can come too," I say. "We can't leave him on his own like this. We'll sit in the back together."

Outside, Jimmy is leaning against the bonnet of Gabriel's pale blue Wolseley, his whole body tilting to the left, as if he might just slide to the ground in a moment. It's an incongruous sight, this raddled, red-faced farmer wearing yesterday's clothes, slumped on a car so spotless and shiny it looks as if it's come straight from a showroom.

"Into the car, then," Gabriel says. He is curt, a little sharp, the voice of an irritated parent, not an equal.

Jimmy lifts his head to look at him. "You talking to me?"

"Yes. Let's get on with it, shall we?"

I have not seen this side of Gabriel before.

"Who d'you think you are?" Jimmy's voice is thick with alcohol, he is slurring like a cartoon drunk. "You can fuck off."

"I've brought Beth with me, like you wanted. So, please. Do us all a favor. Get in the car."

To my surprise, Jimmy complies. Perhaps he is responding to Gabriel's tone, which is crisp and authoritative; perhaps he is exhausted and just wants it to be over.

Gabriel glances at me, raises his eyebrows a fraction; he wasn't expecting it to be this easy. *We're through the worst of it*, his look says.

The drive from Meadowlands to Blakely Farm takes only a few minutes but tonight it feels ten times longer. Jimmy, slumped in the front, asks the same question, over and over. "Why d'you do it, Beth? Why d'you have to do it?"

"I'm sorry, Jimmy, I'm so sorry."

"'S'not right. After ever'thing you and Frank have been through. Why d'you do it?"

I don't know how to answer him except to say that everything we've been through is the reason why. I know it. And Frank knows it. The day Bobby died ended something more than just his life.

Leo is gripping my hand so tightly it's beginning to hurt. He is eleven, still a little boy, really, and he has seen far too much.

"Here we are," Gabriel says, falsely bright, as we turn into our yard.

The last time he was here was for the wedding. A week ago today, almost impossible to grasp how much has happened since then. Since Jimmy stood in the barn, his brother next to him, watching his bride walk toward him along a roll of red carpet.

Gabriel parks outside the farmhouse and I leap out to help Jimmy.

"Here," I offer him a hand.

Jimmy looks up at me with a lazy, drunken smile, his eyes half-closed. "Tired now," he says, dropping his head down.

I pull him toward me but Jimmy resists, slumping back into his seat.

"Here, let me help you," Gabriel says, switching off the engine. He turns to his son in the back. "This will only take two seconds."

I see how Frank flinches when we come into the kitchen, Gabriel and I, with Jimmy between us. It is the first time he's seen us together since he learned of the affair.

"Wasted a whole day and half a night looking for you, you idiot," he says, turning to his brother. To Jimmy, Frank's voice is warm and affectionate. He doesn't look at us. "When are you going to stop scaring the life out of me? You're a married man now. Going to be a father one of these days."

"Sorry," Jimmy says. He topples into Frank's outstretched arms, leans his forehead against his brother's. For a long moment, they embrace.

"No more of this, OK?" Frank says, softly. "My heart can't take it."

"I'll get going, then," Gabriel says, and Frank looks at him for the first time.

"Thank you for bringing him home."

Frank, thanking the man who has been sleeping with his

wife. Somehow his voice is controlled. He really does sound thankful.

But the effect on Jimmy is incendiary, as if he's been slapped. "Not havin' that," Jimmy says, swiveling sharply so he is only a foot or so away from Gabriel. His voice is strangely distinct now. "Thank *you* for nothing," he says. "You've ruined my brother's life."

"Now, look," Gabriel says. "Let's not go through all this again. I've told you how sorry I am."

I hear all kinds of things in Gabriel's voice: frustration, sadness, regret. But Jimmy registers only the note of slight condescension, or at least, that's what I imagine. There's no knowing what Jimmy is thinking in this state, or if he's even thinking at all.

He reaches out and grips Gabriel's throat with his strong hands, as if to throttle him.

A scream rises from me, long and bloodcurdling. My nerves are shot to pieces.

Frank yells, "Jimmy, no—" and darts toward him.

"All right, all right, keep your—" Jimmy says as he releases his hands from Gabriel's neck and takes a step back, but the rest of his sentence is lost as, just then, the door bursts open.

It's Leo.

Leo with a shotgun aimed at Jimmy.

Leo, staggering backward from the force of the gunfire.

Horror seconds, nothing making sense. Jimmy on the floor, silent, motionless, blood pooling across his pale shirt. Frank, kneeling beside him, his palm pressed to the shot wound, trying to contain his sobs long enough to blow air into his brother's lungs. The child's screams. Over and over, he shrieks. His face bone-white with shock, shotgun dangling at his side. Gabriel, not moving to comfort him, not at first. As if we have been frozen into some awful tableau, and for a moment, none of us can break free.

"I'm calling an ambulance," I cry, coming to my senses.

But Frank gets up from the floor. There is blood all over his hands, his face. His right sleeve is soaked in it, all the way up to his elbow.

"Not yet, I need a minute to think. He's gone. Jimmy's dead, Beth."

At this, Leo begins to cry. "Have I killed him? Dad? Have I killed him?"

Gabriel swoops his son up into his arms and Leo wraps his legs around his waist like a small child. Buries his face in Gabriel's neck. "It's all right," Gabriel says, rubbing the small of his back.

But it isn't all right. It will never be all right again.

Frank is crying too. Silent tears course down his face but his voice is terse, businesslike. "Get the boy out of here," he says to Gabriel.

"What are you talking about? We have to call the police."

"I'm sorry," Leo whimpers. "I'm sorry, Dad. I didn't mean to."

"Beth." Frank's voice is sharp. "Get them out of here, you go with them. I'll deal with this. I'll say it was an accident."

"I'm not leaving you."

"Right now. I mean it. You must do as I tell you. *Please*, Beth." He yells to make me understand, trying to penetrate my shock, and perhaps his.

"We have to tell the truth about this—" Gabriel says, but Frank cuts him off.

"No. The boy will end up in court. He's eleven, isn't he? They will make him testify. Is that what you want?" He looks down at Jimmy's body. "He's my brother, let me deal with it my way."

All Gabriel can ask on the car journey back to Meadow-lands is why.

"Why would Frank do that? Why would he take responsibility for something he didn't do?"

I'm crying too hard to answer him.

My foolish, noble husband, with his misplaced sense of guilt.

1969

Farming does not give time off for tragedy, heartbreak, or prison terms: I am exhausted physically, mentally, emotionally as I haul myself around our land, but it is one of our busiest seasons. There are late-born lambs to console me that arrived when I was away, and a few last ewes still waiting to birth. I check their rears for any signs of labor, press my palms to their bellies in search of a breech, the act now as routine and meditative to me as it once was to Jimmy and Frank when I first watched them. I mix their feed and the sheep swarm around me, allowing me to trail my fingers along their wiry, woolen coats. After the days in court, the release of being here is like a shot of adrenaline.

It is little more than a year since a dog tore into this field and attacked our lambs, igniting a sequence of events none of us could have imagined. That Leo would appear, looking a bit like the boy I had lost, needing a mother when I was still so desperate to be one. That Gabriel and I would be together again day after day and we would realize the feelings we had kept tamped down inside ourselves had been there all along, just waiting to reappear. That this man I had obsessed over, this boy who once opened me up to desire then abandoned me, or so I thought, would turn out to be not the villain I'd created in my mind but someone I still cared about, someone I still loved.

When I see Gabriel walking up the field toward me, I think perhaps he is an apparition, some kind of hallucination from my tired, fragile mind. But the man keeps on coming, his tall, willowy form unmistakable to me.

"Beth." He stops a couple of feet from me.

I push back a strand of hair with a hand coated in sheep feed.

"I had to come."

"OK," I say, although it isn't. It's the opposite of OK. I am not ready to see Gabriel. I am not ready to see anyone.

"I never thought he'd go down for it. Robert was meant to be the best there is, everyone thought he'd win. I'm so sorry, Beth. I've let you down."

I don't want to have this conversation. This pointless, hopeless conversation.

"How long will he get, do you think?" Gabriel asks.

"Robert says to expect eight years. But he could get out sooner. Maybe even in five, if we're lucky."

I grimace at the word, so does Gabriel. Lucky, we are not.

"I'm sorry," Gabriel says again. "I should never have let Frank do this. I didn't want to at the time. Do you remember—" He breaks off, floundering.

I am a wall of silence. I know I need to speak. I need to help Gabriel deal with his guilt. It's just that I am so tired. Tired of all of it.

"Robert let us down too," Gabriel says.

"That's not fair. He did what he could. The story never really added up. He didn't have the full facts."

"I'll never understand why Frank did it. Why would he take the fall for a child who wasn't his?"

It must be the exhaustion, there's no fight left in me. No resistance. Words begin to form in my mind, words I must not say, but they're rising, unbidden in my throat, in my mouth, rushing out of me, into the air. "He couldn't save your son."

"What are you talking about? He did save him. He's gone to prison for him."

My heart is hammering so hard I feel I might pass out. "Your first son."

It takes a second, that is all.

"Bobby?" he says, voice faltering on his name.

I incline my head, the merest breath of acknowledgment, it is as much as I can do.

"My *son*. He was my son?"

He roars in pain. I have never heard anything like it. This howl. This long yell of torment and rage and sorrow as, at last, it all falls into place.

"Gabriel."

I move closer to him, but he backs away. "Don't come near me."

I watch as Gabriel covers his face with his hands and begins to sob. This thing between us, this shocking, hidden thing, it is unforgivable. I've always known that. And so has Frank.

He looks at me again, brushing tears from his cheeks. "Leo looked like Bobby, didn't he? I see it now, that photograph of yours, the one Leo liked so much. Christ, poor Leo. You cheated him out of a brother. And me out of a son. You stole him. You and Frank."

"He was my son too. And you weren't there for me, remember?"

"But—" Gabriel's voice rises to a wail. "I would have stood by you! I loved you. Why didn't you tell me?"

"I wanted to. Your mother knew. And I hoped she'd tell you for me."

"My mother knew? My mother?"

The horror in his face. I am almost too afraid to carry on.

"I didn't tell her, she worked it out. I thought she might want to help me, knowing it was your child I was carrying. But all she cared about was protecting your reputation. She made me promise never to tell you. She paid me off, Gabriel. A big fat check for my discretion."

"No," he says. "No, no, no. She wouldn't do that to me."
The pain in his voice, the doubt, it is heartbreaking.

"You know she would. When did your mother ever care about anyone other than herself?"

There is a long silence. And then Gabriel looks at me, eyes like ice. "All those stories you told me about Bobby. That was your guilt, wasn't it? You'd kept him from me all these years, and you thought you'd throw me a few snippets to make yourself feel better."

Rage explodes within me. The last bit of stored anger breaking free. A wild, wild woman screaming in her field of sheep. "Frank is in prison because your *son* murdered his brother. He took the fall so Leo didn't have to. So *you* didn't have to watch your son stand up and testify in court. So *you* wouldn't have him taken away. And, yes, it's because he got to be Bobby's father and you didn't. And, yes, he felt guilty about it, especially after Bobby died. But where were you when I needed you? Where were you when I was asked to leave school, pregnant and unmarried at seventeen? Frank took on me and another man's baby without a second thought. Because he loved me. And Frank"—I'm crying hard now—"was the best father to Bobby. Better than you could ever have been."

I sink to my knees, bury my face in my hands.

After the shooting, we tried our best—Gabriel, Frank, and me—to convince Leo it was an accident. We knew he never meant to shoot Jimmy, we told him. Hadn't he just been trying to protect his father? Any son would have done the same.

Even so, Leo became more and more depressed as the months went by and the trial drew near. In the end, Frank went to visit him at Meadowlands, knowing it was a risk in a village full of gossips as it meant breaking his bail conditions, but he did it anyway.

"What's the point of me doing all of this, if the guilt still poisons him?" Frank had said. "I'm going to make him understand, once and for all, that he's just an unlucky kid who got tangled up in an adult mess that was way beyond his comprehension."

"I'm sorry," I mumble at Gabriel from behind my hands, I cannot bring myself to look at him. The rage has left, I am ashamed. "I'm an awful person. I do terrible things. No wonder you hate me. I hate myself."

I sense Gabriel kneeling down on the damp grass, feel his hands on mine, gently lifting them from my face.

The way he is looking at me, this stare that has everything in it, grief and sadness and passion and loss, innocence and anger and a light slowly fading. A lie that has been at the center of everything. A lie that has always been too big for absolution. And yet, what I read in Gabriel's eyes is not blame or hate, as I expect, but love.

We are embracing—holding on to each other really— while the sky slowly darkens around us and sheep mewl and chunter and birds swoop to their nests, in the place Bobby, our son, most loved to be.

Before

I know I am pregnant even before I miss my period. It is not because my breasts are tender or the feeling of nausea when I wake up, or any of the other telltale signs I have been reading about furtively in the library. I just know.

The last time we made love—how it hurts to remember—was in the middle of the night when I stayed with Gabriel in Oxford. It was that magical semiconscious intimacy, our bodies taking over before our minds could catch up, reaching for each other in a dream. Afterward, I couldn't remember if my diaphragm was in. Later, at home, I realize it wasn't—the diaphragm is sitting smugly in its case—but by then I am far too heartbroken to care. Gabriel and I are over and all I want, all I can think about, is finding my way back to him.

As each day passes without my period arriving and with new, incontrovertible evidence—my breasts swollen and mapped with blue veins, the constant need to urinate, an intolerance for aromas I have always liked: frying bacon, coffee, even perfume—I know I must tell my parents. But, somehow, I can't find the words.

I think about Gabriel almost constantly. I pick up the phone to call him a hundred times, two hundred. But he hasn't been in touch since we broke up and I fear there is only one reason for that—he is in love with Louisa. Without realizing it, I gave him the ending he wanted.

What would Gabriel make of my pregnancy? He's honorable, I do know that. He might offer to marry me. But would I want to marry him, knowing he loved someone else?

At night I write letters to him, pouring out my regret and sadness. How sorry I am for the things I said. How I wish I could take them back. How desperately I miss him. Also, there's something you should know . . .

I think I might be pregnant.

No matter how many times I write that sentence, the words always look too shocking, too final. Every time, I rip the letter into tiny pieces.

After two weeks of indecision, I walk over to Meadowlands, knocking on the front door before I can change my mind.

I am expecting Gabriel home for the Christmas holidays, but it's Tessa who answers, and she looks startled to see me. "Beth. What can I do for you?"

"I was hoping to talk to Gabriel."

"He's not here, I'm afraid."

"Oh," I reply, and a lump forms in my throat as I try to work out what to do next. I hadn't thought about the possibility that Gabriel might not be home.

My breathing quickens and Tessa must notice because she says suddenly, "Why don't you come in, Beth." She turns and heads inside, and I follow her automatically.

In the little pink sitting room where Gabriel and I once lay head to toe on the velvet sofa drinking wine, Tessa motions to the armchairs in front of the fire. "Sit."

I perch awkwardly and wait as she pauses to examine me.

"When will Gabriel be here?" I manage to ask, breaking the silence.

"Next week, I expect. Although I must admit, I'm a little surprised to see you. My understanding is that you and he are no longer together."

I am lost for words. Wounded by her casual confirmation of our breakup. And the fact that she knows.

I don't know what to do. Or where to turn. I'd hoped

Gabriel would be here and I could tell him about the pregnancy and together we'd decide what happened next.

Unconsciously, I rest my palm against my belly. Thinking of the embryo growing within me. No more than a quarter inch long, the library book tells me.

Tessa is watching me, with her eyes narrowed.

"For heaven's sake. Are you pregnant, Beth? Is that what this is all about?"

Before I know what I'm saying, I gulp out a "Yes."

As soon as I admit it, I feel relief. Someone other than me knows the truth. Surely, Tessa will want to help me now she knows I am carrying her son's child?

"How did it happen?"

"I—we—were careless in Oxford."

Tessa tuts. "How irresponsible. I'm rather surprised Gabriel hasn't thought to tell me himself."

"He doesn't know yet."

It's strange how Tessa's face floods with sudden light. She leans forward to pat my hand. "You're keeping it from Gabe, sensible girl. We don't need to worry him with it, now, do we?"

"Actually, I was planning on telling him today. That's why I'm here." Tessa gets up and begins to pace the room in tight little circles. "Let me think for a minute. Do your parents know?"

"Not yet."

"Even better."

"They might begin to notice after a while."

Another snap change in Tessa's lovely face. "Surely you're not thinking of keeping it?"

"What else would I do?"

"My dear, I sometimes forget that you're a village girl and have seen nothing of the outside world yet. There are places we can go to sort the whole thing. Nothing backstreet, don't worry. All one needs is money and a willingness to travel abroad for it. I'm so glad you thought to bring this to me."

I stare up at Tessa in distress. "Are you talking about abortion?" I whisper the word as if even saying it out loud could offend my unborn child. I was brought up a Catholic. Not a very good one, it's true—my pregnancy is evidence of that—but the years of indoctrination have made me sure of one thing. This tiny fertilized egg inside me will one day become a baby. And I will love that baby and give it the best life I can.

"Yes, that's right. Far easier than you might think. There is no need for you or Gabe to wreck your lives over one stupid little mistake."

"I don't think this baby is going to wreck my life . . . or Gabriel's."

A pause.

"You seem determined to tell him."

"Don't you think he'd want to know? He might want to be involved, it's his child we're talking about."

"Ah. I begin to see where you're coming from. Did you think you could talk Gabriel into marrying you? I can't see that happening, Beth, I really can't. Don't take this the wrong way but Gabe seemed rather relieved when he said you'd broken up. I think it was a strain on him, to be quite honest, trying to keep the thing going when you never saw each other. And of course, he's got a whole new scene at Oxford. Lots of new friends."

My resolution to be brave has vanished. "Is he still with Louisa?" I choke out the words.

At this, a look passes over Tessa's face that I cannot read. Is it confusion? Or relief? Or something else? "Early days, of course, but they *are* a good match. And Louisa's father can do so much for Gabriel's writing career. I know you wouldn't want to get in the way of that." She laughs a fake, tinkly laugh. "Perhaps they'll move to Hollywood when they leave Oxford. Perhaps we all will. Get away from this beastly weather."

I shiver, despite the warmth of the fire. I should never have come. I need to get as far away from Tessa Wolfe as possible. I need to lie in a quiet room and cry for everything I have lost.

"Oh, are you leaving?" Tessa says, when I stand.

I nod.

"Hold on two secs, I have something for you."

I watch as Tessa sits down at her desk beneath the window. I remember coveting it the first time I saw the desk with its pretty mother-of-pearl inlays, the secret hidden drawers with their dainty gilt handles. *One day*, I thought, *I will buy myself a desk like this and fill it with treasure. Love notes and rare feathers, strangely shaped pebbles, secret poems. Ribbons and stamps and bottles of bright-colored ink.*

Tessa crosses the room and hands me an envelope. "No need to look at it now. But it will help, whatever you decide."

I open it, of course. Inside is a check for a thousand pounds, the name left blank. I gasp. My parents earn less than this in a year. "It's too much."

"Nonsense. I insist you take it. A lot of girls in your situation choose adoption. I can recommend a very good agency in Knightsbridge."

I stare at the rose-pink carpet, dangerous feelings whirring through me. "My" situation. Not Gabriel's. This is how it works in this world of hers.

"Beth?" Tessa waits until I look up at her. "I ask one small thing in return. Promise you won't tell Gabriel about the pregnancy. His life at Oxford is just beginning, I couldn't bear for this to ruin his prospects. And if you do decide to keep it, could you be discreet about the baby's father?"

I don't answer her. I can't. It's fine for my life to be derailed so long as her precious son's remains intact.

"Is that a yes?"

I nod my assent. It's the only way I can get out of the room, the house, the entire toxic universe of the family Wolfe.

Outside, I stand on the steps for a moment, taking in the paradisial acres, the lake with its gliding white swans, a glorious setting for our short-lived love story. Turns out, it was nothing but an illusion.

I draw fresh air deep into my lungs. Breathe out all the ugliness of the past thirty minutes.

It is over. It is over. It is over.

On the last day of term, I am called to the headmistress's office.

"What now?" Helen says, worried.

She is my best friend and I have always told her everything. But the secret growing inside my belly is mine alone, for now.

My thoughts are no longer on Shakespeare or the Brontë sisters or St Anne's College, Oxford. I am not interested in Charles Dickens and his depiction of the industrial revolution. I do not care about the Christmas parties I have been invited to, nor the dresses my classmates plan on wearing to them. I gaze out of my classroom window, knowing my life is about to change forever. But, for a short while, there are only two of us in this private bubble of mine, me and my unborn child. It feels sacred, somehow. I don't want to share it.

I knock at the headmistress's door thinking how much I have changed in a matter of weeks. There is nothing she could say to hurt me now. It's strange but I feel protected by the tiny, precious secret within me.

"Elizabeth. Come in and sit down." She gestures to the chair on the other side of her desk.

She has a small Christmas tree in her office, decorated with red, silver, and gold baubles by some of the first form. Once upon a time, I was one of those girls, eleven years old and thrilled to be invited inside Sister Ignatius's private enclave.

"I considered bringing in Father Michael, the school governor, for this meeting but I decided, in the circumstances, discretion would be best. This matter is for you and me alone."

For a moment we regard each other, the nun and I, my head spinning with questions. Does she know? How could she? There are only two people in the world who know I am pregnant. Me and Tessa Wolfe. It can't be Gabriel's mother. All she cared about was keeping my pregnancy hushed up for as long as possible.

"I have written to your parents this afternoon to inform them that regrettably you won't be returning to the convent next term, Elizabeth."

"I don't understand."

"I think you do."

"Please explain it to me."

"You're courageous, I admire that about you. The school has decided it is no longer appropriate to keep you here. Places are discretionary and fiercely sought after, as you know. We have decided to offer your place to a pupil who is able to adhere to the school's moral code of conduct. We expect our girls at the top of the school to set a strong example for the younger pupils. And you made no attempt to conceal your unseemly behavior, Elizabeth, quite the opposite. However, this is not an expulsion as such and I have explained that to your parents. We invite you back to sit your A level exams here in June if you should so wish."

She stares at me, hard. "Although I think that most unlikely. Don't you?"

"Who told you?"

The words are out before I can stop them.

"I had a visitor yesterday who gave generously to our donation fund for the new science block. She was most anxious your delicate situation should not be found out in school. Better to have you off-site as soon as possible, before the rumors started."

"She bought me off, too," I say, tears stinging my eyes. "You can do that when you're rich."

To my surprise, Sister Ignatius laughs. A genuine laugh that appears to have actual warmth in it. "You're better off without people like that, in my opinion. You know, I'm not too worried about you, Elizabeth. You're smart. You're full of grit. You'll come out on top in the end. I don't doubt it for one second."

Frank arrives at our cottage a few days after Christmas. How different he looks without his school uniform, as if the mundanity of black blazer and gray trousers concealed the well-madeness of his form. His hair is still damp from his bath, and the scent of soap clings to his skin.

"There's something I'd like to show you," he says.

"What is it?"

When Frank smiles his eyes scrunch so tightly together, they almost disappear. I've never noticed that about him before.

"If I told you that would ruin the surprise, wouldn't it?"

Outside the cottage is an old Land Rover, its original color hidden almost entirely beneath layers of dried-on mud.

I notice Frank's hand on the steering wheel, tanned and strong looking but with surprisingly elegant fingers, the nails cut short. When he changes gear the muscles of his forearm move beneath his skin.

We turn into a long dirt track leading to the Johnsons' place, Blakely Farm. I know where Frank lives even though I haven't been here before.

"We're going to your house?"

"Nope." He parks the Land Rover beside an iron gate. "We've arrived," he says, grinning at me.

I follow him around the perimeter of a long, sloping field until we reach a vast oak tree at the far end. "What a tree," I say, to be polite. "It's enormous." If Frank Johnson thinks I'm a tree-hugging kind of girl, he's got another think coming.

He points to a dark hole at the throat of the tree, just above my eye level. "Look in there," he says. "But don't put your face too close."

At first, it's so dark I can't see anything but then I begin to make out the shape of a nest and within it two tiny birds, barely covered in fluff, their minuscule yellow beaks open.

"A nest. Isn't it the wrong time of year? It's so cold. What are they?"

"Blackbirds, probably. They've come early. I think they've been abandoned. I've been checking in on them for a couple of days. They're starving."

"Will they die?"

"Not if we save them."

"We?"

Frank smiles. "Or you? I thought you might like looking after them. It's kind of a full-time job at the beginning. And I'm working all day on the farm. But I'll take the nest home and chance it, unless you want to."

"I'll do it," I say, decisively. "Why don't we take them now? They might not last the night out here."

"I had a feeling you'd say that. I've got everything we need in the back of the Land Rover."

He makes to go but I reach out to halt him, my hand on his arm. "Do you love me, Frank?"

He doesn't seem in the least surprised by the question, even though I have asked it out of the blue.

"Yes. But I'd settle for being friends."

"I'd like that."

"Friends, you mean?"

"Or more than friends. When we know each other better."

It seems so simple and innocent, his sudden laughter. *So this is Frank Johnson,* I think, a little wistfully, *with his wholesome, uncomplicated life.*

Frank calls for me at the cottage when he's finished on the farm. First, we inspect my nestlings, who are thriving; every day they gain weight and a few more feathers. Then we drive around the country lanes in the thick winter dark, talking. We talk about our families, the friends we like from school, the ones we don't. Music, our favorite records, surprised to discover we have similar tastes. Frank doesn't ask me about Gabriel or why I have left the convent, or whether I still plan on going to Oxford. I don't ask Frank why he didn't stay on to finish his A levels.

I notice he is most animated when he talks about the farm, even boring things like the stray sheep that took him hours to find or how he is so used to the stink of slurry he doesn't notice it anymore. I see how this is his world, his oxygen, and when he's outside it he struggles to feel like himself.

"Show me," I say to him one evening.

"Show you what?"

"Your favorite place on the farm."

This smile of his, so broad and comforting, like a shot of

euphoria. It makes me feel happy just seeing it, and I want to keep flicking the switch.

"I have Sunday afternoon off," he says. "You need to see it in daylight."

I should have known he would bring me back to the oak tree.

We stand beneath it looking out at a stripped landscape that seems rigid with cold. But I see how the field slopes gently downhill, offering a view of beyond, a patchwork of brown-and-ochre squares bound by hedgerows, the rise of a hill in the distance, a feeling of infinity. I see why he loves it.

"Does all that land belong to the farm?" I ask, but Frank doesn't answer me.

He says my name. Softly.

I know instantly from the way Frank is looking at me what is about to happen. My whole body is alert to it, even the air feels dense with expectation.

Frank steps closer until we are only inches apart. He is going to kiss me.

"Wait." I hold up a palm. "It's not that I don't want to," I say quickly, when his face falls. "I do want to. But there's something I need to tell you first."

"All right."

He stands there, calmly waiting. Unconcerned.

"I'm pregnant. I'm keeping it."

Frank's face does not change. He nods, considering what I have told him. Takes his time. Seconds pass, perhaps a whole minute.

"And the other fella. Doesn't want to know, I suppose?"

"Doesn't know. And never will. We broke up so . . . "

"Ah. I see. Well, in that case . . . " He smiles at me until I find myself smiling back. The two of us grinning like idiots when I thought I had nothing to grin about, beneath an ancient oak tree on a wintry afternoon. "Isn't that something to celebrate?"

Frank opens his arms wide, an invitation. And laughs as I step into them.

Part Five

Grace

1975

Grace is weaving down Top Field with two ewes and a cluster of newborn lambs. She knows how to tack back and forth across our field in a slow zigzag, making sure her babies walk in the right direction. She knows when to stop and wait so the lambs stay close to their mothers. She chats to them incessantly, just like her uncle used to, and her brother, Bobby. She is five years old.

One of these lambs is more special to Grace than the others because yesterday she birthed it by herself. When its legs began to appear she knelt beside the ewe, grabbed the ankles in her small hands, and tugged, waiting for each contraction to ease it out a little farther each time.

"Pull hard now, Gracie. Give it everything you've got," my father said, when the lamb's little black nose first appeared.

I knew he was fighting the urge to help her. I was too.

Grace yanked hard, grunting like a heavyweight wrestler, and at last the lamb slithered free. I wish I'd had a camera on me. Her face. I wish Frank could have seen it, the mixture of pride and awe when she turned to grin at me and made a thumbs-up sign.

She was born, not on the kitchen floor like her brother, but at Dorchester Hospital, eight months after the trial finished. I waited until the risks of early miscarriage had passed before I told Frank I was expecting his baby. I knew how much it would mean to him, another child, his own flesh and blood this time.

"Guess what?" I said, the next time he phoned. "I'm

pregnant. Thirteen weeks yesterday. We're having a baby, Frank."

In the short silence before he spoke, I pictured him in the prison telephone box, fighting his emotion. I heard his rapid breaths, the croakiness of his voice when he spoke.

"How?"

"I threw my diaphragm away, a few months before the trial. I didn't want to tell you in case it didn't happen."

"We're having a baby? You're pregnant? We are going to have another child?"

Frank was shouting now. Shouting and laughing. Repeating my news until it had sunk in.

Remembering the joy in his voice when I told him consoles me on the loneliest nights.

When I first saw our daughter, I felt such a rush of elation. She had been born at exactly the right time to be a woman.

"For you," I whispered to the tiny baby at my breast, "the world is changing."

You have a daughter, I wrote to Frank that same afternoon. *She's the most beautiful thing you've ever seen. Will you choose her name?*

His reply came by return of post. *Let's call her Grace.*

I thought, *Yes, Frank gets it. She is our second grace. She is our new beginning.*

I hoped Frank would let me visit him in prison once our daughter had been born. But, every time I asked him, he said no.

"Please, Beth, let me get this done in my own way."

I railed at him sometimes. "Why is it all about what you need? What about me? What about me needing to see you?" I shouted, flaring up on one of our weekly Sunday-night phone calls. "You're ashamed for me to see you in there?

You'd rather go years without seeing your wife or being able to hold your child in your arms because you're ashamed of what I might think? Then I'm ashamed you think so little of me."

I hung up on Frank before he could answer and was filled with remorse for the rest of the night. I'd wasted our phone call. And, worse, I'd upset him. And now I had to wait a whole week before I could talk to him again.

Two days later, his letter arrived.

Dear Beth,

I have this picture in my head and it's the thing that sustains me, every single day. I imagine myself coming back to the farm one bright, spring afternoon. A cold, crisp, sunny day, the kind of weather that has always been our favorite. There are new lambs in the field and all Bobby's favorite birds are back for the summer chittering away, making a racket.

I step onto our land and breathe it all in. I'm home, I say to myself. I'm home. That's when I see you with Grace, for the very first time . . . and it feels so pure, Beth. I don't want this place in your head or hers. I know I'm being selfish. Please try to understand—?

Frank

My father visits Frank every month to keep him updated on the farm.

When Frank was sentenced to eight years in Wandsworth Prison, both my parents resigned instantly from their teaching posts in Ireland. Within three months they were back in Dorset helping me manage the farm.

It has been joyous seeing the way the farm has changed them. And how they have changed the farm. My mother, whom I couldn't have imagined without her books and her marking, is out with us in the fields all day. She lives in an old pair of my father's cords and has a permanent outdoor tan. She looks years younger.

My mother found an old handwritten recipe for cheddar muddled in among the farm accounts. She spent months perfecting her version of Blakely Cheddar and then she began selling it at the local Saturday market. The cheese is sharp and salty but creamy, and distinctive in its purple wax coating; every week it sold out within an hour. Now we've converted a shed into a cheese dairy, invested in new machinery, and the cheese sells throughout the country. This tiny experiment has become our staple income.

My father likes to save up problems for his visit to Frank. When something baffles us—usually a piece of equipment breaking down—he always says: "No matter, Frank will know how to fix it. I'll pop up and see him, shall I?" In this way, he tries to keep Frank engaged with our life at the farm.

Aside from my dad, the people who have visited Frank in prison most often are Gabriel and Leo.

It took a long time before Gabriel was able to talk to me again, and I understood it.

He turned up at the farm, out of the blue, one afternoon.

My father answered the door and came back into the kitchen, his face full of meaning. "It's Gabriel," he said.

I went out into the yard to talk to him, shutting the front door behind me. At first, we just stood there, watching one another. It was the first time I'd seen him in months.

"I need to ask you something," he said, eventually. "But you won't like it."

"Go on," I said.

"I'd like to tell Leo that Bobby was his brother. I think it might help him process what happened if he understood why Frank did what he did. The worst thing for Leo is knowing Frank is in prison when he feels it should be him."

Ours was a complicated tale with many pieces to fit together. All of us were to blame in some way—Gabriel and me, Frank, Leo, and Jimmy too. Everyone played a part in the tragedy.

And everything was about Bobby, really, when you dug deep enough.

Gabriel and Leo visited Frank every week and for a whole hour they would talk about Bobby. It hurt Frank to begin with, spending time with the man who had briefly stolen his wife. Recounting memories of days on the farm with Bobby. Telling Leo exactly what had happened on the day of the accident. And why he felt responsible. But slowly, he began to look forward to it. Slowly, he began to heal. And Leo finally understood what had driven Frank to make his noble, foolish gesture. Saving Leo was really a way of saving himself.

One Sunday on our phone call, Frank said: "I'm ready to let him go."

He could have been talking about Jimmy, but I knew he wasn't.

"Aah," I said, though it was more an outlet of emotion than an actual word. Sadness or gladness, both probably.

That night, I began to write a poem for Frank, the first time since Bobby died I'd felt the urge to put pen to paper. I thought it was going to be about Grace and our new beginning, but it wasn't, in the end.

Gabriel's novel came out a year after the trial; I thought it a rather sad book. There was nothing of him and me in it, the girl and boy we had been when he first had the idea, but it was tinged right the way through with yearning and regret, a quest for second chances. That did belong to us. I worried the adverse publicity around our affair would affect his career, but it didn't turn out like that at all. Scandal and notoriety are good for book sales, it seems.

Gabriel and Leo are living in California now. Leo is at an American high school. He writes me postcards about baseball and burgers, and he sent Grace an LA Dodgers T-shirt for Christmas. She refuses to take it off. Leo is seventeen now and from the occasional photos Gabriel remembers to send, every bit as handsome as his father was when I first met him.

Sometimes, when I'm out walking with Grace, we pass by Meadowlands on our way to the woods. There's a spot in the road where you can see through the trees and have an almost perfect view of the lake. I stand there for a moment remembering the girl and boy who once fell so passionately in love. They don't feel like Gabriel and me anymore. Their innocence as they swam among the water lilies and brewed coffee on a camping stove believing themselves creatures of great fortune is too poignant, and I cannot contemplate them for long.

Not so long ago, Leo made a noble gesture of his own: He went to visit Nina. He didn't ask our permission for the tale he told her, although he did swear her to secrecy before he began. No one needs Frank facing a new sentence for perjury.

I was in the yard hosing down my wellies when Nina turned up. I watched in amazement as she got out of her car, even more astonished when she stood up and I saw her swollen belly. She was seven months pregnant. I'd heard tell of the new man Nina had met in the Compasses one night— an accountant of all things, with an office in Salisbury.

"I know," Nina said.

I didn't need to ask her what she knew: Her face said it all.

"Frank's story never made any sense. I'm sorry I hated you."

"You were right to."

We embraced for a long time, both of us crying.

Nina had a little girl. And although her daughter belongs to another man, not Jimmy, I can't help but feel there's a symmetry to that. Too much has happened for Nina and I to ever recover a friendship but, who knows, perhaps our daughters will become friends one day. Jimmy would like that, wherever he is. Bobby too. He always did adore Nina.

Grace is halfway down the field now, murmuring to her ewes just as Bobby did and her uncle, Jimmy. I once told Grace her brother used to have names for all the sheep, so she does the same thing. Bugs Bunny. Madame Butterfly. Mavis. I hear her gently chastising Mavis for taking too long. "Would you have us wait all day, Mavis?"

Beyond Grace I catch a flash of navy blue. A man has arrived at the bottom of our field. I watch him place a hand onto the fence and hoist himself over in one go, swift and effortless. Frank looks tall and strong in the wedding suit, walking in his own land, home to me, to Grace, to the start of another day. I knew he was coming out soon, but not this soon. He always did say he wanted to surprise us.

"Do you see that man walking up the field?" I call to Grace, and she stops to look.

Shields her eyes like Little Bo-Peep. "Who is it?"

"Can't you tell?"

She has a photograph of Frank on her bedroom wall. She always wishes him good night, the last thing she does before she falls asleep.

She pauses for a second or two, assessing the man walking up the field toward us. Then she screams, "Daddy!" and she begins to run, her sheep abandoned.

I watch her racing down the field, elbows pumping. She is wearing pink shorts and red wellies and her hair trails behind her in a dark cloud. I watch Frank as he opens his arms, as she flies into them. As he swoops her up and spins her around. I can hear them laughing. I watch as Frank throws his head back and yells at the gray clouds passing overhead. "I am home. I AM HOME." As Grace tries it, resting her neck against her father's shoulder, face upturned to the sky. "I AM HOME. I AM HOME." As they laugh and yell and laugh some more, this father and daughter who are meeting for the first time. Then they turn to me. Frank stretches out his right arm and Grace, cottoning on instantly, holds out her left. A giant man and girl scarecrow.

I glance at my father, who is standing by the tap, pretending to fill a bucket of water for the sheep, but really, openly gazing. He is crying as he watches them, but he's always been like that, my dad. These are joyful tears.

"Run, my darling," he says to me. "Run."

Frank stays rooted to the spot, arms wide open, waiting. Thinner than I'm used to, and older, but still Frank.

"Run, Mama," my girl shouts, still laughing.

So, I do.

For Frank, Love Beth

If the man could hear me, I would tell him this:
It was instant, Dad
It was instant.
No pain
The sorrow was all your own.
Enough now.
I would tell him that.

Lives should be measured in intensity.
Remember mine
For its glory-stretch of furious light and wondrous
    beauty.
The world we love-lived
Is earth
Is dust
Is me, Dad.

Acknowledgments

Thank you:

First and foremost, to my brilliant agent Hattie Grünewald. For believing in *Broken Country* on the strength of a ten-thousand-word submission and helping me shape it through your thoughtful edits into the vision we shared. Thanks, too, for your calm and wise advice and your constancy; it has been a joy working with you.

To the unstoppable Liane-Louise Smith and Kathryn Williams for championing *Broken Country* around the globe—it has been quite something to watch the two of you at work! At the Blair Partnership I am also grateful to Jordan Lees, Alex Ford, and Rhian Parry for their continual guidance and support.

To my editors: Carina Guiterman at Simon & Schuster US and Jocasta Hamilton and Abi Scruby at John Murray in the United Kingdom for your forensic interrogation of the manuscript and making the process so enjoyable. Not to mention being quite the loveliest people in publishing.

The entire Broken Country team at Simon & Schuster, who have been such a joy to work with, and in particular Maggie Southard, Danielle Prielipp, Wendy Sheanin, Liv Stratman, and Anna Hauser. Thank you Natalia Olbinksi for the glorious cover.

I would like to thank the foreign editors who fell in love with *Broken Country* and wrote such beautiful letters to say so. The way you connected with the story means so much to me.

I am grateful to the farmers who allowed me to accompany them in their daily lives when I was researching *Broken Country*. Your passion and instinctive understanding of the land and its wildlife was the fuel I needed to write the novel.

Thanks to Al Sykes, Lisa and Frank Reeve, and Peter Shallcross. And, of course, Keith and Nina Maidment, who have been farming the fields surrounding our house for half a century.

To Graham Bartlett, former detective turned crime author, for fielding my endless questions on policing and criminal justice so graciously.

Broken Country has unexpectedly introduced me to some truly inspirational women. Elizabeth Gabler and Marisa Paiva at Sony 3000 Pictures, Reese Witherspoon, Sarah Harden, Lauren Neustadter, and Ashley Strumwasser at Hello Sunshine: Thank you for your warmth and your passion for *Broken Country*. And Josie Freedman at CAA—thank you for making a long-held dream come true!

I chose to publish *Broken Country* under the name Clare Leslie Hall to honor my late parents, Jean Leslie and William Hall. We did not have them for long enough but the mark they made on the lives of my sisters and me has been everlasting. To Jane and Anna, as always, for being my twin rocks.

To John for literally everything. Thank you for your unwavering belief and your big heart; I am so lucky to have you by my side.

And to Jake, Maya, and Felix, who have grown up to be everything I hoped you'd be and so much more. You make me very proud.

The last mention must go to Felix, my youngest. You inspired this novel with your devotion to your puppy, Magnus. It's been a long time coming—you are almost an adult now—but I always wanted to write this story for you.

About the Author

CLARE LESLIE HALL is a novelist and journalist who lives in the wilds of Dorset, England, with her family. Under the name Clare Empson, she published two thrillers in the United Kingdom and Germany. *Broken Country* is her North American debut.